D0442833

The Exact Nature of Our Wrongs

ALSO BY JANET PEERY

What the Thunder Said

The River Beyond the World

Alligator Dance

The Exact Nature of Our Wrongs

JANET PEERY

St. Martin's Press
New York

This is a work of fiction. All incidents and dialogue, and all characters with the exception of some well-known historical and public figures, are products of the author's imagination and not to be construed as real.

Printed in the United States of America. For information, address St. Martin's Press, 175 Fifth Avenue, New York, NY 10010.

www.stmartins.com

Selections from this work have appeared in different form in *StoryQuarterly*, *Idaho Review*, and *Image: Art, Faith, Mystery*.

Designed by Kathryn Parise

THE LIBRARY OF CONGRESS CATALOGING-IN-PUBLICATION DATA IS AVAILABLE UPON REQUEST.

ISBN 978-1-250-12508-8 (hardcover)
ISBN 978-1-250-12509-5 (e-book)

First Edition: September 2017

10 9 8 7 6 5 4 3 2 1

For GMS, who willed it

Spiritus contra spiritum

Carl Jung, letter to Bill W.

The
Exact Nature of Our Wrongs

One

Even a hundred years past the town's founding a visitor to Amicus might guess it had been laid out by rival drunks. A flatland hamlet between the Chisholm Trail and the Santa Fe tracks, the place had no true center but was an array of storefront concerns and modest houses ranging over the six square miles that lay within its boundaries. A fitting figure for her family, Hattie Campbell sometimes thought, especially on days when she was torn among conflicting desires, by her husband and six children vying for attention or love or favor or whatever prize it struck their unfathomable fancies to vie for.

In this way had grown their helter-skelter prairie town. A stretch of melon field would open onto an outcropping of peeling clapboard bungalows and these would give way to a stand of cottonwoods. A mile or so away, past the Farmers and Drovers Bank, another clutch of houses, only a bit tidier, would appear, and then a stunted peach orchard, and then a pump jack dowsing crude oil up from bedrock. Yet another mile from these you'd come upon the grain elevator, the hardware store, and the water tower, so leak-prone that in a big wind water would sheet out like a gusher from a derrick. From the roadside billboard depicting the whitest of white hands clasped in hearty greeting and the words "Welcome to Amicus," it was a good hour's walk to the bermed-up boxcar that served as the civic tornado shelter. On the western edge of town the land opened up and the Great Plains began their slow rise toward the Rockies.

Haphazard and down on its heels as the place was, her family had prospered here, and Hattie liked it fine. Her husband, Abel, ran his law practice out of a low-roofed adobe building that had first been the land office and then a pool hall and punchboard dive. During Prohibition the structure, because of its thick walls, had been put into service as the jail. After repeal it was turned into a Phillips 66. This, too, she thought, was a fitting figure, at least where it concerned her husband, a man in whom the law was ever at odds. When Abel bought the building he had the gas pumps and the buried storage tanks removed. Out of wrought-iron rod he welded the letters L-A-W O-F-F-I-C-E, hung them over the arched doorway, and set up shop for what would be a long and satisfying practice. In later years he sat as town judge, a post that called for settling ordinance matters, presiding over civil disputes, and deciding fault in traffic offenses. Hattie was on the library board and served as treasurer for the Amicus Garden Club. She joined the women of Dorcas Circle in charitable works, played the piano for the First Presbyterian Sunday School, and sometimes led a lesson for the youth.

The Campbells were known and respected, and she had been proud of this, but in the past few years, with Abel's retirement and the rise of the next generation, she'd begun to fear that their standing was slipping. No one had said anything outright, but from time to time she saw a crooked look pass across the face of someone she was meeting for the first time. "I'm Hannah Campbell," she would say, using her softer given name to keep from having to utter the flat-sounding rattle that was the name she went by, but almost before she could add, "but call me Hattie," there'd be that flicker, that shadow. The Campbell name had once meant respectability and a certain stature, but lately she wasn't sure exactly what it had come to mean. Scofflaw, maybe. Wayward. Something not very good.

Often she shook her head in despair—or as close to despair as she ever came, which amounted to a sinking sense of bewilderment—at her children and their problems. Public intoxication (all four sons), drug offenses (three of them), DUIs (three), firearms violations (one son), speeding tickets (no firm count, as their father *would* fix their tickets), habitual lawsuits and embarrassing public confrontations (one daughter), foreclosures (same daughter, two sons), divorces (all of them, even Doro the good daughter), and the periodic estrangements that came if anyone mentioned their offenses. From the boys and the girls alike—those who were still alive were baby boomers past the early stirrings of middle age—the trouble she and Abel endured with all but one of their six offspring was almost biblical, and it was clear the felling blow would be dealt by Billy, the baby, now in his middle forties and wearing every misspent year.

For over two decades her youngest had lived under a sentence that had once meant death, positive for the terrible virus that left his immune system in ruin and would lead, in less time than any of them suspected, to his end. Many times during the ordeal that was his adult life, on any given night, he'd feared he might not last until morning, but of course he had. He was a firebird, his sister Doro liked to say, a phoenix. After every close call he went on living, sometimes in better shape than before, at least for a while. But eventually he would relapse. Those who loved him more or less coped, and Billy himself endured his fate with a shifting array of denial, humility, gallows humor, despair, and hope, but from time to time things could get dicey, for in addition to his precarious health he was an addict.

Painkillers, black tar, methadone, drink—any substance at hand. Cough syrup, cigarettes, codeine, cocaine. On a lean day even candy. He favored gigantic chocolate bars with high sugar alcohol content, and he claimed when his choices were limited, five big Butterfingers could at least give him a right smart buzz. From the Big Book of Alcoholics Anonymous he'd learned about the use of sugar to quell cravings, but he suspected his appetite for the huge bars probably wasn't what Bill W. had in mind.

Hattie adored him, and she lay awake nights worrying that when she died—she was in her late eighties—there would be no one to care for him. His never-ending needs and habits had driven away all his old friends and most of his family. He lied, he stole, he worked angles. That he committed these acts with a loving heart and an infectiously bright spirit did nothing to diminish the seriousness of his crimes, but his habitual ebullience made it easier for her to overlook many of his offenses and to believe they were merely stumbling blocks on a path that would straighten out at any minute. But lately, even she had to admit that things were getting worse.

"He's flat killing you," her daughter ClairBell said. Had said on more than one occasion. ClairBell was known for stretching facts to the fraying point, but in this case she was probably right. Hattie had suffered a heart attack a few years before, a silent heart attack she'd thought at first was indigestion from the short ribs she'd barbecued for dinner or maybe gallbladder distress from the months-old peanut brittle she'd found when she was cleaning out the holiday cupboard. Thrifty to the marrow, she hated to see her good homemade candy go to waste, and so she'd stood there eating it, piece by sticky, stale piece. Later that night she'd had a bout of chest pain, for which she blamed the candy. She didn't get around to looking into her condition until three weeks after the event, too late for a stent. Too late for anything other than to marvel that the infarction hadn't killed her outright. An artery was ninety percent blocked.

Daughter of pioneers and ranchers, she kept going, weaker than before and with a new little throat-clearing cough that reminded those close to her of what she'd been through, but determined to carry out her mission of easing Billy's way through the world, for she believed the Almighty had spared her for that purpose.

Caring for Abel in his dotage had taken a toll on her energy. On her nerves as well. Her husband had never been easy. He was what people used to call a man's man, but even this description didn't go the distance. He was a grab bag of contradictions, a dervish of crossed purposes. A sensitive, swaggering, foolhardy rakehell, a perfectionist, a savant, a daredevil with a penchant for recklessness, intolerant of incompetence, especially his own. How many times had she heard him mutter to himself when he did something that didn't measure up to his exacting standards, "Stupid, stupid, stupid"? But he was far from it. The man knew everything under the sun. If he didn't know the answer to a question, he would make one up, bluffing like a cardsharp to keep from having to say he didn't know. His poker face was legendary, and even after sixty-two years of marriage he could fool her. Maybe it was true that she was easily fooled, but still. Half the time his humor went over her head, and often she couldn't tell if he was joking or serious. "Oh, the tragedy of the literal mind," he would say, simply to madden her.

Sometimes he was a stubborn old crotchet with strong opinions and precise specifications for the right way to do certain things—a ripe tomato must be sliced a quarter of an inch thick and the abomination that was Miracle Whip must under no circumstances be permitted in whiffing distance of a BLT, which should be made with butter and never margarine—but other times he was an affable jokester, a generous host and party wit, a hail-fellow-well-met. A midnight lover whose hands . . . oh, she blushed just remembering. But whether he was Genghis Khan or the Miller of the Dee or the Sheik of Araby, you never knew which of these he'd wake up as. And lately he seemed to be getting even more erratic. She needed no more stress—that much she was certain of. Billy was nothing *but* stress, his brothers and sisters told her for the umptieth time after an awful birthday celebration, Abel's eighty-ninth.

For the event, Billy had taken the crosstown bus from his boarding-house in the city, the county seat some miles north, to the bus stop nearest Amicus. In her pale blue twelve-year-old Skylark, Hattie had gone to pick him up. On the way home he had talked her into stopping at the phone store and out of the ninety-five dollars she had concealed, against such a possibility, in her pocketbook's secret compartment. The deviation from her schedule as well as the confusing cash transaction Billy brokered—he could talk so fast!—had rattled her. In the past few years her thinking, it seemed, had slowed. She was frazzled by the time the other family members arrived for the birthday dinner.

The eldest at sixty, Doro had flown home from Boston, where she lived a life as far removed from the goings-on in Amicus as a librarian's from a rodeo clown's. By day she was an associate dean of students at a tiny liberal-arts college. By night and under a pen name she was a writer of western novels. She remained unmarried even thirty years after divorcing her doctor husband, and this caused Hattie to worry. Was her eldest too hard to please? Too modern? A feminist? She was certainly not a lesbian; there were her three grown children as proof.

Late as usual, son Jesse pulled his Silverado into the driveway just as dinner was called. Despite the home-to-work restriction on his driver's license stemming from a DUI a few years back when he was still a roaring drunk, and his general testiness when faced with a social obligation that required him to take off his hat, he had chanced the two miles from his farm, a boarding stable and drywall operation in the bend of the Big Slough where it flowed into the Ark River. Jesse and his father had a strained relationship resulting from Abel's ongoing campaign to improve him. That the evening's occasion was his father's birthday was grounds sufficient to cause Jesse to kick the truck's front tire before he entered the big stone ranch house.

ClairBell and her new husband, Randy Billups, had driven over from their country place in their white Coupe de Ville. Randy suffered from a polio injury that left him with a limp and a brace, but he managed to work as a mechanical engineer to keep a roof over the heads of ClairBell and her grown sons and a backyard swimming pool under her buoyant body. As to whether Randy was a saint or a dupe, the jury was out, though his kindness and the affection in which the family held him—the man could manage their bristly ClairBell—would billet him with the saints. Hattie liked him very much, and often she had envied her daughter's luck. What might marriage be like with a mild-tempered man?

All the Campbells save Gideon, who was living off the grid in a straw bale hut in the Sangre de Cristos and hadn't been heard from for months, were gathered around the table. Toward the end of the meal, after the birthday song was sung by Hattie, Doro, and ClairBell and mumbled by Jesse, as the birthday cake was served, Billy began to monopolize the talk. Walleyed with morphine and Retrovir, he rambled from subject to non sequitur subject, and in the middle of a monologue about the correct way to say that one was sick to one's stomach—Billy insisted that "nauseated" was preferable to "nauseous"—he had fallen asleep, his forehead coming to rest in his plate of devil's food cake.

Jolted awake by a poke from ClairBell and called by his father to account for himself, Billy laid the blame for his drowsiness on his prescription medicines. He outlined the pills he required, their effects, and why no one should trouble to wake him if at the dinner table he nodded off. Even if he wobbled or swayed. Or breathed like Darth Vader. Not even if he drooled. Why no one should shush him if he talked too grandly. "Or too longly." Billy tittered at his lunatic adverb, but no one else laughed.

"Oh, honey. How many did you take?" Hattie fretted, tucking a salt-and-pepper curl back into her French twist. Her tight permanent wave had gone bushy with the heat and exertion of preparing the birthday roast, and she worried that her head, because of the way she'd bobby-pinned her hair at the back, looked like half a blown-out dandelion. "If only you'd watch how many you take . . ."

Muttered Abel, balling his napkin, "Oh, for crying out loud." He pushed back his chair and rose to full height, which now that he was an old man and had shrunk—his last VA hospital physical measured him at only five and a half feet—did not have the effect he'd hoped for. To make up for his lack of presence he made his voice gruff and inserted an epithet, "Happy dang-blasted birthday to me."

"Papa, sit down and eat your cake," ClairBell said, reaching over to tug at his hand. ClairBell alone could upbraid her father, and from her and her alone would he accept blandishments. Had anyone else told him to sit down or tried to cajole him, there would have been hell to pay. Hattie had long ago given up trying to manage him. He could not be managed. He resisted even the subtlest handling. Hints, pointed looks, coming sideways at him—none of these methods had worked. Not once. If he was in a balky mood there was no hope; he was a mule, a man-size lump of tar on a log with its arms crossed and its chin set.

His sisters had once told Hattie that when Abel was young they'd nicknamed him the Little King, after the ermine-robe-trailing monarch in the funny papers who insisted on having his way. Abel was the first-born boy after a run of daughters and his parents had favored him. As a child he was a spoiled-rotten customer. A very bad hat, the sisters told her, a stinker. He pouted. He threw heroic fits over nothing, a nickel slug, say, or a licorice jellybean or a half-empty bottle of flat root beer. They shook their heads; how the Little King had become a second lieutenant in the United States Army, a war veteran, an attorney-at-law and officer of the court, a respected member of society, they would never understand. As a boy he had heeded no rules but his own. Now, at ClairBell's word and another tug at his hand, the officer of the court sat down meekly, but taking care to affect a look that would promote the impression that sitting down had been his own most excellent and reasonable intention.

Insulted by his family's scrutiny, Billy wiped his forehead of cake crumbs and got up from the table. He set a staggering course toward the bedroom wing. He meant to dramatize his angry departure with a flounce followed by a head toss, but his body—he was no taller than Abel and much slighter—would not oblige. His attempt to storm off looked like a crazed dance, a spasm.

Only ClairBell laughed at his failed display. Jesse and Doro sat silently, hoping that with Billy's departure the meal could resume, that their father would calm down and their mother would be spared the storm they feared was brewing.

"Go to your room," Abel barked needlessly after Billy, forgetting that his son didn't live at home but uptown in an apartment, forgetting he was forty-six.

"Bark!" shouted Billy, unchained by the pharmacological storm in his system. "Bark, bark, bark!"

Hattie fled the table and took refuge in the living room. If only Abel wouldn't bait him! If only he would be kind! If only Billy would watch his tone.

Abel rose from the table. Prepared to stand up for himself against his wife's constant judgment of the way he dealt with his son, he went after her at a rapid hobble. He planned to tell her there were limits and then to outline precisely what those limits were.

Seeing this and feeling protective of his mother, Billy changed his coordinates and lurched after his parents.

Bracing for an altercation between father and brother, both parties known for blowtorch tongues and no fear of heat, especially if blame was the name of the game and Hattie was the prize, Doro and Jesse and ClairBell brought up the rear.

Randy Billups had learned from blistering experience to keep his opinions to himself when the Campbells squared off, and so he pulled up a stool at the kitchen counter and settled in with a toothpick and the *Auto Weekly*.

They seated themselves on couches and chairs in the living room. Billy took a stance with his back to the fireplace stones, gripping the mantel behind him, arms extended in a pose of crucifixion until he snapped out of a nod to declare, "For your information, *ma chère famille,* I know exactly what I'm doing." Billy had been told, in Paris no less, that he had quite the accent. He took pleasure in strewing French phrases throughout his speech. He was hurt by his family's constant monitoring, by the looks he saw pass among them, and he planned to show them how efficiently and carefully he could manage his prescriptions. Pulling an orange vial from the pocket of his thrift store blazer, he crossed the room to dump a pile of blue capsules into his mother's aproned lap. Next he dropped in some peach-colored tablets.

"These, if you must know," he said, warming to his subject in an adenoidal voice, the result of past abuses to his sinuses, "*cannot* be taken with food and must be spaced over the day not to exceed six in a twenty-four-hour period, O heaven forfend." He grinned drunkenly, luridly.

Dropping white tablets into the mix, he shook the apron so the pills danced like jumping beans. "And these are Percocet and must be taken not to exceed two hours of the previous dose of the blue and peach. For my pain. Do you see?"

Hattie cocked her head, trying to focus her gaze on the tablets, but a cataract made a blurred spot and she couldn't get the image she was seeing to make sense—the nest of tablets and capsules looked like the spoils from a doll's Easter basket.

She and Billy were at one of their impasses regarding his medicine. Medicines plural, she should say. Out of her household account she had agreed to pay for those obligations that Medicaid and the Ryan White Foundation didn't cover as long as he kept his drug usage down, as long as he took his prescriptions sensibly and as directed. But his habits were more than she could keep track of or handle. She knew he pulled the wool over her eyes on many occasions, but what could she do? It was so hard to tell what was pain and what was excess. She had determined to walk the fine line between doubt and belief, but mostly to give him the benefit.

The whole issue was especially troubling because her son and her husband were at odds. Billy couldn't bear the way he claimed Abel treated her. "Sharia law," Billy sometimes said, always under his breath. Her son refused to hear her explanation that this was simply their generation's way and that she'd accepted the bargain when she'd taken the vow to love, honor, and obey. And little did Billy know, she'd often thought wryly, the myriad ways she'd learned to get around her seeming subservience. She could be foxy when she had to.

For his part, Abel resented the boy's hold on his wife. He had tried, but he couldn't get past his son's—he couldn't, he *couldn't* say "gayness," couldn't say "homosexuality," could barely bite out "proclivities." It wasn't so much the fact of the matter—he'd seen enough of humanity in his practice to understand and even to empathize—as it was his son's flamboyance. Billy was a peacock. A showboat with flags and bunting unfurled, brass bands playing on all decks, grand feeling on parade. He made no attempt to tone himself down but rather, wherever he went, made a spectacle. Spectacle making in any form was roman numeral one on Abel's unwritten list of everyday sins. And the way he went through money. And his froufrou French. And the way his mother doted on him.

Were Hattie forced to choose between the two men, husband or son, duty would see a tack toward her husband, but love would send her wandering back toward the opposite shore. She had long thrown herself between Billy and the world, not only to protect him from Abel, who could be dismissive and even caustic in his criticisms, but in the hope of forestalling the ruin Billy was bound for. Try as she might, though, she could not tell him, "No." Oh, she wanted to. She knew she should. But she always felt like Pilate washing his hands, or Peter before the cock's crow. It was easiest to smile and go along, to look on the bright side and to believe the best of people.

"And this big pink lovely is methadone, which I crush finely and then using a razor blade carefully form a line—" A bout of hiccups interrupted Billy's spiel, but he forged on to explain how he cut and snorted the powder.

Abel, too, had been trying to track his son's sleight of hand, thinking that somewhere in the display would be a clue to the beta-blockers he thought might be missing from his nightstand, but for all he understood of the recital, his youngest son may as well have been a sideshow grifter fast-handing walnut shells over a dried pea.

Bewilderment was Billy's aim: if he baffled his elderly parents, his mother would say, "I give up," and once again he'd have sole charge of his drugs, with none of her well-meaning interference. This had worked in the past. Had worked off and on since his positive HIV test at twenty-one; he had convinced his mother that any hitch in the ready cavalcade of drugs might signal his end.

He loved Hattie, but he also knew he could use her. He hated this dishonesty in himself, but the appetite that drove him had grown stronger than love. She would believe anything he told her, no matter how outré. While he was in her care the world was his and the fullness thereof, for she couldn't bear it when he suffered pain. If he told her he needed to go to a ramshackle house in a sketchy part of town because some unspecified someone there owed him money, off they went in the Skylark, Hattie with her hands at ten and two as Abel had endlessly instructed, peering over the wheel, pocketbook by her side, as Billy had lost his license after a third driving-under-the-influence. If he told her that a prescription was accidentally flushed down the toilet, in her quavering voice she'd call his doctor to vouch, in her innocence repeating his apocryphal tale of the mishap in exacting detail. But this time, as she stared at the pile of pills in her lap, she sighed, and then she raised her head, turned to her older children, and said weakly, "This can't go on. I'm old and I'm tired and sometimes I can't even think straight. We have to do something different."

"Well," said Billy, trying for humor, "in that case I'd better take control of these." He bent to scoop up his pills, clumsily dropping them into his pockets. A blue capsule fell to the floor. Everyone looked at it but no one would move to pick it up. Billy hadn't seen it and when he turned to leave the room, he accidentally ground it beneath his shoe, leaving white powder on the nap of the dark Persian carpet.

Thinking to lighten the mood, ClairBell said, "Let me get that." She mugged a greedy, salacious face, put index finger to nostril, and pantomimed a spectacular snort. She was hurt when nobody laughed.

"You *would,*" Billy said when he realized who was mocking him and why. He and ClairBell were often at odds. ClairBell had accused him of purveying drugs to her son Garrett. Billy had countered that it was the other way around, that Garrett was stealing from ClairBell's stash of prescription painkillers and selling them on the street. No one who witnessed the argument could determine guilt or innocence. "It's your chicken and your egg kind of deal," Jesse was known to say.

Billy left the living room. When the rest of the family heard the glass patio door slide in its tray, they knew he had drifted outside into the south yard to light up a Maverick.

Hattie shook her head. "I don't even know how to think about this."

"I do," Abel said pointedly, getting up to make his way to the backroom den where the History Channel was waiting, one mind-numbing click of the remote control away.

Hattie rose from the sofa and left the room. She went to the kitchen to survey the wreckage of the birthday dinner and get things put right.

In the living room the others discussed the new development. The dilemma was always the same and so was the conversation. They went over the outrages Billy put their parents through. Money, shame, legal quagmires, fear that he would be killed or that he would die of an overdose. But this time was different. This was the first time their mother had asked for help. So rare was the occasion that they decided to step in.

When they were agreed, Jesse called Hattie to the room and explained their intention.

"Leave it to us," ClairBell said, cobbling her fingers through a bowl of Gardetto's to pick out the rye chips. "We'll get him on the right road."

"Do you think you can?" Hattie asked dubiously. "I just don't know . . ." Her voice trailed off.

"We'll get it done, Mom," Jesse pledged. "Don't worry."

For years Jesse had wanted to ride to his mother's rescue, to relieve some of her misery. He was protective of her against his father, who dominated her, he thought, and against Gideon and Billy, who took advantage of her trusting nature. He'd learned during his last few years at the Sunset Limited AA group that Hattie was a classic enabler, and he'd tried to tell her she contributed to her own dilemma and to Billy's habits. But he hadn't been able to get her to see how she made him worse. She genuinely believed she was helping. Jesse sighed. The way he did with Patsy, his sometime lover, who drank herself to life every afternoon and into oblivion every night at the Pay Dirt.

Hattie went to the sliding doors and peeked outside. Billy slumped in a lawn chair on the patio where years before a swimming pool had been, now filled in with dirt and paved with flagstone. His chin rested on his chest, a forgotten Maverick burned between his fingers. Quietly she opened the door, tiptoed across the flagstone, and removed the cigarette from his hand. She stubbed it out and put it in the ashtray and then slipped back into the kitchen, where she started on the dishes.

As the eldest, Doro conducted the meeting to set the agenda for how to deal with what they had long called the Billy Problem.

"A mercy kidnapping?" she suggested, trying to wring some humor out of a situation that wasn't really funny. She was disappointed when Jesse and ClairBell didn't laugh. Among friends and colleagues she was known for humor. Back east she was considered a card. People thought she was funny, or at least amusing. She loved to liven up stodgy committee meetings. But here on the plains in her hometown it was as if she spoke another language, as if she were a washed-up comic, bombing in a hostile room. She pushed up her glasses, cleared her throat, and went on. "We need to get him some help," she said, "before this gets worse."

After a long discussion they decided that it was too late this night but that the next time Billy called expecting their mother to fetch him home for another Lost Weekend, a posse would ride. The posse would intercept Billy and take him to the ER.

"Haul his scrawny bew-tox to detox," said ClairBell. She put her fingertips together and in a sinister voice said, "Excellent."

Jesse laughed at their sister's clowning, and Doro remembered—again—that when she'd moved east she'd made herself an outsider. She had to be careful not to come on too strong, too bossy. As it was, her brothers and sister thought she was a Goody Two-Shoes a know-it-all, and a meddler. She needed to watch her step and try not to offend them. She needed to remember that their refusal to laugh was their way of circling ranks. She knew they called her "The Coastal Elite."

"Sounds about right," Jesse said. "It's way past an intervention. We've been down that road before."

ClairBell said, "Speaking of roads, remember that time Billy ran Honky into the Forty-seventh Street ditch?"

"That sorry Chevette." Jesse shook his head. "And we had to pull it out so Hizzoner wouldn't find out . . ."

ClairBell picked up the tale. ". . . and there was old Billy Boysie, dressed in his waiter's tuxedo, all bow tie and cuff links and that pleated thing around his middle, wandering down the road, chatting up those Hondurans who ran the cantaloupe stand and saying how they should wrap this fancy-ass bacon around a piece of melon . . ."

"Prosciutto," Doro supplied without thinking.

"Gesundheit," said ClairBell, smirking, giving Doro the side eye. "And we made him promise to stop drinking and he signed this pledge he wrote up and decorated to look like the Bill of Rights?"

"Might as well have burned it," Doro said, hoping to move past her gaffe. She thought of telling about the time Billy called her from jail, sobbing that he needed bail money, but this would just lead them down their well-worn path of cataloguing his misdeeds and it would make her look like a jerk for refusing to post his bond. "So what are we going to do?"

After they talked out the difficulties they made a plan to commit him to a drug rehab facility so Hattie couldn't undo with her endless forgiveness what had to be done in his, and of course her own—Doro had said this so often that Jesse and ClairBell sighed when they heard the words—best interests.

They concluded their business by electing Jesse to return Billy to his apartment later that evening. "That way, if he needs to be carried . . ." ClairBell began, but just then their father, having shaken himself from his post-dinner nap, presented himself to announce that he would be turning in for the night.

ClairBell hastened to fill him in on their plan. He nodded. At times of high feeling, Judge Campbell relied on sayings of the great English barrister William Blackstone, confounding to most hearers. "I have tried," he said magisterially, "since time whereof the memory of man runneth not to the contrary to effect this very change. But in vain. Oh, in vain since the ages ornate." He meant that he had long tried to get Hattie to butt out of Billy's life.

ClairBell petted his arm. "It's all right, Daddy. We got you."

The next morning after breakfast Doro sat at the kitchen table with her cell phone, making arrangements. She dealt with the county social services, with Medicaid. She worked out the details so that if she happened to be back east when the time came Jesse and ClairBell would have a protocol to follow.

As it turned out, they had to wait only a few days, and Doro was still in Amicus wrapping up her visit when Billy's come-and-get-me call came. She mustered the others and they set off toward the bus stop in her rental Focus.

Jacked up on a brilliantly calibrated pill cocktail that unfortunately he couldn't remember the recipe for, Billy stumbled down the steps of the crosstown bus. Hoping to earn a laugh from the greeting party—two silver-haired sisters and one graybeard brother, God woot!—he plucked a cheap advertisement sign from the weed-grown easement to flash over his head: "CASH MAGIC!" He cut a crazed jig and then flourished the sign like a courtier doffing a cavalier hat. *"Monsieur et mesdames!"*

He was funny, their baby brother, adept at self-parody, inventive, witty and sweet-natured, prone to displays of temper under only two circumstances: if someone showed disrespect for his mother, whom he loved without reservation, or for Doro, whom he loved madly despite her refusal to lend him money; or if someone maligned his intentions, which were *always,* he insisted, *always* good. But now his siblings didn't dare to laugh at his antics or he would be encouraged to greater effort. He was flying too high. Even from a distance his pupils looked like dark pools. "Look at those eyes," ClairBell muttered. "World's Largest Hand-Dug Wells."

Doro pulled the Focus around the lot, stopped the car, and into the backseat went their brother. Ray-Bans shielding her eyes and silver-gray chignon loose and whipping in the oven wind of August, Doro hit the gas and the car took off. ClairBell—shorter, plumper, cracking wise, her platinum clip-on wiglet a corkscrew cascade—rode shotgun.

Straw summer Resistol cocked back on his head, Jesse manned the rear seat so he'd be on deck, ClairBell had whispered, in case the captive needed a body block by a silverback cowpoke with a bunged-up knee, ha ha, no offense. "None taken," said Jesse.

Billy settled happily, not suspecting where he was headed. "My sisters, my brother, my saviors," he said royally from the backseat as the Focus pulled onto the right-of-way.

"You don't know the half," ClairBell turned around to say, but Billy had nodded out.

As outlined in the plan, they stopped at a strip-mall pizza joint. "Let's get some food on your stomach," Jesse explained as he shook his brother awake. So wrecked was Billy on his cocktail of prescription as well as street drugs that he didn't notice their grim expressions. At Papa G's he flirted with a teenage counter boy in a ONE LOVE T-shirt. The kid lifted his lip in a languid sneer and rolled his eyes, but Billy didn't notice.

Billy had once been handsome. He'd been told he looked like a smaller, skinnier Marco Rubio but with a buzz cut going gray and better politics. Or like Robert Downey Jr., smaller and more delicately made, but with the same dark, soulful eyes. He'd had good teeth and a dazzling smile, an endearing way of sweeping grandly into rooms, as his pitch for irony was perfect, tastes that ran to gold collar stays and French cuffs. But now he wore a soiled olive drab T-shirt and wrinkled madras shorts that hung on his thin hips. He was unshaven and hollow-eyed, and the effect of his licking his grizzled chops over the counter boy made him look, ClairBell said later, like the Little Bad Wolf.

As they piled back into the Focus, Jesse's bad knee seized up. "Shit fire and save matches," he said through gritted teeth, working out kinks that each year grew worse, the effects of the skywalker stilts he used to hang drywall. He was fifty-six but his body felt eighty.

Billy touched Jesse's arm and asked in a slurred voice, "Can I give you something for that, brother? Vicodin? Percocet? Opana? It's new."

Jesse was tempted. If his sisters hadn't been there, he'd have taken his brother up on his offer. He liked painkillers as well as the next person. Sure, not enough to go out and seek them, but if a pill or three happened to roll his way, he wouldn't turn them down. But this didn't seem like the right time. "It'll pass," he said, massaging his knee. "But thanks."

ClairBell craned around, dramatically putting one hand to her forehead and cupping the other toward Billy. "Headache. Maybe I'd better have some."

Billy drew back the hand that offered the pills. Doro pretended interest in the road and Jesse took off his hat and examined the hatband. The subject of ClairBell's history with opiates was forbidden by threat of a ClairBell fatwa. Some years before, Doro and Jesse had tried to talk to her about her problem, but she'd cut them dead, citing her many illnesses, some real and some phantom. She concluded with an exacting audit of everyone else's vices. Nicotine for Doro, who was forever trying to quit smoking, add booze and the occasional pill for Jesse and Gid, and for Billy all three, plus fentanyl patches, morphine, the kitchen sink, and whatever-addictive-else. Everybody was an addict, she said. Every last one of them. And at least she, ClairBell, didn't smoke. The silent treatment she gave them had lasted from Easter until Christmas. No one spoke of her problem again and so it had ceased to exist. But the truth was that she could mimic diseases so successfully tailored to the drug she wanted that she never lacked for stores. She had undergone elective surgeries in the hope of doses. She was blackballed in two of the city's emergency rooms and had recently begun to frequent the pain management clinic in the old bowling alley. People said the place was a pill mill—one of the doctors who staffed it had just been indicted.

When Billy continued to ignore her, she turned around, crossed her arms, and slumped in her seat.

Next on their secret agenda was a shakedown for drugs Billy might try to smuggle into the hospital. "Why don't you show me what you've got," Jesse said, playing off his request as if he had reconsidered Billy's earlier offer.

Billy obliged, and from his pockets spilled rainbow stores. While Doro explained what was to happen next, about the ER and the arrangements she'd made, Jesse collected the stash in a napkin.

Billy sighed, settling back in the seat. "I see how it is," he said in the voice of Grover the Muppet, using the childhood pet name from when he was the beloved baby of the family. "It is detox for Boysie?"

Firmly, sadly, in unison, hearing in their answer the long-learned inflections of their father's voice, the posse said, "It is."

Again ClairBell leaned around her seat and held out a hand to Jesse, gesturing toward the confiscated pills. "You want me to take those home and bury them in the burn pile? Set fire to them, maybe? I'd be happy to. We can't just drive around town with them. What if the cops stop us?"

Jesse said, "Better not, Bell. Some animal could get at them. Your coyotes and your raccoons and whatnot." He dumped the take into the remains of cherry limeade, shook the cup until the pills dissolved, and then poured the pink slurry out the window to splatter onto the hot asphalt of East Harry Street.

"Litterbug," said ClairBell. The rest of the way to the hospital she glared at the roadside, thinking dark thoughts. Nobody appreciated her. It was all Dean Doro Do-Right and Jesse the Beloved and the Prodigal Favorite, O Where Have You Been, Billy Boy? She, ClairBell, was the Forgotten Child. She tried to work up a few tears but could get none to fall. At least, she thought, she had Randy. Doro had run her husband off, even a medical doctor not perfect enough. Well, there was the matter of his drinking, but still—a doctor? ClairBell would have made a different choice, but Doro had to have things just right. Spoiled, she was, ClairBell thought. Prissy and spoiled and stuffed up like a Thanksgiving turkey with book learning, educated way past the need of any common everyday person to get along in the world. She, ClairBell, was salt-of-the-earth and she loved it. So there.

Jesse the Beloved's wife had divorced him. Same reason: drink. Plus some ugly business with a shotgun that neither ClairBell nor the courts could figure out. Had Jesse turned the weapon on his wife or on himself or on the barn door he eventually shot full of holes? Whatever, he was nevermore allowed to own a gun in the state of Kansas, the United States, and possibly the universe. Despite his sobriety he was keeping company with Patsy Gaddy, barflooze extraordinaire. He thought he was hiding it, but everyone knew. Still, Jesse acted like the woman wasn't shacked up in his spare room, cadging rides and smoke money and bleeding him white. One day when the rest of the family was out in Jesse's tomato patch, ClairBell had sneaked into his house and she'd seen the piles of women's clothing on the floor—little bitty raggedy cowgirl jeans and pink plaid pearl-snap shirts and the fringed vest Patsy wore everywhere. Oh, Brother Bear wasn't pulling one over on ClairBell.

Gid's latest common-law hookup was the usual hot Gideous mess, all crystals and chakras and incense and sweat lodges and New Age ugga-boo. Plus an aquifer of booze. Finally there was the Prodigal's life partner, Leo, a retired Navy chaplain turned AIDS counselor Billy'd joined up with in what they'd called a commitment ceremony but which looked for all the world like a two-groom wedding cake with punch and shrimp cocktail in the basement of the Metropolitan Community Church. She'd liked to have died when the two grooms gave each other that Pac-Man tongue-kiss for a full minute in front of Daddy. Reverend Leo had beat feet west the second or third time Billy fell off the wagon, but not until after they'd taken a few trips to Europe and a cruise to South America. *A half-life partner,* ClairBell thought, cracking herself up. But seriously, only she was still married. Go figure.

When she thought of her first two marriages, she softened. Fact was, every last one of the Campbells was messed up from the bassinette on and every bit of it was Hattie's fault; their mother played favorites. The order went this way: Billy first, always, foremost, followed by Jesse the Beloved. Their brother Nick probably would have been next because he was male, but he was long gone, dead at twenty-three of a sick heart, and so it was Doro the Exploro in third place, and then in fourth place Gid, who was a man-child so he should have at least beat out Doro, but somehow that part of her mother's favoritism didn't play in Gid's case and Gid didn't care about favorites anyway. This left ClairBell to waddle along at the tail end of the line like the last quacking duck in a wooden pull toy. A hot, satisfying tear brimmed over.

After Billy had gone through triage, to which he submitted docilely, supplying information about his consumption that widened the eyes of a student trainee, Jesse walked with him and the hospital attendant to the detox intake.

The sisters went outside to wait in the parking lot. They leaned against the car's hood, Doro waiting for her heart to slow down. She'd forgotten to take her beta-blocker that morning and she felt a pounding in her neck and beneath her breastbone. ClairBell opened the car door, found the warm remains of a Reddi Mart Pepsi, and sipped through the straw. Her mouth was dry. She'd been ramping up on some of the oxycodone she'd snagged from her father's top drawer, a prescription he had for the bouts of back pain he suffered even years after the war. She'd swallowed three while the others were at the intake desk. Feeling the buzz come over her, she watched the late afternoon light play like water on the chrome of the parked cars and thought, not for the first time and she hoped not for the last, how beautiful light could be, how refreshing wind could be, even if it carried a faint smell of engine oil and hot tar and maybe a whiff of the sewer plant on South Hillside, and how good life was, really, and how much she loved her dumpy, clunky-tribal-jewelry-wearing, know-it-all big sister, poor old Goody-Two-Orthopedic-Shoes, who was standing off a ways, gazing at a bus stop bench through her fancy Hollywood sunglasses with a queasy look on her face.

An elderly woman in a flowered headscarf waited for the bus on the bench beneath a redbud tree, shopping bags at her feet. The woman looked at her watch and then drew a cigarette from her fanny pack and lit it. The smoke blew their way. The cloud hit Doro like the divine afflatus, and she breathed deeply. She took an involuntary step toward the woman. She was on her third quit, she had told everyone about it as an insurance policy, and for the past weeks she'd been doing well. The day had been difficult, though. Despite all her hard talk about getting help for Billy, despite the danger he put their parents in, the financial drain his habits were, and the damage he was doing to himself, she felt as if she were betraying him. She would bum a smoke, just one. It would calm her. Only ClairBell would know. Then she remembered that whatever her sister knew, the world would soon know. Jesse would know. The clerks at Dollar General would know. Hattie and Abel would know, along with embellishments calculated to make Doro look worse. By the time ClairBell finished reporting the incident, the tale would be that Doro had scrounged through an overflowing ashtray frequented by lepers and lit a crumpled butt, spendthrift that she was, with a flaming ten-dollar bill. She took a step back.

"You okay?" ClairBell asked, looking at her sharply. "You look a little sick."

"Good." Doro took a deep breath. "I'm good."

ClairBell snort-laughed. "Everybody knows you're good," she said. "I asked if you were okay." She cut her eyes toward the headscarf woman and then back to Doro. "You looked like you were having a nicky."

Doro pretended to notice the woman and her wreath of smoke for the first time. She knew she should admit to her weakness, her temptation, but she couldn't. Something in her, a part of herself she didn't like and was trying to work on, wouldn't let her give ClairBell the edge. "No," she said shortly. "I'm just tired."

ClairBell rolled her eyes to throw shade on her sister's pitiful excuse. "Right."

In the barred room of the hospital basement where Billy was to stay for his detox, Jesse made his good-byes. "Thank you, my big brother," said Billy. "Tell Doro and ClairBell I understand. I know you want what's best for me."

Of the Campbells, Jesse was most sentimental, and he was moved by his brother's surrender. He loved the flighty little punk and it ripped his heart out to see him this way, sick and down. Not to mention that Jesse'd been there himself, but with booze, saved only by a sponsor who kept him straight, and his own banged-up white knuckles. He shook Billy's hand, thinking not for the first time that if his brother weren't such a high-flaring flame ball of the kind the barstool jockeys at the Pay Dirt would want to beat up, he'd like to have taken him, back in his drinking days, for a beer. They could have compared notes about what it was like to be sons of Abel Campbell—Attorney-at-Law, Municipal Judge, and King of Kansas. At this last unkind thought, he told himself, almost by reflex, *Easy Does It. Keep the bitterness down.*

When Jesse arrived at the car and relayed Billy's message, ClairBell's anger, simmering all day and muted only a little by her meds, boiled over. "That little skunk. What I really want is for him to pay me back for everything he stole. Last time he came over he kyped a bottle of Lortabs from my train case—which was locked, by the way—and a jug of quarters from the pantry. Not to forget Randy's best Stetson he wore to gay rodeo night and did anybody ever see it again, yee-haw?"

As she carried on, Jesse and Doro pretended interest in the western sky, now piling up with thunderheads. When ClairBell made claims, it didn't pay to question her word. The more far-fetched her accusations were, the more fiercely she stood by them. In this way she was like their father—every argument was a hill she was prepared to die on. Besides, they reasoned separately, silently, these particular charges probably hadn't been fetched from that far away. Billy's rap sheet was long.

On the ride home they were quiet. The sky darkened, lowering. A fresh, ozone-y wind came up. As the first gouts of rain splashed across the windshield, ClairBell quietly took up the ever-nourishing matter of her abandonment, Jesse considered the odds of a request to use Abel's log splitter being met with a simple yes or no, with no dramatic reading from the List of Tool-Borrowing Offenses, and Doro reflected on how to pack for the next morning's flight, on the relief it would be when the plane skimmed over the harbor and touched down at Logan and she was done, at least for this visit, with family matters.

At the house in Amicus, Hattie had waited for word, and when the party returned she asked for an accounting, sighing as they filled her in on the day. "So he's safe," she said. "For now."

Two

The child was an accident, a slip on a snowy March midnight in 1963, Hattie and Abel tipsy on champagne and staking their fates on a diaphragm so brittle it should have been tossed away months before, whispering under blankets so not to wake the five children asleep in rooms down the hall.

They had recently come back from the city where Abel's job as a claims adjuster had taken them, to their homeland among the farm towns of southern Kansas. To Hattie, the time they'd spent in Chicago had seemed like exile. Abel's health had gone bad there—a hiatal hernia and maybe an ulcer and all of it most likely caused by nerves and worry. Homesickness, Hattie suspected, but she kept her opinion to herself. She was glad when he decided to return to the slower, quieter place where they'd grown up, glad to return to family and to ways she knew. The champagne was to celebrate their homecoming, their first night in the first house that wasn't a rental, and to mark the new leaf in Abel's career.

After the war ended he'd gone to law school on the GI Bill. There'd been a glut of new lawyers in the year he graduated, and so he'd decided to wait to start a practice. Before they knew it Theodora and Nicholas were toddlers and the child who would be Jesse was on the way, and in no time at all Claire and Gideon came along to make five. Thanks to Hattie's frugality and a boom economy, they got along all right, and at last, a decade after Abel had passed the bar exam, they were able to put a down payment on a stone house on three acres in the outlying village of Amicus, where Abel had been hired as town counsel. Another purpose of opening the bottle, though neither would say it and both tried hard not to think it, was to blunt the recent, terrible news—the diagnosis of their eldest son's heart defect and his diminished life expectancy.

Nick was a skinny thirteen. He had soft brown eyes and long lashes, sand-colored hair, a high forehead. On his cheek below his right eye spread an oblong birthmark the color of Mercurochrome. His nail beds were blue, his fingers had started to club, and when he tried to run he wheezed and had trouble catching his breath. He would probably not live past twenty, the doctors said. Neither Hattie nor Abel could bear to think about this. Nick had been Abel's hope, his first true joy since before the war, and he made no secret of this. In his son he saw traits he wished that he himself possessed—Hattie's patience and kindness, for two—in addition to a good mind and a sense of justice. It had been Abel's worry about Nick's health rather than Hattie's—she was pragmatic about illness and tended to brush off sickness or to expect time to do its promised work—that led to the cardiac catheterization and the diagnosis: tetralogy of Fallot. A defect of birth. Four holes in their boy's heart.

As winter turned to spring, the weather warmed, and Hattie missed first one and then two of her monthly cycles, she wondered if maybe she was entering the change of life. She was forty, and she was eager to see the end of her moon-ruled days. She'd put her education on hold to marry. Back in the days right after the war everyone was getting married—her sisters and brothers, her friends, everyone—and the world had turned into a whirl of bridal showers and weddings. She and Abel were married in Hattie's church, First Baptist, with the aisle and dais lit with candles, with sheet cake and frilled nut cups in the church basement, a honeymoon trip to the Ozarks. They hadn't made their destination that first night for the rise of desire that in all the years they would be together would not diminish, a desire that caused them to turn the shoe-dragging, tin-can-clanking Studebaker into the first highway tourist court they came to after leaving the city limits. They parked and hurried to check in, the white painted letters scrawled on the car's sides announcing—for all the world to see and to Hattie's maidenly embarrassment—Abel's lustful ambitions: "Hot Springs Tonight!"

Now, with the childbearing part of her life drawing to a close, Hattie intended to go back to school and finish a degree in elementary education. Maybe teach school part time. She knew well that her work was her husband and children and house, and she didn't question it, but often through the years of infants and young children she had looked up from the stove or the sink or the washing machine to imagine the day she would be free. She loved the children, but still she had counted the years.

When other signs that something was going on inside her came on—tenderness in her breasts, morning queasiness, an odd blurring of time, the longing for an afternoon nap—she thought again, until the reason for these changes dawned on her like a slow and terrible change of mind. After disbelief came dread. She remembered the sleepless nights, awakened by a baby's cries, her exhaustion, how confined she'd felt, how haggard, tethered to a newborn, to infants and toddlers, her life become urine-drenched and soiled, the reeking diaper pails, the calf mash smell of Karo syrup and evaporated milk, curdled and everlasting spit-up. Magazine articles and glossy advertisements made motherhood look like bliss, like an enterprise the resourceful woman could control with the latest products and could even take delight in, cooking balanced meals, greeting her husband at the door in a pinafore apron, freshly bathed, a steaming crown roast held out on a platter. What a laugh, if it hadn't been so sad. Not one of her friends would admit to a similar sense of doom, and so she felt alone, beleaguered and worn to a nub. Her doughty little mother had given birth in their farmhouse in the same bed she'd conceived seven children in, nursing each baby until another was due. How had she done it?

Abel was a camera buff and he loved to photograph her, artfully staging her or, worse, catching her when she wasn't expecting him to aim the camera. He didn't seem to notice her distress, but when Hattie saw candid photographs of herself in those years, even long after they were over, she had to look away. The haunted look in her own eyes made her feel sick. She had moved through the days of early motherhood as though—it was silly—as though she'd committed some unknown sin and she couldn't get away from what she'd done, as though she were laying offerings at the altar of an unknown god.

Every Saturday Abel had stayed home to watch the children while she took the car to do the week's marketing, and sometimes she imagined pressing her foot on the gas pedal and driving away, driving and driving and driving as far as she could go. On one particular Saturday, deep in the frigid Chicago winter when she was desperate to get away, if only to sit in the cold car in the stillness, Nick and Jesse had hidden in the backseat, planning to pop up and surprise her and trick her into taking them along to the store. She'd driven only a block when they shouted, "Surprise, Mommy!" She'd screamed in shock, and then turned the car around, sent them to the house, and gone on alone to the store. When she returned home and parked the car in the alley, for the longest time she couldn't make herself go inside. She'd sat in the car until night fell and frost flowers bloomed on the windows and the lights in the bedrooms went out.

She wondered if something was wrong with her. Maybe it was that as a girl she'd been a wanderer, lonely as a cloud and happy, in pastures and creek beds, a poetry lover, easily seized with romantic ideas. She had often consulted her heart to see if she had a religious calling; sometimes on her long walks she talked to God, and more than once she thought she'd heard Him speaking back. Through the rustle of wind in cottonwood leaves, a meadowlark's sudden swoop, a cloud over the sun, but definitely God. Maybe in order to consider the things she liked most to think about, the great mysteries of faith and love and hope, and to feel like herself in her own skin, she simply needed great stretches of quiet.

When she hinted at her tiredness to her closest sister, Sammie agreed that having babies and young children was difficult and, really, just ridiculous for what it put you through, but from her laugh and her jolly pink face Hattie could tell that she didn't feel . . . what, what was it?

She tried to take inspiration from Proverbs, the thirty-first chapter. She'd known the words from girlhood, if not by heart entirely at least by familiarity, but their meaning set her back all the more—all that virtue and spinning and weaving and vineyard buying, the rising up in the dark of morning and all the candles not going out by night made her weary, and what did the virtuous woman get for it, besides a swell eulogy? In the only act of sacrilege she'd knowingly committed she'd hurled the King James Bible her parents had given as a wedding present against the kitchen wall. It lay on the floor, pages fluttering, for almost a minute before, wracked with guilt, she seized the book and sent a sorry prayer heavenward. But finally, blessedly, she had gotten through the difficult years and was ready to begin her life again.

When a third month passed without a cycle, Dr. Cobb confirmed her pregnancy with a rabbit test. It was after the manner of the time and place to wait to announce the news, even to a husband, and so she kept her own counsel until later that day. After supper she made a pitcher of lemonade, musing bitterly about the phrase—it seemed that no matter where she turned she couldn't outrun platitudes—and took two glasses out to the south yard where Abel planned to put in a swimming pool.

He lounged in a metal lawn chair, wearing khaki pants and a white V-neck T-shirt, smoking a Winston, glasses on the end of his nose, contemplating the shape and dimensions of the pool to come and sketching his plans on graph paper. He loved nothing so much as a mechanical problem. She pulled a chair beside him and they sat quietly amid their children's activities.

Fifteen and suffering the dual miseries of an awkward adolescence and a solitary nature, Doro sat in a crook of the sycamore, reading *Look Homeward, Angel* for what was surely the fourth time. Beneath the tree, Nick and Jesse tossed sycamore balls, trying to hit their sister's dangling legs. Hattie knew she should stop them but they'd just find some other devilment, and anyway Doro needed to learn to get along with them, stinkpots though they were. The girl alternated between stormy and standoffish. She was, Hattie had determined, too sensitive, wound too tight. Like her father.

ClairBell at eight and Gideon, seven, had dragged an old mattress to the cinder-block patio wall Abel had built and were jumping off the wall onto the mattress, bouncing and bobbing for attention, and then climbing up to jump again. ClairBell yelled, tirelessly it seemed to Hattie, and in a screech that set her last nerve quivering, "Look at me! Look at me!"

Gideon was in his Mighty Mouse phase. He wore a ragged bath towel around his neck as a cape. "Here I come to save the daaay!" he called as he jumped—again, again—from the wall.

"Six?" Abel asked when she'd gotten the words out. "I can barely support you and these five." He took a sip of his lemonade and made a face. "How far along are you?"

His reaction irked her but she was determined to put up a good front. "Maybe three months."

She smiled. It was funny, but if she'd been unsure that she wanted a new baby, after Abel's negative reaction she was now having another think. Maybe the life growing within her was a kind of second chance. A chance to be less worried, less overwhelmed, a better mother. A chance to do things right, and—oh, heavenly days—maybe this was her old pal God, speaking to her in His inscrutable language! Without knowing she was even considering it, she heard herself saying, "I was thinking that if it's a boy we could name him after your brother."

In truth, she'd thought Samuel would be fitting, given her own first name, Hannah, and its biblical implications.

Abel's mind raced. He felt conflicting, arguing voices coming at him from many quarters, all seeming to crowd into his own dry, constricted throat, and he was at odds with every one of them. He wanted to tell Hattie about the osteopath who had fixed unwanted pregnancies for several clients, but he wasn't sure he should bring this up now. He wasn't certain how Hattie felt about the subject. Abortion was against the law, so maybe there was his answer; Hattie was law-abiding to the core. Maybe he could sidle around to the subject later. He needed to think. "Come to the ham shack," he told her with a nod to the yard full of children. "We can have some privacy."

Off the garage he'd made a room to house his amateur radio equipment. Among the transmitters, transceivers, receivers, condensers, the vacuum tubes, and Morse code keys was the first little glowbug he'd built as a boy, all his salvage, Collins and Hallicrafters and Hammarlund and Heathkit, his radio paradise. He'd put two stools near his workbench, plugged in an old refrigerator, and installed a cast-off couch. Outside he'd built and erected a forty-five-foot antenna. The antenna was a city code violation but if anyone on the council said anything he planned to argue the ordinance was a breach of his rights under the First Amendment.

He locked the door behind them and went to a cabinet above his workbench for the bottle of Dewar's a client had given him. Into one of the baby food jars he saved for storing parts he poured two fingers for himself. He extended the bottle's neck to Hattie but she declined. "How about some crème de menthe?" He had a bottle of that as well, another client gift.

"All right, but only a little," she said. She drank only rarely, but this night she felt the need, though she wasn't sure why, to join him. Lately Abel had been drinking more, she'd noticed. She blamed his clients and his law school buddies. As well there was a group of doctors and pharmacists and businessmen, World War Two veterans all, that he'd taken up with. A fast crowd, she thought, big talkers, big drinkers. This bunch went pheasant hunting on the Nebraska line, elk hunting in Montana, was contemplating buying a boat to moor in Gulf Coast Florida, where they'd invested in a shrimp cannery. She wasn't sure of the details, but the cannery involved a bond issue and some other civic finessing. Pie-in-the-sky plans, she suspected, though Abel meant business on at least some of his enthusiasms. He'd already brought home three motorcycles, a BSA 650 for himself, and a Honda 50 and a

Honda 90 for the boys to ride around the yard. It was illegal for Nick and Jesse to ride on the street, but Abel told them to keep to the dirt roads outside the town limits and they'd be fine. She wondered what he was teaching them about the law and how he could possibly construe that it didn't apply to him. He had a saying that infuriated her—"If you're not cheating, you're not trying"—and she wished he'd quit using it in front of Nick and Jesse and even Gideon. They were already wild boys, cut from his cloth. They didn't need a standard like this to march under. She had given up on the dream that one of her sons might have a call to the ministry, but she would at least like to see them abide by civil laws.

Abel poured her a capful and handed it to her. He hadn't known he would do what he did next, but he extended his jar to her capful and, remembering one of his father's toasts, said, "May we get to heaven before the devil knows we're dead."

At first Hattie's eyes widened at the mention of the devil—she took hell and its high angel seriously—but then she laughed. She felt strangely spirited, a little like she had nothing left to lose, so why not throw caution to the winds? They clinked cap to jar, and Hattie slugged the crème de menthe and felt the slow syrupy burn.

Abel downed his Scotch and looked at his wife. She was a beautiful woman. In the domestic clamor of their daily life he sometimes lost sight of her loveliness. Her squared jaw and chin, her high, broad cheekbones, the warm color of her wavy hair like brown sugar candy—these had slain him from his first sight of her when they were children. Her dark eyes were canted, one more so than the other, and though her ancestry was English and Welsh, she looked as though she'd blown straight off the Russian steppes. Kyrgyz eyes, he thought. He'd picked up the phrase from some long-forgotten novel. If she had a flaw, it was the whitened scar at the end of her nose. A girlhood accident with a barbed-wire fence had ripped the fleshy tip of her nose and the line still showed white, especially when she was upset.

She'd nursed five infants and her breasts had fallen slightly, but her figure was the kind people turned to watch, something about the way the small of her back curved, her posture. She had the most beautiful deep-clefted derriere he ever hoped to see. And she was modest, not aware of her beauty. Because her ways were demure, nothing carnal about them, this made her irresistible.

They met at grammar school during the Great Depression when he was twelve and she was ten. Having set off a firecracker in a classmate's lunch pail, Abel was racing one way around the schoolhouse and Hattie, engaged with her friends in a game of Run, Sheep, Run, came barreling around the other. They collided at the corner, knocking the wind out of both of them. When he saw the female creature with her nut-brown skin and wide cheekbones, her dark eyes at a fetching slant, he was poleaxed. For a long minute they regarded each other, and then they turned around and ran back the same way they'd come. At the time he'd had what he later, when retelling the story, called a "reaction," his elaborate enunciation of the word and a look over his glasses giving listeners to know that if the first two letters were reversed, the *e* placed before the *r*, a more accurate idea of the phenomenon that overtook him, physically speaking, would emerge. Nothing more happened until a dozen years later and after the war had ended. When they met again in a college Spanish class he'd had another reaction.

He had one now.

"We need to think about this," he said, "before it's . . ." But it was already too late. He kissed her, and down onto the ham shack couch they went while outside their children jumped and raced and shouted as dusk shadowed the yard and the cicadas set up their squall and the fireflies came out. No more was said of choices.

That November, on the day Abel finished digging the hole in the south yard where the pool would go and Hattie had her eight-month checkup and learned that she should prepare for a Christmas delivery, the President of the United States was assassinated, just down Highway 81 in Dallas. In Amicus, all was ready for the new baby—the cradle in Hattie and Abel's bedroom, a bassinette against the wall, a new oaken rocking chair, as the pitiful, creaking old one she'd had for the first five was good for little but kindling, but it seemed that in the sadness and upheaval of national events, everyone forgot about the child to come.

On doctor's orders, Hattie went to bed, letting Doro take charge. When she wasn't shrinking from human company Doro could be bossy and officious enough to get the younger children off to school in the mornings. Her sisters Sammie and Alma brought casseroles and did the laundry and cleaning. The neighbors pitched in. Hattie had Abel move a television set into the room, and she lay watching the funeral cortege as horses drew the caisson slowly through the capital's streets, followed by the caparisoned riderless horse. She had not voted for the man and she was not given to tears, but this terrible tragedy defied her usual reserve—somehow it was tangled up with her own doomed Nick, who probably wouldn't grow to adulthood, and with the new baby to come and her fears for it—and she sometimes rose from her pillow to find it moist. Saddest of all the sights on the screen was the little boy in short pants and a blue coat on his third birthday, saluting his lost father. Into what kind of world was she bringing another child?

Christmas came and went, but finally, on the last day of the year when Abel was about to leave for an office party, her water broke. They left the younger ones with Doro and drove to the hospital, where a few minutes before midnight their infant boy entered the world. They named him William Blackstone after Abel's brother Bill and the British barrister who was Abel's hero. And—Hattie did not tell him—William Wordsworth.

In the early morning hours Abel left Hattie and the baby at the hospital and drove home to a houseful of sleeping children. He let himself in the back door, cocked his ear to listen for any wakers, but all was still. He went down the hall to the back bedroom to check on the boys and then poked his head in the door of the girls' room. He went outside to the ham shack and poured himself a Scotch and stood in the dark. Idly he flicked on the power switches and the vacuum tubes began to crackle and hum to life, signals to be heard, their high-frequency squeal sounding ghostly and faraway, evidence of the world outside the narrowing boundaries of his own. He looked through the window at the frost-covered ground, and for a moment it appeared that a massive shadow loomed over the yard, an ominous-looking cloud, a black hole, a frozen star at the boundaries of which time stopped. He rubbed his eyes and looked again and understood that he was seeing only the empty pool.

Hattie had finished her pregnancy in the shock and sorrow of the assassination, but now the baby's new life seemed to wash away her grief. She stayed on bed rest for a while, and the children flocked to the bedroom where she recuperated. They gathered around her, clamoring to hold the baby. They rocked him, sang to him, played with him, and it seemed that with the turning year her happiness knew no bounds, the infant days that had once stretched lonely and long now almost glowing. Around the little boy the family grew up a second time, reordering itself with Billy at the center. He was funny and sociable, a gigglebox, an endlessly diverting new toy. He loved it when they nuzzled him. He flirted with them to entice them into his baby games. Hattie felt she'd entered a second youth. She had loved the others, of course, but never like this. Here, maybe, was the child she could train up in the way he should go. Here, maybe, was her little man of God, her Samuel.

Away from the center of things Abel entertained himself and slowly grew away from the messy goings-on in the house. He worked and tinkered. He built a cabana beside the pool and then a machine barn. He brought home more Hondas, another BSA, and a Ducati. He still turned to her in the night, and his appetite was strong as ever, but Hattie knew that with the new baby some balance between them had tipped.

From an early age, Billy knew how to get what he wanted. His ways were fetching and funny. He was interested in beautiful things—jewelry and statuary in particular caught his infant eye—and he loved best to play in Hattie's jewelry case, in Doro's makeup box, with ClairBell's pop beads and plastic barrettes. He was lively, a miniature showman, a clown, dapper in dress from an early age. From his mother and her Singer he commissioned a business suit like the ones his father wore, complete with vest and tie, to be sewn from mint green polyester double-knit in a herringbone pattern. Hattie happily ran up the little garment on the machine, and everyone laughed and admired the suit when Billy put it on. He wore his tiny suit to church, to the grocery store, to the Dairy Queen for a cherry dip cone. He rode directly beside Hattie, standing up on the bench seat of the white Lincoln Continental

Abel had taken in trade from a client who couldn't pay his fee, his arm around Hattie's neck. "He looks like a game show host," Nick said once, laughing.

"A tiny polyester butler," ClairBell said, "or Richie Rich."

Hattie worried a little, but not much, and they all doted on him.

If Billy did something cute and someone took notice, he repeated the action until the joke grew stale and it was clear he needed to be called down, which he rarely was. Hattie lamented, "You children are spoiling him!" But the truth was that she too indulged him. Only Abel tried to bring order and calm to his youngest boy's upbringing, to put the quash on the wholesale adoration.

When Billy was three he fell facedown in the deep end of the pool, drained for the season except for six inches of black leaf-and-twig-littered water. On that September evening Abel was at the town hall for a council meeting and not due home until dark. In the kitchen preparing pork chops, her mind on whisking lumps out of the gravy, Hattie had no clear view of the pool, for her back was turned to the glass wall that took up the south ell of the house. She failed to notice that Billy had ridden his tricycle onto the apron of the pool and had parked it at the brick coping that rimmed it.

In the big central bathroom off the kitchen, home from college for the weekend, Doro made ready for a movie date to see *Doctor Zhivago.* Nick and Jesse rode their Hondas around the property, playing a charge-and-dash game called Spartacus. The object was to snatch a towel wrapped like a toga from a gladiator-boy who stood in a clearing, facing his mounted attacker. Though Jesse was the stronger rider, Nick usually won because Jesse would lose his nerve and at the last minute he would dodge the oncoming opponent. ClairBell and Gideon played on the banks of the creek that ran behind the house, trying to entrap a garter snake. ClairBell had just pinned the creature's head in a forked stick and they were watching it writhe. It was Gideon's idea to transport the snake to the big bathroom and let it loose on the slick tile floor to scare their big sister and maybe send her running in her underpants through the house. ClairBell and Gideon snickered for a while about that possibility, exciting themselves with the imagined vision of their prudish sister exposed, and then ClairBell picked up the snake and they made their way up the bank.

Left alone by the pool, Billy contemplated his own prank. The family cat loved the sandpaper-like texture of the diving board and she often lazed on its rough surface. She was drowsing there now. Billy's plan was to catch her and drop her into the black water below.

He climbed up the low board and made his way to where the cat lay, a task he'd done often enough through the summer, though always with a brother or sister waiting to catch him when he jumped and always with the beautiful blue water rippling below. Ribbon was an old marmalade kitty, manhandled by children and accustomed to being picked up under her forelegs and dangled limply, helplessly. At first she submitted patiently enough to Billy's will, but when he got close to the edge of the pool, she drew up her hind legs and clawed the air, flipping herself over. She made her escape from Billy's grip, but fell ten feet down into the muck at the bottom of the pool. In the struggle Billy toppled over, cracking his head on the brick ledge. He fell, unconscious, into the filthy water.

No one had witnessed the accident. Hattie's first indication that something was amiss came when she caught sight of Ribbon, muddy and yowling at the patio doors. Wondering what had happened, she hurried outside. Scanning the pool, she saw nothing out of order. The shallow end was empty except for a plywood plank and a homemade skateboard one of the boys had abandoned. There at the deep end was Billy's tricycle parked on the apron. The dark, debris-clotted water at the pool's bottom lay in shadow. At first it revealed no clue, and she had almost turned to go back into the house to resume her dinner preparations when she caught sight of a patch of dirtied white fabric, half submerged—the training pants she'd put on the baby not twenty minutes before.

She didn't remember afterward how she got down into the pool, whether she'd jumped into the dry shallow end or hastened down the steps, or how she pulled the still body from the water and laid him on the dirty concrete. Standing there, she knew only that she had to think of what to do.

Only think.

But she couldn't. No thought would come, and it would be this way all her life, that in dire times she would freeze and be unable to summon a thought. Something would shut down in her brain.

She stood, trying, trying.

ClairBell and Gideon had made their way to the south side of the house, to the door nearest the big bathroom, garter snake at the ready. When they saw their mother standing alone in the deep end of the pool, and that the bundle at her feet was their baby brother, they dropped the snake. Yelling, they banged into the house and barged into the bathroom and then ducked out of the way so Doro, who was dressed in madras shorts and a white blouse with a Peter Pan collar, who had worked summers as a lifeguard, could race past them to help. Nick and Jesse had come in to wash for supper, and they called the police, who dispatched an ambulance.

Doro knelt in the bottom of the pool over the baby's body. His skin was cold and blue. She turned him so he was on his side, stuck two fingers in his mouth, scooped out a clot of matter, leaves and sticks, turned him on his side. Black water poured out. She put her mouth to his blue one and began to blow the way the Red Cross had taught. Another murky spring of water gurgled up. As sirens sounded in the distance she kept breathing into him, not sure she was doing it right, worried that she was pushing more of the foul-smelling water into him. Her only practice had been on the rubber mouth of Resusci Annie. She looked up once to see that neighbors stood around. The woman who lived next door brought a blanket and she put it over her brother, tucking in the edges, and then the ambulance was there, the attendant lifting him to secure him to a gurney. He was unconscious.

At the Town Hall, Abel had heard the police call come in. He raced home to find fire department, police, and ambulance on the property. Neighbors and gawkers, drawn by the sirens, stood around. When it was clear that his son was breathing, he fell to his knees in the empty pool, his face in his hands, not to pray but to cover the horror at the terrible bargain, the profane prayer his mind had too suddenly, too easily supplied: *Take this boy, spare the other.*

By the time Hattie came out, grim-faced, shattered, dressed for the drive to the hospital, he had composed himself.

Billy recovered, no worse for wear. Abel labored for several years to forget his unholy exchange, to forget the sick feeling he'd had when he found himself thinking the unthinkable. When Billy was six, the pool's concrete cracked in a bad freeze, and though Abel groused about cheap materials and a capricious water table and his own workmanship, he was relieved when the bulldozer drove the last of the fill dirt over the hole where the pool had been.

Three

Winfield was a hill town in the shadow of the dormers and chimneys of the former state asylum, where even into the middle years of the twentieth century chains and leg-irons were used to restrain patients. It was to this place, now a drug rehabilitation center, that Billy went when his detox was completed. A student of architecture, he led his recovery pod in historical appreciation of the Victorian-era buildings and in sick jokes about their current incarceration, but he did well on the program. Given his upbringing, Hattie's teaching, and his own spiritual leanings, talk of surrender to a Higher Power was second nature, and when the time had been accomplished he was released.

Clean, sober, clear-eyed, he went first to a halfway house and then to a job at a Bible publishing company. Hattie was ecstatic. The manager was a deeply kind man who recognized suffering when he saw it and who lived a loving creed. In this man's presence Billy flourished. He made decent friends and he made enough money to rent a bright studio apartment in an Art Deco building in Riverside Park, which he furnished in tasteful castoffs from Hattie's attic and the Goodwill, and where he was happy and productive for almost a year, until sickness and hunger and need again drove him down.

He went down fast. All his old haunts he revisited, his old sources he renewed. He tricked the PA at his doctor's office into a double prescription for methadone. He lost two apartments. The pretty Deco one he'd set fire to in what he said was a cooking accident—"But cooking what?" ClairBell wanted to know—and from the second place, no more than a flop, he was evicted for operating a massage parlor without a license. "It was probably a front," said ClairBell late one night on the phone to Doro as she brought her sister up to date on Billy's relapse.

For all her sister's education—to ClairBell's way of thinking a mighty waste—Doro could be a big dunce. "A front for what?"

ClairBell made her voice dire. "Happy endings?" she repeated until Doro at last caught her drift and said, "Oh, no, I don't think so."

"Well, he looks like death warmed over," ClairBell said. "Who'd even want a massage from him?"

Doro sighed. "I don't know," she said, but then suddenly, sadly, she did.

It was a wonder he was getting around at all. The side effects of antiretroviral treatment had weakened him, and the hip replacements he'd had in more stable times had gone bad. He limped painfully. Macular degeneration and a bout of shingles had left him blind in one eye. For suffering that was genuine and unbearable he took the prescribed methadone, which he supplemented with benzos and oxy and vodka, cough syrup if these substances were scarce.

ClairBell tried to crack wise. "Looks like the Little Bad Wolf has checked himself into *re*-tox," but nobody laughed. The situation was grim. No one could live this way for long, least of all such a small man who was so sick already. From all appearances Billy had begun a decline that he couldn't recover from.

Because he would otherwise be on the street, Hattie, bucking all advice and Abel's glower, invited him home to live in the guest bedroom.

Jesse shook his head. "He's forty-fricking-seven, Mom."

ClairBell huffed. "Enabling again? What happened to tough love?"

Outraged, ClairBell phoned Doro, who said, "And we're surprised?" though if Doro were to tell the truth, she was. She had believed he could beat the beast. It was no comparison, she knew, but she had quit smoking. Going on almost a year. She crossed her fingers and wished she had a cigarette to celebrate with.

All were against the residency plan. Billy would burn down the house, either with forgotten Mavericks or with his midnight flambés or his crème brûlée torch, and the old ones would go up in smoke. Probably Billy himself, the very god of second chances, would escape the fire and live on. He'd deal drugs from the deck. Lowlifes would traipse through the yard. He'd turn Hattie into his drug runner. He would sell her, ClairBell said, for a nickel bag.

But Hattie only smiled. " 'Inasmuch as ye have done it unto the least of these . . .' And it's only until he gets back on his feet."

It was late November. Abel was growing more feeble, drawing his age about him with the tartan blanket he wrapped around himself like a stooped Highland laird. His youngest son's voice at the dinner table, droning in terrible monologues about food and wine and books and his plan to enroll in a fly-by-night massage "academy," set his teeth on edge. So did the clatter-bang-crash of Billy's late-night cooking and the missing beta-blockers and painkillers from his medicine lockbox, money from the wallet he left on his nightstand. He'd had to hide things all over the house and outside and then he couldn't find them himself. Any man would bark. As Abel waxed in anger and Billy in backslide, Hattie recited the Beatitudes. *Blessed are the peacemakers,* she whispered for strength, *for they shall become the children of God.* She'd settle for less if only the two wouldn't snipe.

A week into his stay, a certified letter arrived, addressed to Billy. It was a bench warrant for contempt signed by Judge B. Gerald Jameson, a colleague of Abel's. The year before, during the decline that led to detox and rehab, Billy had failed to appear in court on a forgery charge. He had stolen a blank check from Hattie's book, made it out to himself for two thousand dollars, and signed her name.

"Why can't we just forgive the debt?" Hattie had wanted to know when Abel discovered the theft. "He can pay us back."

"With what? The money you sneak him behind my back? He spends his disability check the minute it hits the bank."

To teach Billy a lesson, Abel pressed charges, badgering Hattie until she joined suit. Billy was served a citation, which he ignored, hence the warrant, now catching up to him.

Abel saw his chance to clean house. "We'll hand him over," he decreed from the kitchen stool where he stirred a bowl of fudge ripple ice cream to the consistency he liked. He'd been choking a lot lately and he'd been trying to keep his diet soft. "He'll have to go to jail. The law requires it."

Her back to him, Hattie washed dishes with a pointed slosh and splash. "The law now," she muttered. "So now it's the law."

When she made no audible answer, Abel persisted. "We need to show him we're in accord."

She scrubbed at a scorched pot. "Well, you may be in accord with yourself, but I'm not." She was treading on thin ice, she knew, but she didn't care.

"Then I'll get one of the children."

Abel stumped down the hallway to his boar's nest to think. Jesse was out of the question. He was currently sober but his time in the county DUI work-release program had left him with a grudge against the court system. ClairBell was square with the law except for a pending personal-injury lawsuit brought by some ambulance chaser she'd hired after a fender bender. The case was doomed, yet another of his daughter's nuisance suits to clog the docket and fan the flames of her martyr's fire. What she sought was the usual emolument, the healing application of a greenback poultice. For all her maddening ways, she was his favorite, but she wasn't a good candidate for the job. One, he couldn't control her; two, her jealousy of Billy might ignite; three, her habit of stump lawyering too often made her mouth run ahead of her hindparts. Gid was out. He'd come back from New Mexico after his bale hut burned under suspicious circumstances, but he had a hollow leg, a foul temper, and a hatred for what he called "the police state."

That left Theodora. If there was one thing he could depend on, it was that his eldest would try to please him. As a child she'd been a shy creature, sensitive and quick to cloud up. Early on, he supposed, he'd made her afraid of him. He knew this and he regretted it. When she was three he'd had to question her about Hattie's wedding and engagement rings, missing from the nail in the linen closet where she often kept them. It was the early fifties and they lived in a postwar crackerbox house near the law school. There'd been a terrible drought that summer and the bare dirt yards had cracked, leaving crevices that went down ten or so inches. He had a hunch that the child had dropped the rings down one of them. He searched with a flashlight but finally gave up and came inside. Hattie was in the nursery putting Nick and Doro to bed, listening to their "Now I lay me"s. He asked her to go over the last time she'd seen the rings.

"I put them on a hook in the linen cupboard last night, when I was soaking diapers, and now they're gone."

The rings had set him back a pretty penny. He'd been saving to buy a horse and he had his eye on a little roan, but instead he bought the rings so he could propose. To see that money buried in the dirt . . .

In summer pajamas printed with figures of Goldilocks and the three bears, Doro lay in the top bunk of the army-issue beds he'd painted blue. A hot breeze blew through the open window. Outside, locusts sawed.

"Sister, look at Daddy."

The child, frowsy-headed from near sleep, sat up, alert and watchful.

"You took Mommy's rings from the hook in the linen closet and you played with them, is that right?"

She shook her head and looked down. He went on. "But you saw the rings. They were pretty, weren't they? And you wanted them." He reached for her hands and held them and looked into her eyes, and there it was, the crack, the guilty flicker, the child's darting gaze. He had hit the truth.

He badgered her then, cross-examining the way he might a witness, employing the rhetorical strategies he'd learned in law school—Did you or did you not? Were you telling a fib then or are you telling a fib now?—trying to trick her into confession until she was mixed up and crying and finally Hattie had stopped him. "Abel, that's enough. She doesn't know where they are." The next day Hattie found the rings when she put away clean laundry, tucked among a stack of washcloths. He wasn't sure his daughter remembered the night—she'd been only three—but it seemed to him that since then she'd been ginger around him, skittish and wary. But he knew he could count on her to do right. Or at least do what he told her to do. He began to plan his strategy, and when she arrived from Boston for her pre-Christmas visit, he deputized her.

"Well, hot damn. It's tough love at last," ClairBell said when she heard about Abel's plan to turn Billy over to the court system. "Daddy's cracking down on him even if *she* won't. I'm proud of you, sister."

Doro's heart sank. When ClairBell was proud of her, it usually meant she was about to do something that would turn the bad-girl spotlight, the one that usually illuminated ClairBell, onto herself. This seemingly new problem—whether or not to help her father get her brother to jail—was the age-old coyote trap of her parents' crossed wills, and once again her do-gooding paw hovered over the snare. No matter whose will she upheld, she'd be wrong.

She spent the next day making herself scarce, claiming a bogus trip to the library and a lunch with friends in order to avoid Abel, but at last she decided to make good on her word. She told herself she would be a help to her brother, a buffer. She told Billy the same. She laid it out plain—it was this or the police would come to the house to arrest him, why not spare himself?—and he agreed to turn himself in.

Hattie was a mild woman, but she had a limit beyond which smart money didn't bet, and now she was angry past tolerance. Not at her husband, or at least not any more angry than usual, but at her daughter for taking his side. On the morning of the jailhouse trip she wondered aloud to Doro what would it hurt to drop the charges. Or not to have pressed them at all. Or to have *given* Billy a cash gift in the amount he'd stolen. "Or you?" she said darkly. "You could help. You've done well."

Doro studied the shredded wheat in her bowl. This was true—she had a good job, a light-filled apartment in Brookline, and her sagebrush-and-snakebite novels sold surprisingly well—but the time was wrong to say she'd done well by curbing her impulse to toss dollar bills into bottomless wells. Which wasn't true anyway, as she had indeed tossed her share, if well-made clothes and books and plane tickets and beautiful dinners counted. And the time wasn't right to admit to her famously frugal mother the alarming credit card debt she'd racked up. Not that she would, anyway—admit it. Certain things were best kept quiet. Doro dipped her spoon into the cereal and fished up a mouthful, which she used to forestall further talk. "Mm-hmm," she mumbled.

"Well, *I* have a date with a two-dollar ham" was Hattie's last dispatch as the jail-bound party made ready to leave. At the market the day before she had sorted through the bargain bin and found a whole boneless ham her Depression-era childhood wouldn't let go to waste. Ham cradled in one arm, she hugged Billy with the other and told him, "Honey, you don't have to go. They can't make you."

Already feeling the effects of the pre-jail dosing he'd done, Billy said, "It's all right, Mother."

Because her feelings often took on a surrogate, when Hattie vised the clamp mount of the cast-iron meat grinder to the kitchen counter and tightened the screws it was lost on no one that they bored into Abel's hard head and Doro's soft one.

Deciding that his little Dakota truck was too small for the errand, Abel took the wheel of the Skylark. Doro settled herself in front and Billy sat in back. They left town and drove north, taking Old 81. "America's Main Street, this road was once called," Abel said hopefully, instructively. "Runs from Minneapolis to Dallas, following approximately the Sixth Principal Meridian."

Doro thought something seemed off with the mission. Her father was too intent, as if this were his last chance to win the battle with his son, yet another hill to die on. Couldn't he see that Billy was a wraith, too sick to be jailed? Her brother weighed less than she did. He could barely walk. Surely the time for punishment was past. But she also believed that no one stood above the law, having learned this truth at Abel's knee. How many times had he said, "Do not presume to think you're above the law," as she and her brothers were growing up?

Hundreds, if it was one. And what if this time was the charm and in jail her brother would get help and the cycle would finally cease?

As they crossed the John Mack Bridge over the Ark River, Abel said, "Did you children know that in the thirties Indians coming up from Tonkawa refused to pay the bridge toll? Forded on horseback, they did. Right here."

"I should research that," Doro said, her mind elsewhere. Her work on pulp novels had made her alert for the plot twist, for the captive to bolt for the scrub. She stole a look to see if Billy showed signs of making a getaway, but he appeared to be sleeping.

Lulled by the warmth in the car—his father kept it cranked to Bikram level—Billy rested his head on the seat back. The opiates in his belly and the methadone in his nostrils assured him that time would pass no matter where he was, behind bars or in bed. Soon enough he'd be back at his blue-sky trades. This was a side trip, no more. He closed his eyes and entered the realm he thought of as Joyland, not an imagined place exactly, but a state of exquisite awareness that allowed him to range in memory, in present and past, to ponder the mysteries of blood and the story of himself on the planet.

Billy longed for illustrious ancestors. Not the yeomanry from whence he came, oh, no. Persons of good taste and an interest in art and music. His research into his genetic underpinnings yielded little in the way of a claim to brighter heritage, however. On a genealogy website he found family members who were descendants of the *Landed Gentry of Ireland in the Time of Cromwell,* Brian Boru, Anna of Hungary and Ferdinand I of Spain, Wenceslaus, Strongbow, and a long run of Spanish Habsburgs, but these lines appeared to wane in social class until they resulted in Hattie's mother's people, the Hensleys, who mingled with the Ennis line, which began in Ireland when a Sir John Ennis stowed away on a ship bound for the New World. Billy considered that this nobleman might be the seat of an auspicious connection, at least where a taste for fine things was concerned, but too soon he learned that Sir John had fled Ireland after murdering the tax collector. Billy had sighed so loudly that the library's other computer users had looked up.

The Hensleys and Ennises were farmers who moved west to Missouri, digging sassafras and ginseng and farming the flinty soil along the White River. One of the few early pictures of Hattie's mother showed a thin girl in a flour-sack dress posed on bare dirt, tornado-stripped trees spiking the white background sky, and three dog-like shapes in the shadowy foreground that on closer look were revealed to be free-ranging razorback hogs. Again he'd had to face things: hillbilly blood ran in his veins.

Hattie's mother at eighteen went to a church social where a stranger with high cheekbones, bad teeth, and brown eyes, one of them slightly inward-turned, bid high on her sour apple pie. Lorenzo Dow Davies had come across the plains and down into the Ozarks to buy some mules. His young first wife had deserted him, took their infant son and fled, and he was in that year of 1918 as much in the market for a wife as he was for a mule. His line began in the New World with a conscript from Cardiff, who embarked on a career of swearing so foul that it was noted in the annals of the Maryland penal colonies. A bounder, this conscript served only four years of his indentured servitude before he bolted. Whether the darkness that showed up in the family later, in a few cousins who suffered from mental illness, was the legacy of the first criminal it was impossible to say, but Billy's grandfather Davies possessed a hesitancy of being that spoke of some kind of family shame, as though he'd been burned early and badly.

Anyway, if he followed the chain of mitochondrial DNA he found clear title to membership in Haplogroup U5b1c, a genetic bottleneck that united Sami reindeer herders with Basque shepherds. And if he took the longest view, he could trace the chain of being that began in Africa and moved to an Iberian seacoast or the Arctic tundra, that traveled through Byzantium to the British Isles, bearing slowly westward, until it yielded the girl who would become his mother, who would come to a turning point in a school play yard in the cattle town of Wichita when she met a boy as scrappy and outspoken as her unknown great-great the foul-tongued conscript, a jug-eared, green-eyed, bandy-legged daredevil who was Abel Campbell and who would become her husband.

The Campbell line was Ulster Scots, sired by one Alexander, an old-school Presbyterian and a dour messenger of doom. His offspring became farmers, preachers, teachers, husbandsmen accustomed to the habits of hard work and thrift that led to plenitude in Lancaster County. Land proud and industrious, they liked their own ways so well that over the generations they took to marrying each other, until enough first cousins had conjoined to yield thirty-eight students to the Ohio School for the Deaf. Despite their mild inbreeding, the family ran to smugness, temperance, and piety, even zealotry. From this line came Billy's paternal grandfather, Oliver. In Oliver ran, along with piety, a terrible streak of mischief. In his youth in East St. Louis he learned the fighting Irish code of silence, to scrap and swear, to love a cold beer and a good fistfight. A big family story was that Oliver and a pal named Frankie McBride determined to disrupt a Billy Sunday revival by smuggling fireworks into the tent, planning to blast them off at altar call. The idea was to stampede the faithful like so many sheep and make the holy Joes think that Old Scratch himself was paying a visit. But the Campbell bent toward religion came out just in time when the preacher's words rolled away the stone that was young Oliver's heart and instead of the wild conflagration he'd planned he went forward, bawling like a motherless calf. On his way out of the revival tent he saw Alice Eliot handing out fliers for the Sunday School movement. She smiled and he was smitten.

The Eliots lived in a fine house on a shady street. They had household help, music lessons, and good horses, but there the niceties ended. Alice's father, Guy William Eliot, was a drinker and a rascal. He came of clannish folk that traced their history to the Border Reivers, criminals most. Alice's mother had a horror of spirits, and eventually developed a horror of her husband. After her last child was born, she drove him from the house. Rather than fall upon alms she made a meager living baking and selling pies. Alice forbade alcohol and all low activities.

So there was madness on the Davies side, striking some, missing others. Hensleys were shy and practical and not given to extremes of feeling. Campbells were proud, pompous, pugilistic. Eliots ran to extremes where drink was concerned, and also to gab and argument and guile. No matter how Billy put all these strains together, he wound up with mulligan stew. At the end of the line his parents, heedless of the perilous fit of alleles, mingled their DNA, begetting Doro, Nick, Jesse, ClairBell, Gideon, and himself. Surely, surely, surely, in all the souls that came before, there must have been some outlier, some kinsman, who would understand how it was with him. Someone to whom he could reach across the generations, for at times he felt like a lone boat adrift in a vast sea. A lone boat, he realized as the car pulled to a stop at a light, on its way to the county jail.

"All Great Plains rivers are a mile wide and an inch deep," Abel said to break the silence in the car, but no one responded. While his daughter gazed out the window and his son drowsed, he tried to still his jumbled thoughts, which centered on how hard he was finding it to drive. The well-traveled road seemed foreign, and it was as if another man, a weaker, older man with rabbit wire where once his mind had been, steered between the yellow lines. Among taco joints and tire stores he looked for the landmarks of his former life, the cattle auction grounds, the peach orchards, the salvage yard, but it was as if they'd never been. To ease his mind he flicked on the radio and the rest of the way as the prairie blurred past and the first clapboard bungalows appeared on the city's outskirts they listened to the public station's daily airing of *Boléro*.

He had once known the courthouse complex, but so much had changed that the map in his mind was off. He undershot the right street by a block, landing them in front of the old courthouse rather than the new. He parked anyway, playing off his error as intentional. He grabbed his cane from the foot well and said briskly, "I thought we'd take a look at the grand old lady."

Built of dressed limestone, the courthouse dated from the days just after Wyatt Earp. While they stopped to admire the stonework arches and arcades, Doro kept an eye on Billy, scanning the area to see which way he might hobble off. But he stayed close, drawing his Mavericks from his shirt pocket and shaking the pack her way. When she declined, he said, "Oh, that's right." He grinned devilishly, a flash of his old humor. "Quitter."

She had quit, but her mouth was parched. The gravity of what they were about to do lay heavily on her. She was putting her sick brother away, sending him to jail, and all for the privilege of doing right. Or was it because she wanted to please her father? Make peace in the house? She didn't know. Just one puff would calm her, would set her mind straight. But she'd vowed not to yield, even in the cuckoo's nest that was home, and so she shook her head. When Billy stubbed out his smoke they walked on.

The lobby had been newly blocked into zones and this, too, rattled Abel. They would have to pass a checkpoint. His children went to stand in line and he followed, watching so that when his turn came he would know what to do. His daughter set her handbag in a plastic tub. Her sunglasses and watch she put in a felt-bottomed container that looked like a church collection plate. His son placed his cigarettes, lighter, and wallet in a similar vessel. The children walked under a gantry and passed through to gather their effects. It was his turn.

There were three types of memory, he knew from reading an article in the journal *Science*: semantic, skill, and episodic. Somehow the obstacle he now faced was a puzzle of all three types and he couldn't think of what to do first. He fumbled with his tweed cap, and then decided to unbuckle his belted jacket. He took off the jacket and put it in a bin to go through the sensor. He rested his cane against the conveyor belt and dug in his trouser pockets.

An alarm sounded. At first he thought his hearing aid was squealing, but then the officer held up a horn-handled pocketknife, the boyhood rabbit-skinning knife he carried for luck. He tried to master his feelings, but his heart hammered against his chest wall. His cane clattered to the floor.

"Here, Pops." A female guard pulled him out of the line and patted him down, running her hands along his legs, groin, flanks, chest. His knees weakened, his belly pitched, his eyes went teary as he tried to remember the Fourth Amendment, the standards for unlawful search and seizure.

"It's almost over, old-timer," the guard told him. She helped him put himself back together and then handed him his cane.

When he was safe on the other side, Abel growled, "I've practiced here since the waters drew back and the ark came ashore. I'll old-timer *her*!"

Billy placed a hand on his shoulder. "Papa, do you need to sit down? There's a bench over there. Let's sit down a while." Billy led him to the bench, waited until he sat, and then took a seat beside him.

This kindness unmanned Abel. Billy's finest trait was compassion. To the halt, the suffering, the needy, the broken-winged, the boy's heart had always gone out. This nicked at Abel's own heart, as he shared the trait and had long tried to hide it in the interest of manliness. It wasn't too late to put a stop to the errand he just now couldn't remember the importance of, to turn around and go home. For a long moment he considered, but then he remembered the principle he wanted, even at this late date, to stand for. "Let's get done what we came to do."

Back at home, Hattie had come to the end of the ham. Her grinding arm quivered, her blouse sagged with sweat, and pink mounds of ground ham rose high as her sorrow at the cruelties her youngest, her gentlest boy had endured. He'd been bullied in school. In their cowboy-and-roustabout town he'd been mocked. And his treatment at home, by his own father, was callous. Abel hadn't wanted their late-in-life child, held disdain for the purses and jewelry and dolls, the Easy-Bake ovens the little boy loved. His father and brothers and sisters saw only his crimes, but she saw past the shame to his suffering. She wasn't a crier, but she put her face in her blistered, fat-slippery, ham-smelling hands, drew a deep breath, and let it out in slow, ragged spurts.

At the courthouse, the elevator doors opened and the delegation rode up. Doro thought she might have to do the talking when they reached the jail's intake counter, and so she stepped briskly toward it, but after his slump her father had recovered. He handed over the warrant to the officer, his voice again strong. "This is my son, presenting as ordered."

When Billy stepped forward, extending his wrists for handcuffs, his fingers for the ink pad, Doro had to turn away. He looked so small, so thin. He was the baby brother she'd sung to, the infant whose plump cheeks she'd kissed with a love so strong it had weakened her knees. She understood suddenly that while Billy was doing this for their mother, to lighten Abel's pressure on her, he was also doing this for her, so that he might do right in her eyes. The words "like a man" came to her, the highest praise of their male-centered family applied to its least so-called manly member, and even though she saw the words as retrograde and even insulting, somehow they applied. Courage, it was, rather, or gallantry maybe—his choice not to make a scene. Or was it grace? When she turned back around to wave, he was gone.

Already on his way out, Abel hurried along the hallway. Doro followed him as he took the elevator to a lower floor and stopped at a courtroom's double doors. When he saw B. Gerald Jameson's nameplate he removed his cap and entered, motioning her to follow. They took seats at the rear.

Abel intended to speak to his old colleague. It seemed wrong to be in the city after so many years away and fail to pay a courtesy call. As he settled into his seat, a rise of almost-forgotten power returned to him. He wasn't sure what it was—rightness, order, the satisfactions of ritual?—but whatever it was he had missed it. Why had he left the practice of law? He was as fit-minded as the day he'd been admitted to the bar. And it mattered, the law. In the ruin of his family life, the sorrows and disappointments, the low doings of his children, he sometimes forgot.

Before the bench a tattooed longhair with eyebrow piercings was being arraigned on a charge of growing five or more marijuana plants, a felony. "Why didn't the stupid kid stop at four?" he whispered to Doro. "If you're going to break the law, aim for the misdemeanor." He had nudged his daughter to make certain she took his point before he remembered that she was the only one of his children who needed no instruction. Like her mother, she would obey a law even if it was wrong. Or so he told himself; sometimes he wondered if behind her law-abiding mask there lurked a criminal mind—she was certainly smart enough, and some of the plots in her shoot-'em-up books might point to a nefarious streak.

When the docket was empty he hooked his cane over the seat back and stood. "Your Honor, may I approach the bench?"

Judge Jameson took off his reading glasses. "Why, if it isn't Abe Campbell," he called out warmly. "Approach."

Though it made his neck ache to look up at his former colleague as they spoke, Abel felt readmitted to the inner circle of justice. They talked of times gone by in a town that revered its rogues, the fighting Hallacy brothers and the Pappas boys. The arsonist Gus Pappas had recently died, not by the sword he lived by, but by falling down his basement stairs at the age of ninety. Old Pappas had been convicted of gambling, racketeering, assault, burglary, larceny, and arson, but he was generous, charming, beloved of waitresses, widows. He'd written his memoirs, had run for city council, was mourned. "By God, they don't make crooks like that anymore," Abel said.

Talk of the sainted old outlaw had loosened his tongue and he found himself saying, "Your Honor, a boy of mine's up on the sixth floor for failure to appear. When he comes before you, deal with him as you would any other. I ask no special treatment."

With his spine held straight he took his leave, retrieved his cane and his daughter, and went down to reclaim his knife.

All the way home he was in high spirits. His mind had returned to working order. He flexed his hands on the steering wheel. "I ever tell you about the Clutter murder trial out in Finney County? Hickok and Smith?"

Doro's mood rose to meet his. He'd spoken of the trial many times—she'd been eleven when the murders gripped the state—but she wanted to hear the story again. She'd read *In Cold Blood* more than once and could recite the opening lines. And she loved it when he told stories, her ear tuned for sixty years to his syntax, his figures of speech, the timbre of his voice. It was then that any uneasiness she felt around him went away.

"Nineteen sixty," he began. "My partner Red was the best trial lawyer in the region, bar none. A bona fide barn fire, he was. Out there on the high plains the local guns were having a shoot-out with due process and Red decided to pin a star on himself and out west he went with his chest puffed up like a little cock grouse. High-handed around, I'd lay odds, and hound-dogged those farm girls, no question. Took off at a trot when the whiskey bell rang."

"He met Truman Capote, didn't he?"

"Hated him on sight and the feeling was mutual. Had nothing to do with the trial. They were both little squirts, around the same stature, and this made them so peeved with each other there was no remedy but to square off and fight."

"They had a fistfight?" Doro supplied the line he waited for.

"Venomous-look fight. But a damned bloody business. Two bantams."

When they passed a Harbor Freight Tools store Abel considered a stop to buy his daughter a miniature flashlight or a lady's set of screwdrivers to reward her for her loyalty, but decided against the plan—it was late and Hattie would have dinner waiting. His wife could be angry, she could hold a grudge, but night after night for more than sixty years she had laid a fine table. Eagerly, he resumed speed.

Doro looked out the window as the fields and farms of the countryside appeared. There was a bridge, she saw, from the topic of their conversation to her telling him—or at least alluding to—the truth of her being, the half closet she could not bring herself to come out of, not even to Billy. It had gotten too late to tell her brother. So many years she'd failed to tell the truth that to do so now would be like admitting a lie she'd been telling for years, which would make it worse. And would her silence be a rebuke of his choices? Would her telling? It was confusing. At the bottom of it all she felt as if she were betraying him.

As for her father, she wasn't sure how she would sound saying it, what words she would use, how he would react. He wouldn't like it, that much was certain. Would he pretend equanimity but secretly judge, and would this add yet another layer to the strangeness between them? To come out and say it now would be a mark of honor, she supposed, an acknowledgment more in keeping with the principles she wanted to live by, at least in the abstract sense, of honesty and disclosure. But in the walkabout world things weren't always so clear.

Too much time had gone by, she decided. Her father was too old to hear it. Her mother too. It would only hurt them. And what would they do with the knowledge anyway? And what did she have to prove? She should have done it long before, but the truth was also that she hadn't really known who she was until she was well into her fifties and finally came into herself, safely away from her family. She lived a quiet, celibate life, happy with friends, happy with work. Her children knew; she had told them. But the Amicus family? Nobody had asked. It was as though what constituted her innermost self was immaterial to her existence, at least in their minds. Still, she couldn't blame them. To them she was Doro, big sister, who tried with all her might to be perfect but always fell short.

To keep her father on subject, she said, "So was it a fair trial, eventually?"

He took a long time considering. "No," he said, "probably not. But it was a fair hanging."

Dusk was coming on when they reached the driveway. The porch light was off. Inside, Hattie sat at the barren kitchen table, mending one of Billy's shirts. "What's for dinner?" Abel asked, casing the open refrigerator. "Where'd you hide all that ham?"

Hattie smiled grimly. "Frozen. Rock-solid. But there's tomato soup"—she nodded toward the counter—"in that can." She bit off a thread. "You know where the can opener is. And there are sheets on the couch. For you."

In the middle of the night Doro woke up and couldn't get back to sleep. She drew on her robe and crept down the hall to snag a Maverick from Billy's spare pack. She found a book of matches and then slipped outside. The night was chilly, the heavens clear. In a few days she would board a plane back to the life she'd made, a life unclouded by messes legal or moral, a life that fit her better, where she didn't have to pretend to be something she wasn't. Still, the day, for all its tensions, had had its moments. Seeing, in the midst of addiction, the ghost of her brother's old dignity. The companionable ride home with her father, and the absence, for just a moment, of the shadow that sometimes clouded their interactions, the shadow that made it hard to meet his gaze. Being of use, doing right.

Standing behind the armillary sphere her father had welded, its iron arrow pointing toward Polaris, she tried to remember the explanation he'd given when she was twelve of the difference between true north and magnetic north. Then she wondered what he had meant about fair trials and fair hangings. Failing at both mysteries, she resolved to think large thoughts about families, about fathers and daughters and mothers and sons, the secrets they kept from each other and the impossibility of knowing each other, but her mind was running on fumes and eventually she gave up, lit the cigarette, and smoked, enjoying it as if no time at all had passed since her last one, seeing stars. Words that had stirred her when she first read them came into her mind. *Which of us has known his brother? Which of us has looked into his father's heart? Which of us has not remained forever prison-pent?* She tried to blow a smoke ring but a breeze came up and tore it away.

The next morning when the telephone rang, Hattie answered. "Oh!" she said, covering the mouthpiece to tell Doro that Billy had been released from jail. Into the phone she said, "Oh, honey, honey, honey! That's just wonderful news!"

Doro smiled weakly, smiled falsely. She took her coffee to the couch to brood, the couch newly vacated by her father, who had moved to his den. Why had they gone through the painful charade only to see Billy released the next day? Once again she'd been lured into trying to help. Next time she would heed her daughter's warning: "Mother, give up. It's Amicus. It's your family. Where two's company and three turns into an intervention."

So, okay, she knew this, and maybe the quip was funny, but at the next crisis her drunken, enabling, junkie, jailbird kin could deal with themselves on their own. To think she could help them was folly. And why was she the only one not mired in drink or drugs or criminal behavior? It beggared reason and it beggared chance. And if she lived to be a hundred, she would not know why she was not the favorite. Quickly, she brushed away this last thought. It was juvenile. Favoritehood was ClairBell's bailiwick, her life's song. But, really, she was weary of being the only halfway-adjusted one. Sneaking a smoke? That was bush league. Back east, when she spoke of her family, people thought she was embellishing, casting them as colorful misfits. She'd begun to hide the truth that all three of her living brothers as well as her dead one were felons and that her sister was an opium-eating professional plaintiff who claimed, in utter seriousness, to breed rabbits with cats. Cabbits. Doro still couldn't get over that one. The stuff of their lives was too crazy to be made up, too comic if it weren't so heartbreakingly true. But nobody laughed, except for her, sometimes, when she tried to get through a tale so low-rent and ridiculous it would actually hurt if she couldn't bend it toward farce. The time ClairBell's tract house collapsed onto the warren of rabbit tunnels beneath it. The time Gid, tanked up on tallboys, ran his hoopty into a snowbank and in fear of cops finding his stash began hurling the beers into snowdrifts, accidentally hurling his car keys as well, not to be found until thaw. The time Jesse, drunk-jealous, broke into a romantic rival's house and installed a spavined old buckskin gelding in the other man's bedroom. Her father blowing hot and cold, her father and his on-again, off-again grudges, prototype for ClairBell though no one would say this aloud, her father with his sliding scale of crime, declaring no one above the law and then handspringing over it as though it were a vaulting horse. Her father, talking of how to get around the law, of knowing the law so you knew how to break it. No wonder his children were messed up. And the everlasting adventures of Billy, free spirit and freelance masseur, and his church-lady sidekick, her mother. What else was it but farce? She'd tried for years to figure out how her family had gone so wrong. And then she felt guilty for holding herself apart. The fact was that there was simply no way to be in any of it. Except maybe absent. Part of their troubles she blamed on crackpot ancestry, an amalgam of outlaws and saints, libertines bred with teetotalers, evangelists with madmen. Part she blamed on the town, on scrappy little hardscrabble

Amicus, a town that had never figured out what it wanted to be when it grew up, and part she blamed on ordinary bad luck. But fault didn't matter; they were who they were and nobody changed.

And maybe the worst of all of it was that she knew she was as bad as the rest for not changing. At the next sign of trouble she would mount her white horse and take to the skies, touch down again on the plains, her same sorry, duty-bound self, clan member as cracked as the next come to save their small world from itself, that worry—and not only worry but need, specifically the need to be good—no, it was worse, the need to be *seen* as good—would see her trolling Orbitz late of a sleepless night, paying too high a price for a too-crowded flight to a place where the most unchanging truth of all was that the darker her brothers' and sister's deeds the brighter her gleam. No, she didn't just have to be *good*; she had to be *better*. Even worse, she had to be *best*.

This sudden sad truth scalded her up off the couch. What *was* this old need? Where had it come from? What did any of them want but to be loved and how was she any different? She went into the kitchen to try to atone.

Her mother hung up the phone. "Billy needs a ride from the bus stop," she said, reaching for her handbag and trying to tuck wayward strands into her French twist. "I won't be long."

To reset her good-daughter button, Doro stepped forward. "Would you like me to go, Mom? I'm happy to." Appallingly, *appallingly,* this last was true.

Her mother's smile was radiant. "Oh, no, I want to." Her look darkened. "Besides," she said flatly, "you've done enough."

Hattie had set aside the brisket she was trimming, but before she got on the road she decided to take Abel a conciliatory treat, some V8 juice in his favorite drinking vessel, a squat iridescent green salmon can he'd rescued from the recycle bin. "Much good use left in this worthy little can," he'd said. He'd buffed the can's rim to perfection and soldered his initials onto the side, and he maintained that the can held the cold better than any juice glass. The ridiculous can irritated her and she hid it in a high cupboard so he couldn't find it, but now she fished it out with a wire hanger, washed it, and filled it. She went to his den and kissed his temple. "Thank you, Abel," she told him, patting his arm.

"Thank *you*," he said, pleased. Tears welled, the easy tears of old age, he knew. His wife wasn't given to showing affection and the truth was that for all the years of their marriage, no matter how bristly or cantankerously he'd behaved, he had craved it. He smiled and reached for her hand. "To what do I owe this heartwarming change?"

She was too happy to draw back her hand. "He has a new court date! He's free. His bail was only a dollar!"

Dimly Abel recollected the day before. "But I didn't . . ." His voice trailed off along with his vanished thought. He meant to say that he'd done nothing to tamper with justice but then he wasn't certain he hadn't. He thought he'd told B. Gerald he wanted no special treatment. Maybe his old colleague hadn't paid attention, or had assumed he was angling for clemency. Hell, if he *had* done something to fix the outcome and his bride was this happy, he'd wear that laurel wreath gladly. He would sooner perish than let her know the power she held, but his most guarded secret was that despite his bravado, despite his insistence on cock-of-the-walk, he had lived all the years of their marriage—he lived still and he would to the end—to be large in her eyes.

"You didn't what?" Hattie searched his face for a clue as to how he'd meant to finish his sentence but saw only a look that was part pride and part puzzlement, a lost, yearning look, his eyes hooded, confused. A memory lapse. She'd been watching him for signs, had seen many in the past years, but this was the first one that moved her to pity. To cover the sudden sharp ache in her chest, she gave a bright, brush-it-off look and said, knowing it cost her nothing to let him save face, and feeling, in the moment, like the most blessed of peacemakers and all's right with the world, "You can't fool me, Mister Fox. You knew all along it would turn out just fine!"

Abel beamed.

Later that morning as Hattie settled Billy in the guest bedroom, she hummed a low song whose words only she knew. They had to do with her devotion and its wellspring. Her last-born was more than her child. He'd been her companion, her joy. Not once in his life had he spoken an unkind word. With his bright ways and lighthearted wit he alone made her laugh. Truly laugh. He teased. With easy affection he could sling his arm over her shoulders, pull her toward him like a boon companion. With him she forgot to be stern and contained, but rather returned to herself as a girl, her lost self. And somehow he drew from her the love she'd prayed all her life to be filled with, helped her know that such love was made not from sacrifice but from grace, the mirror of heavenly love she'd pledged as a girl to live by. For such beauty what else could she give but her all? It was true that he was an accident, a slip, and she had brought him into the world against her better judgment, but it wasn't guilt that led her to soften his falls. It was love, and it bore all, believed all, it hoped all, endured all. Her self-help-book daughters could talk of tough love until heaven fell down; hers was tougher. She had guarded his birth; she would be there for his death, whenever, however, it came. She hoped she would be forgiven for praying that it would come soon, as a mercy, for he would never be—never be—well. She would not again stand in his way. He could take what he wanted, he could do what he wanted, no matter the cost and no matter how wrong. His death she would bear as her troth. She was that weak and that strong, called to one purpose, one only, and this was to be his mother, not his counselor, not his conscience, not his judge.

When she returned from the kitchen she saw that he'd dry-swallowed the pills and was at rest, breathing slowly and deeply, his hands folded over his narrow chest. His cheeks were sunken and there was new gray in the stubble on his jaw. She placed the water glass on his bedside table and then took a long time neatening the prescription bottles, lining them up like watchmen at vigil, like bearers of myrrh at the tomb, and quietly closed the door.

As she passed Abel's den on her way back to the kitchen, she heard him call out to her, "Hattie."

She stood in his doorway. "What is it? Are you hungry? Can I fix you something to eat?"

"I know what you're thinking."

Her heart seemed to jump in her throat. "You do?"

He flicked off the television set and the picture died. "I do." He looked at her over his glasses, the better to frown on her plan. "And he can't stay here."

Four

Many years before he was diagnosed with the disease that would take him from the world, Abel had made a plan to end his life. If Hattie went first, or when he'd lost enough of himself to see no other way, he would go out on his own terms—Brahms on the machine barn radio, his Sig Sauer P238's chamber loaded, 8-mil polyvinyl sheeting laid out on the concrete floor. Instead, on a snowy Sunday morning in his ninetieth year, he lay bed-bound in the ICU of the Robert J. Dole Memorial Veterans Administration Medical Center, too weak and confused to do away with himself.

No one imagined he would have lived so long; he'd been a sickly child. When he was ten he'd come down with pneumonia, for which there was no cure. He was put to bed in the farmhouse kitchen, next to the stove, tucked in with an ailing Poland China piglet his older sisters had named Lizzie Glutz. Boy and pig had lived, and the illness hadn't stopped him as a youth from acts of daring or as a man from taking risks. Twice he'd broken his back, once on Saipan during the war and once years later when he'd brought a little Cessna to a soft crash landing in a Mississippi cotton field but had then pinwheeled into a levee. He'd survived strafing from Zeroes, septic shock from a chainsaw gash. Walked five country miles with an appendix near rupture. Screaming a 650 BSA with a wide-open throttle down a macadam road, he'd hit an armadillo and gone flying, his leathers scraped to lining but not one broken bone. He'd been a rakehell, to his family larger than life, but now he lay stricken by myasthenia gravis, a disease that a few months before he'd not known existed, and felled by the pneumonia bacterium that had nearly claimed him as a boy.

Doro and ClairBell sat quietly beside his bed, a temporary truce called in their long war to win his regard. Hattie, too worried and fretful to sit down, tried to aim herself in two directions at once—to fetch a box of tissues and to turn off the glaring overhead light. She couldn't make up her mind and so she rocked in place, her skirt swaying about her still-trim knees as if the bluebirds printed on the fabric might carry her away.

In the high-ceilinged hospital room, with its frosted glass and wire-mesh window, the anticlot stanchions around his legs gasped and wheezed, their rhythm seeming to close in on him in a way that felt urgent, imparting the sense that before he died something monumental needed to be said. Of his four sons, three were still living, and he wanted to make things right with the two who weren't yet lost to him, and so he sent away the women and called for the boys, who waited down the hall, engaged in the dependably satisfying pastime of cataloging his faults.

Jesse and Gideon had become old men themselves, not quite retirement age but closing in. Of the two, Jesse was the smaller. Some of his stature had to do with legs that had bowed from years of breaking horses, but most had come through heredity; in his youth Abel had been a wiry, compact customer. Jesse's thick hair and beard had gone salt-and-pepper, mostly salt. Gideon was longer-boned and had more girth. He had surrendered to the monk-tonsure baldness of the men of

Hattie's side by shaving the rest of his head. Both men wore glasses in an aviator style popular some decades before. Tipped back in their chairs, boots on the radiator, and drinking hospital coffee from Styrofoam cups—Gid had doctored his with vodka from a flask but Jesse had been sober almost three years and would take no chances, as the court-ordered blow and go had just been removed from his truck and his driving restrictions had at last been lifted—they groused companionably about their father's failings. Speaking of the Danish-designed tractor sitting in ruin in Abel's barn, they discussed ways this Jacobsen might be redeemed and used to scrape the driveway so their mother's Skylark could get in and out during the long Great Plains winter.

Seeking a laugh, Gid had just finished mimicking an announcer's voice to say, "Abel Campbell, Esquire, Attorney-at-Law. Putting the 'diss' in dysfunction for over fifty years."

They snorted, but drew up short when their sisters entered and ClairBell said tearfully, "Daddy wants to see you boys."

At first the brothers feared they'd been overheard. This was an old feeling: The Judge knew all, saw all, his the radiant All-Seeing Eye of Providence that gilded his Masonic ring's ruby.

Powering through a hangover, Gid uncapped his coffee cup and swirled the dregs, peering at the pattern as if to read the future. "What does he want?"

It was Super Bowl Sunday, Packers vs. Steelers, and what Gid wanted was to get ready for the party he'd planned in the game room in Jesse's barn. He'd already thawed five pounds of ground venison laced with beef fat, stocked spirit as well as herbal provisions, and now he needed to head to the market for chili powder and two #10 cans of pinto beans. As a statement of the contempt he held for government and a sign of his outlaw sense of irony, he'd worn his stolen Bureau of Alcohol, Tobacco, and Firearms ball cap, but in the lobby when he passed the statue of Bob Dole, native son and his father's law school classmate, and saw the old warhorse's withered arm cast strong and whole and healed in bronze for eternity, he had thought again. Sudden shame at his own lack of sacrifice for any cause larger than dirty blues, good weed, and cold tallboys led him to remove the cap, which he tucked in his bomber jacket pocket. Now he put it back on as armor to face his father. Already Jesse had hung his black Resistol on the rack so he wouldn't be sentenced to the electric chair for the crime of wearing a hat indoors. Gid would be the one to fry, but Gid had already decided he didn't care. It was his damn hat and his damn head.

"Any idea what it's about?" Jesse asked ClairBell. He feared another of the Judge's confusing potlatches, the contradictory behests that set the brothers and sisters squabbling. Over nothing more than stuff, most of it dinged-up. Bottom of the line on everything except for a few prizes. Of the machine hulks overgrown with bindweed and wild buckwheat rusting in the salvage yard behind the machine shop, he liked to joke that his father had created his own private Great Depression. Of the few genuinely valuable items, his father had made gifts of the same full-quill ostrich dress boots to two sons and a brother, the same Kubota tractor and its implements to one brother, one son (himself), and one son-in-law. He'd promised the same Henry .30-30 rifle to two grandsons, a nephew, and a perfect goddamned stranger who had come to help him straighten out the snafu he'd made of Dish Network. Jesse worried that the Kubota he actually wanted would again be used as a chit in the endless give-and-take-back of his father's forgetful last years. Jesse's claim on the tractor was strong—he boarded horses and farmed fifteen acres in truck—but ClairBell was famously grabby, buzzarding over the inventory of their parents' possessions. She had her eye fixed on the Henry for one of her sons, the boots for another, and the Kubota and its nine shop-made implements for Randy.

ClairBell pinched her nose with a tissue and blew gustily. "Brothers, he's saying his good-byes. He knows it's the end." She broke into tears, turning to Jesse to weep into the collar of his sheepskin barn coat.

Jesse patted her back, his mind on the way the Judge ruled the roost and how the rest of the family flushed at every strut and crow. Their mother's way was to submit to his will, with rare but terrible instances of revolt. Despite Doro's education and the distance that should have inoculated her, their eldest sister mostly played dumb. She would smile sweetly when their father made his grandiose claims—"I've piloted every plane the army ever made"—because it was safer to pretend he was joking than to risk an argument for which the outcome was ordained, the loser certified. Jesse and Gid made do by staying downwind, and with their bull sessions. And probably, Jesse reckoned, with the drug and alcohol problems that plagued them. When he was sober, Billy would sometimes write their father rift-mending letters, saying how he'd always looked up to him. These letters were met with polite but strained thanks, for the Judge eschewed sentiment, especially when expressed in a gush, and so Billy had given up. It wasn't that his children didn't love him—they did, and it could be fairly said that his daughters had elevated him to a stature reserved for folk heroes and his sons had reasons to admire his accomplishments—it was that he was next to impossible to get along with. Even their long-dead brother, Nick, had left a journal detailing his rage at being continually one-upped by the old man. Only sturdy little ClairBell approached him on his own terms, standing up to him snout to snout like a stiff-legged yap dog, fighting him bark for bark.

And only ClairBell showed her feelings, Jesse thought as she sniffled on. Because their father hated emotional outbursts, to avoid displays of feeling or even direct statements thereof they'd learned to hide themselves away to brood or exult in silence. ClairBell wore her moods fearlessly, the way she wore her yard-sale caftans. Today's rig-out was red with black silhouettes of bears and moose and pine trees, and today's feelings, Jesse would bet the Kubota and all nine shop-made goddamned implements, were (1) thrill at the deathbed drama, for ClairBell loved nothing better than spectacle, (2) sorrow at the old man's decline, for she was his pet, (3) resolve to stage an eleventh-hour full-court press for the carved Morris chair she'd long campaigned for, and (4) a nose out of joint at Doro for blowing into town to hog the medical limelight when it was she, ClairBell, who claimed to be a trained nurse. Doro had once been married to Doctor Bob, who before the failure of his health had practiced at this very hospital. For this reason the doctors deferred to her, gave updates to her, and this singed ClairBell's feathers; she had told the fiction of her medical training so often that she had come to believe it herself, even when reminded that her claim was based on a six-week stint as a nursing home psych aide, playing Yahtzee with stroked-out patients. Lately she'd been floating another whopper that she was EMT-certified but that there was some mix-up with the paperwork and this was why she didn't actually have the piece of paper. This was typical ClairBell—another lie standing at the ready when the first was debunked. Jesse sighed. All of them were messed up and the fault could be laid at the Judge's door.

His boots were still wet from his dawn trek to crack the ice in the stock tank, and he wriggled his toes to gin up his circulation. Gid should have done the chore. The deal was that for providing living quarters now that Gid had returned from New Mexico Jesse would get some help with the horses. So far Gid's contribution had been to stock the barn's fridge with Budweiser, stash a Red Man pouch filled with pot under a saddle stand, and station himself in front of the game room television in a burn-pocked La-Z-Boy, presumably to keep the recliner from sprouting legs and walking off.

At last ClairBell broke away to check her image in the vending machine's glass and to rummage in her satchel for a tissue. "Ask him yourselves what it's about," she snapped as she dabbed at a clump of mascara. "Do I look like a fortune teller?"

Jesse blinked. ClairBell's moods could spin like Linda Blair's head.

Gid made a show of eyeballing her festive outfit and putting a finger to his chin in an attitude of comic pondering. "Now that you mention it . . ."

"Stuff it, Gideous," snapped ClairBell. "Is that rotgut I smell on your breath?" She huffed onto a pleather chair. "I wouldn't go lighting any matches." Encouraged by laughter from Jesse and Doro, she went on. "Speaking of matches, how about Gid's breath and buffalo flatus?"

Gid had to laugh. With her North Woods getup and her silver-gray hair done up in a curlicue wiglet their sister looked like a little plump Mrs. Santa with the berserker gaze of Cruella de Vil. He snickered at the image but composed himself when their mother returned from her trip to the ladies' room.

Fiddling with the hasp of her pocketbook in a nervous *pick-click,* Hattie smiled at her sons. "Your father wants a word with you." She *pick-clicked* again, but soon her mind had moved past her husband and onto their missing boy, Billy, lame and cold and sick out in the blizzard on what might be the day of his father's death. She wished she had bought a calling card for the new phone she'd bought for him. Then she remembered he'd lost the phone. She wondered if maybe she should front him some more money to replace the phone, which he'd left at . . . oh, somewhere she couldn't get straight, his tale of losing it was so confusing. She would have to conceal the purchase from Abel, as usual, by using the secret bank account she'd set up for emergencies like these. That was: if Abel lived. The thought occurred to her that if he died she could help Billy with no interference, no lectures, but she quickly banished it. God forbid, God *forbid.* She would happily stay caught between her husband and her son until kingdom come if it meant keeping the peace. *Blessed are the peacemakers,* long habit supplied, *for they shall be called the children of God. Pick-click* went her fingers on the pocketbook hasp.

The brothers left the waiting room. Neither had an idea of what the old man would say. Maybe, Jesse thought, he would give them some last instructions. Take care of their mother, sell the house, auction the contents of his bursting machine barn and shop, thanks, keep the change. What he hoped to hear was apology, a confession that their father had been a tyrant, a blowhard, a know-it-all, and that he had broken his sons as surely as if he'd beaten them with his basswood Indian club.

The night before, in an episode of hospital psychosis, Abel had torn out his IV and tried to yank out his NG tube. "Sundowning," the doctor had told Doro, who kept track of medical developments on her iPhone. "Hospital psychosis. He's seeing shadow people." The night nurses, veteran corpsmen of Iraq and Afghanistan, had to bulldog him.

Secured in a Posey, Abel hectored them about his constitutional rights until he nodded off. Now, waiting for his sons to enter, he drowsed his way upward out of Ativan. Distant voices seemed to play like blurred music, a static crackle, and in the snowy reception of his mind he determined that when the boys arrived he would tell them . . . something. He closed his eyes and gave his efforts to arranging his speech.

He loved the silken song of syntax, the warp and weft of rhetoric, language and its turns, and he tried at first to array his thoughts into the elegant forms of case law. For a time, unbidden, the bloodthirsty oath of Freemasonry played in his mind: *I most solemnly and sincerely promise and swear . . . binding myself under no less penalty than that of having my throat cut from ear to ear, my tongue torn out by its roots, and buried in the sands of the sea, at low water mark, where the tide ebbs and flows twice in twenty-four hours,* etc.

His sons were at odds with him for reasons long distilled: at everything he set his hand to he'd been an ace. A crack shot, an electronics and radio whiz, he'd mastered control of vehicles wheeled, tracked, winged, bladed, and hulled. He sculpted in stone, forged in iron. He'd landed trophy fish in the Dry Tortugas, skinned rabbits and deer, once an elk in Montana, once a bear near Hudson Bay. All game he dressed out and consumed, wasting not. He could butcher a steer. Scald a hog. Name in Latin the insects, grasses, trees, and reptiles of the Great Plains. He'd fought a war, guided the setup of a radio tower on Saipan. He was at home in the limitless geography of space. Quantum mechanics, hydraulics, firearms, particle physics—name a subject and he kept himself informed. He had a prodigious memory. But foremost among his strengths was his command of language, which he could wield as balm or cudgel. Too often, he knew, it had been the latter. When his sons took issue with something he said, with the force of a juggernaut he laid waste to their logic, brought them low, the battlefield strewn with shards of their pride while he prevailed lord of all things, silently hated what he was doing, but couldn't make himself stop. For the boys to be healed of their bitterness, he decided, he would have to speak humbly. To try one last time to talk past his own outsized ego, of which he was well aware and which topped his long list of regrets, to tell them he loved them and ask their forgiveness.

As boys Jesse and Gid had understood that their father meant to teach them how to be men, but decades of failure had weakened their willingness to learn from a man who appeared to think they could do little right. They took his lessons as insults and repaid him in kind. Even if he survived—he was Evel Knievel, Houdini; he *might*—in the dementia that had been worsening for years he was on his way out. He'd already gone past his time as a capable mechanic, and they'd drawn guilty pleasure from the signs of his slowdown, cutting each other looks when he'd wrongly accused them of grand larceny because he was convinced that Jesse and Gid, as they cleaned up a flood of sewage caused by his own jackleg plumbing repair, had suctioned up three gold coins from his homemade floor safe, which consisted of a Hills Bros. coffee can set in cement and secured with a dime-store padlock that any fool with a hacksaw could breach. The coins had been found later, just where he'd hidden them, stashed between the floor joists in his ham shack. Machinery once fine was now a wrack of wrongheaded repairs, the house on the creek a hazard of jury-rigged wiring, of carpentry patches so crude it looked as if a child had played hammer-and-saw. Good angle iron and argon arc welding wire: mangled to fashion contraptions of harebrained design and dubious use. Vintage ham radio gear cannibalized for parts and, from the look of the strewn tubes and gizmos, by squirrels. Over his three-acre domain fluttered Post-it notes in his shaky scrawl, all headed with legalese. *Know all men by these presents that my electronic gear is to be sold to Dish Vance, who will not cheat seller of said gear.* Or, *To all to whom these presents shall come: Let Fred Epps get his hands on a single one of these guns, you'll answer to my glowering ghost.*

Some of the notes brought them almost to pity. One Post-it, timed and dated 2:28 A.M., October 10, 2009, read: *My dearest bride Hattie, I may have accidentally swallowed a hearing aid battery. If by morning I have ceased to draw breath, look no further than this for the cause.* But the impulse to pity would be dashed by: *I have hidden six Krugerrands in a place known only to me. Should I forget the location, a clue can be found in the Latin name of the sharp-shinned hawk and said name will spur recollection by me and no one else.* All he had once known and ached not to forget—lists of stars and constellations, sheaves of runic pages in Morse code, handwritten catalogues of the Greek alphabet and the Dewey Decimal System and WWII radio relay phonetics—everywhere on foolscap left over from his years on the municipal bench was littered the desperate evidence of a once brilliant mind off its rails.

The men entered his room. "Hello, Dad," said Jesse. Awkwardly, Gid patted Abel's knee.

"Same side of the bed, if you would," Abel said weakly. He waited while they drew up chairs. "At ease, men," he said, a nod to the drill commands he'd used when they were boys, an appeal, he hoped, to nostalgia. He reached for their hands, but neither seemed to notice and he had to say, "Give me your hands, boys." When they gave them, he gripped tightly.

Only to shake it had Jesse recently held this hand. Now the feel of it, even taped and tethered as it was to the IV bag, sent a flare to his memory. This hand had shot out to stay him in the days before seat belts when the old man would take them on the wild careens he called Rough Rides, had held him onto the first Honda 50, covered his smaller one to turn the wrench to fit the bigger sprocket, set him in his first shotgun stance, taught him how to crack a breech, skin a rabbit, tie a bowline and bight, fashion a hangman's noose.

Though less sentimental than his brother, Gid was moved as well. He'd had less of his father, for good or for ill, and the few times he'd felt the hand it had been raised in anger over some stupidity he'd committed, but now the grip was different. Chastened, needful, human, weak.

Their father fixed his gaze on them, as though for field inspection. Finally, he said, "Gideon, hat!"

With a show of irritation Gid removed his ATF cap and put it back in his jacket pocket.

Satisfied, Abel began, "Long ago I decreed that I would precede your mother in death and I intend to honor my word." He waited in vain for them to grin at his high diction, at the way humility allowed him to poke fun at himself.

Ears belonging to other men might have heard his mock-heroic tone and self-deprecating humor, but his sons' could not. Jesse swallowed hard. Galled by high-flying language almost as much as he was by the old man's perpetual arrogance, he wanted to get up and leave. His father lay shrunken and small in the bed, a green plastic tube running into one nostril, his whiskered chin jutting like a battered old barn tom's, yet even now he was issuing edicts. Jesse took away his hand and tried to catch Gid's eye, but Gid was looking away, wishing he could pull out his flask. He, too, had released their father's hand.

Hit a man when he's down, Abel thought, and he couldn't stop his face from crumpling, couldn't stay his mouth from stretching into a grimace. So this was the way. All he'd wanted was for them to look up to him, to understand what he had done on their behalf. To teach them, to save them some of the trouble he'd had, so they would be able to stave off the feelings of failure he knew would assail them, their being sons of his. He knew all too well how that felt. For a time he couldn't speak for the thickening in his throat. "Boys," he said finally. "I'm going. This is the end. Will you have no mercy on me?"

Jesse drew in a breath, letting it out slowly to give himself time to think. This was vintage Judge Dad, the question posed in a way that made it impossible to answer, a courtroom gambit. Was the correct response "Yes, I will have no mercy on you" or "No, I will not have no mercy on you"?

Three needs made war in Jesse, the need for his father's approval, the need to forgive him, and the need to protect his own heart, left too often unguarded and open to blows. As a boy he'd become Abel's hope, Nick being unfit for rough and tumble because of his heart defect. For Jesse, who'd been a natural at mechanics and speed sports, Abel had bought motorcycles, entered him in time trials and enduros and motocross races. When Jesse earned National Novice status at the age of seventeen, he entered races at Madison Square Garden and the Astrodome, where he did well but never won, always bottoming out in the last lap for one reason or another. "The will to fail," the Judge had told him, shaking his head. "Son, you have the will to fail."

Hoping to please, Jesse had settled a few miles away from his parents, buying a run-down Depression-era farm and making it into something, rehabbing trucks and tractors from the thirties and forties. But through all of this his father's judgment loomed. Tune an engine, plant a tree, plow a field, break a horse, it was wrong. Only the Judge knew the right way.

Gid, too, was wise to their father's verbal snares—of course the question was a trick—but he was less susceptible than Jesse. He had left town, coming back only when his marriage ended, the recession hit, and he lost his house. His daughters refused to speak to him until he promised to quit drinking, but he would make no such promise. If he had to stand for one principle, let it be his refusal to bend. He had always been less prone to take the old man's opinions to heart. He wanted only to be done with the moment and get on to the game.

Neither son had answered his sidewinding question, but Abel had moved on. What none of them knew, least of all Abel, who believed he was in full control, was that he teetered on the brink of delirium, that at any given moment he would find himself either in robust possession of his considerable wit or adrift in the land of the lost.

The room was quiet except for the monitor's tick. From across the hall came another patient's moan and it tripped something in Abel. Again he broke down. "My sons," he said. He couldn't get his breath. Something was wrong, something was off, and whatever it was it was deep. "Boys," he asked, "where is your brother?"

Assuming he meant Billy, Gid answered, "Snowstorm out there. Buses aren't running." Billy used a cane because of his bad hips.

"I mean Nick. Where is Nick?"

Neither brother could meet his gaze. Finally Gid said, "Dad, he's gone."

"Well, where in red-hot Hades has he gone?" It would be like the feckless Nick to slip out when the going got rough. "He was here last night."

The stanchions kicked in with a mechanical gasp. Jesse cleared his throat. Gid scratched at a patch of tetter on his neck.

The night before, Abel had been laid out on a marble slab—a bier, it was—under the dome of a darkened planetarium, his body draped in gauze, torches—or were they stars?—flaring around him. Doctors and nurses ringed the slab, stuck needles and quills and blades into him. They chanted in a strange language that he realized he, too, could speak, and into all of this he'd gone spiraling. Pig-iron ingots shackled to his legs and arms, a cannonball gate weight attached by a screw eye to the back of his head, he swirled down through shimmering dust past the dead of all eras who waved him on—his father, a favorite brother, FDR and Herod Antipas, John Wayne and Genghis Khan, Cochise and Christ, General Tojo, Marco Polo, the great William Blackstone, men all, the evil, the good—as he spiraled and sank. It came to him that every night, deep in the haunted adyta of hospital time, a switch was tripped so that the wards became caves where mysterious rites were performed. This was the great secret of medicine, a spanking white gloss on the dark world of witch doctors and shamans, and it was given to him to spread this knowledge. He vowed, as he spiraled downward, to remember it all, to remember what he'd seen, what he'd learned, but of course he forgot. It would not be for several months, as he stood on a rise gazing into the summer night sky, that a fragment of this vision would return to him and he would again, if only for a moment, know what he knew.

Suddenly a light had glared into his eyes and in the superior knowledge of the dreamer he understood that the light was ancient, illuminating the IV tubes that ran up his arm and into his gown, causing the monitor to glow through all time onto the man who once had been a boy brought up on the King James Bible but who in one terrible instant on an embattled island in the Marianas had shifted allegiance from God to science, refusing ever after and out of principle to say grace over the meals his wife prepared. And now at the end of his days in one single flash his insight made union of science and faith, its logic immaculate, the elusive Higgs boson he'd hoped would be found in his lifetime residing in him, and this understanding came in the person of a being named Jeff, darkly bearded, garbed in phosphorescent white robes, bearing a psalter, who stood by his bed and put a comforting hand on his forehead. He'd felt exalted, felt sought out and found, anointed and shorn and returned to the fold, the Sunday School boy in wool knickers and bow tie, head smelling of Lucky Tiger hair oil, the coolness behind his ears the all-but-forgotten feel of his mother wet-sprucing his hair.

Now, from the pocket of mind that stored the words to "Invictus" and the floor plan of the train depot in Blackstone, Virginia, from which in 1944 he'd led a signal crew from Fort Pickett to the Pacific coast, from the pocket of mind that remembered the terrible lay of the cliffs on Saipan and the halls of the army hospital on Oahu where he'd lain with a broken back reading Shakespeare's plays came Lear's plea: *O heavens, If you do love old men, if your sweet sway Allow obedience, if yourselves are old, make it your cause; send down, and take my part!*

Believing he had said these words aloud, he again reached for his sons' hands, but both boys had made themselves busy, Jesse by squaring a box of tissues on the nightstand, Gid by flicking the clicker of a giveaway ballpoint that read "Air Capital Computer." What he had actually said, in the cramped tone of a gurgling gut, the word for which—*borborygmus*—he'd known and used in the world-before, was "Wee wye warry wahr."

Over their father's body Gid caught Jesse's eye, but before they could respond Abel shook his head violently. "Haven't I told you time and again that one boy's a full boy, two boys is half a boy, and three boys is no boy at all!"

The phrase came from their grandfather, who used it teasingly to describe the foolery that resulted whenever he hired a pack of young boys to work around the stockyards, but in his own father's voice it sounded like a curse. Jesse's gorge rose. Warmth crept into the tips of his ears.

Abel tried again, thinking he was saying, "All I believed and have failed to believe is united in me, and all the power you ever desired runs through your own veins. And it comes down through the ages through me, through your father to you and to me through mine. Through the veins is the truth revealed to the brain and the heart, do you see? Through the blood. For a long time my brain was not connected to my heart, but now it is. And the beauty of this is that Jeff is in charge. You'll see him around these halls and you'll know."

Jesse studied the ridges and valleys of the white woven blanket that covered his father's body. Gid sucked his teeth. They heard his voice, but they could make no sense of what he was trying to say until he asked, "Now, where did that pig get off to?"

They assured him that there was no pig anywhere about. Big? Did he mean big? Did he want the nurse?

Agitated, Abel pulled at his gown, trying to sit up straighter. "I am telling you there are *indeed* atheists in foxholes!" Then, seemingly out of nowhere, clearly, in full frightening command, he growled, "Don't patronize me. What's wrong with you?"

"Dad, it's all right," Gid said. He had stood up to head for the door.

"Well, it's obviously not all right! Have I been such a bad father?"

Jesse swallowed hard. His mouth went dry. To keep it from quivering, he worked his jaw. *Bull's-eye,* he wanted to say.

Gid looked at his own grip on the door handle and thought, *Frickin' bingo.* He wanted to be somewhere, anywhere, else, but he made no further move to leave.

Abel felt pressure in his left frontal lobe, as though his brain were calcifying, creaking and cracking as it separated from skull and shrank in on itself. *Headshrinker,* he thought. *Hoo-haw.* Only a hotshot could make such a connection. In his sons' scalded expressions, he saw his opening, and he understood with the vision of a soothsayer their deepest need, which was to believe he had ruined their lives.

He considered his boys. Jesse had always been an easy touch. As a child, when someone else cried, he would blubber up. Waterworks like an artesian well. Even a whimpering dog could set him off. He needed to man the hell up. Peel off his "Kick Me" sign. Gid was as tough as the hide on a windfall black walnut. He needed to be cracked so that his concrete head couldn't waylay the rest of him, as it heretofore had.

"Have I?" he asked again.

Heart racing as always when his father's mood turned combative,

Jesse stared at the knees of his jeans, wishing he had the strength to walk away. Gid felt for his flask to reassure himself it would be waiting when this was over.

"You think I've done wrong by you, do you?" Both of them, the soft and the hard, appeared shaken, and all because he had exposed the lie they needed to believe.

Again Gid scratched his neck, this time with his pen. The question was too bald, too weak, but at the same time overheated and paranoid. What was the old man's strategy now? Gid couldn't figure it, but if you turned it a certain way, buried in the question was the admission that he had in fact ruined them. Or at least he knew they didn't trust him. And why. This was enough for Gid; he was done. With the wisdom that sometimes came to him in the shining hour before a buzz gave way to blotto, when the reminder of common humanity came dependably to the fore and his heart opened wide to take in all beings, himself among them, opened so wide it almost hurt, he understood that although his father had cast himself as Oz the Great and Powerful and that fear and idolatry and his own slanted press had caused his children to see him the way he wanted to be seen, the man was mortal, was flawed. He knew it and Gideon knew it. And both of them knew that their flaws were the same.

Chili powder and two #10 cans of pinto beans, Gid recited to himself, proud of his recall, tipsy though he was. "Dad," he began, prepared to tell the old man what he wanted to hear. One final time he patted the old man's knee, this time more firmly. "Dad, it's all right. You've been a good father."

In a way, Gid reckoned, if he took the long view, this, too, was true. Their father was stubborn, confounding, a hero. A gentleman-scholar. A jackass. A one-man wonder and a geezer. A softhearted, hardheaded son of a bitch, depending on mood, but nothing could change him. He was who he was and would be who he was to the end. If there was some kind of lesson in that, then, hey, lesson learned.

Gid took his cap from his pocket and put it on. Touching the bill, he said, "Gotta go," to his brother and with the sense of a burden lifted or at least allayed he left the room. Avoiding the waiting room by taking the stairs, he hurried through the building and made his way to his beater, a whiskey-burned '92 Plymouth, to head south toward Jesse's place. He felt as good as he'd felt in a long time. Ready to drink to his own pardonable faults. And with time enough to make kickoff.

Jesse sat forward on his chair, juddering a leg, wanting to leave as well. Something held him, he didn't know what. After Gid had spewed his lie and bolted, their father had smiled weakly and then had gone to sleep. Jesse sat through several cycles of the anticlot machine and a vitals check from the nurse. Outside, dusk deepened.

Down on South Broadway was a dive called the Stumble Inn, and behind the squat cinder-block building a thicket of thorny bodark trees provided enough cover to hide his truck. The blow and go was gone from his dashboard but his own Breathalyzer cheater, the AlcoHAWK, was still in the glove box. He could be careful. He could watch what he drank—two beers max—stay under the legal limit, and be all right. On the other hand, the AlcoHAWK's double AAs were more than likely dead. He'd have to stop for batteries. How weenie-ass could you get?

And how could the old man just lie there and ask them the million-dollar question and then go to sleep, maybe for the last time? How could he slip, scot-free, the knots of resentment he'd tied? Outrage rose in Jesse at how many times he'd been hurt, at the years of feeling hardly-ever-good-enough and not once perfect. And he had unanswered questions. Had his father ever hated himself? Ever felt guilt? Had he been unfaithful? Had he taken a life? Thought of taking his own? Had he ever thought he was a failure?

His father stirred, opened his eyes, and looked blankly around the room. He rasped a word that Jesse interpreted as "Water."

When Nick was alive and they were little kids and would threaten, during a fight, to kill each other, his father had a method for teaching them the terrible power of words. Mishearing his term for Japanese ritual suicide by disembowelment, they called the practice Harry-Carry. The Judge would frog-march them to the cutlery drawer, pull out a case of ivory-handled steak knives and present them, saying, "You want to kill each other? Gentlemen, choose your weapons." Several times Jesse and Nick had gone so far as to draw knives and brandish them while the Judge stood by, making no move to stop them. Nick was a gambler, his bet always that Jesse would cave first, which he always did, dropping the knife and sniveling like a big Baby Huey at the prospect of murdering his brother.

Did the old man really want water? The doctor's orders were NPO, nothing by mouth. The IV supplied him with fluid. Was he really thirsty, or was this yet another test, another standoff that he, Jesse, would fail?

His father gestured with his tape-and-tube-covered hand toward his open mouth. His tongue was coated, white.

Jesse stood, unsure of what to do. With the sudden rise to his feet, his field of vision blackened, closing in like an old-timey camera's aperture, and he had to wait until the darkness lifted. He was hungry, angry, lonely, tired, all four at once, the conditions AA taught him that could lead to acting on impulses he would later regret, but he didn't care. The words rose from his gut and before he could stop himself he had said, "You sorry old bastard. Who in hell did you think you were?"

The Judge blinked hard. An odd look came over his features, a look that was part shock and part delight, part triumph. "Attaboy!" he whispered hoarsely, trying to raise his tethered hand to pump a fist, failing. "Attaboy!"

"Oh, shit, Dad," Jesse said. "Just . . . shit." He would not be right with his father. He would never be right. He didn't know yet whether or not he would pull his truck behind the bodark trees and yank open the Stumble Inn's door or whether or not he would drive past and go safely home, but he knew he would never be right. He didn't know yet that he would not fall off the wagon, at least not this night, or that when his fall came it would not just come but would be on him like paint, and if there was a reason for it, it would feel more like a miracle cure for the long scourge of blame. He knew only that for the rest of his life he would take from his memory the matter of his father and worry it the way his little blind barn dog worried a possum carcass, rolling in it to keep the good stink alive.

He hadn't for a minute believed that his father approved of his outburst or that the "Attaboy" was sincere. But this, too, was the Judge's way—a last-ditch turnaround that made it appear that all along he had intended an outcome. Against such shape-shifting, no one could win. Jesse laughed. He guessed it didn't much matter what he did. Maybe it never had. The old man would be the way he was regardless. He would always win and it didn't mean jack and this was the great big joke Jesse'd been falling for all his life. He could fight it or he could move on. Without knowing why he did so, he put his hand on his father's brow and in a gesture that anyone with a less troubled history might have said came solely from love and an unguarded heart, surprised himself by leaning down to kiss his forehead.

The kiss pleased Abel in a floating and general way, but he had already forgotten the argument. He had moved on to a moonlit night on a promontory on Saipan where figures scurried far below on the beach. They weren't GIs or Japanese soldiers running sorties; the island was secured. After a last banzai charge by the Japanese army, thousands of the island's Chamorro civilians had jumped from the cliffs to their deaths, but some remained, under American occupation. The little group below, starving women and children among them, was likely comprised of these poor souls, scavenging for food. His captain had ordered him to escort up the hill a chaplain who wanted to be shown what went on at night on the island. On the climb, the beet-faced Church-of-Christer from Kentucky talked of Japanese blood, of torture, how he wanted some teeth, maybe an ear. For a time they watched the activity below, and then the chaplain dared him to shoot, to pick them off one by one. Tired, in pain from a back injury he'd been trying to gut his way through, galled by the cleric's hypocrisy, and never thinking he would hit anything—Abel had squeezed the Enfield's trigger, more to rise to the dare and blast the obscene leer from the chaplain's face than for any other reason. The figures below scattered, all but one, which fell to the sand and was still. The chaplain wanted to clamber down to the body, but Abel shouldered his rifle and walked away. Later he told the captain that he'd fired at a pulatatt bird that had spooked him, but seven decades past the shot still flashed behind his eyes, and he couldn't—he wouldn't—forgive himself.

From the cliff he moved to a late spring afternoon on the Ark River near where he'd grown up, and in his mind tornado sirens moaned and the sky loured darkly and the light went arsenic-green as out into a field of golden wheat he walked, grown older than he'd ever thought to be, to dare a scudding funnel cloud to seize him, take him in the vortex so he could feel its power, send him like a flatland Ahab sailing full speed for the world ahead, where the sorrows of the present world could never reach, where Jeff, who loved him after all—oh, after *all*—waited to take him home.

Outside, darkness had fallen. Sleet sanded the windows. Jesse left his father and went to stand in the doorway of the waiting room. None of the others noticed him. His mother, drained and gray but seated for what seemed the first time since they'd brought the old man in two nights before, as calm as she ever was without Billy in her field of vision, rested her delicate, stocking-clad feet on a chair. Doro spoke quietly into her phone, from the sound of things trying to make an airline agent understand that she needed to postpone her flight. A tearful ClairBell, a box of tissues before her, sat at a table with two tearful young women, diagnosing with great feeling and persuasive authority their father's illness. Gid was long gone, but even in his absence, if Jesse took the long view, here they all were, unchanged.

He made his way down the darkened hallway to the lobby where Bob Dole stood watch in bronze. The clichéd phrase his father had so disdained came to him—*the greatest generation*—but he couldn't summon his usual bitterness. Down marble steps worn smooth he went toward the exit doors and out into the night.

On the hospital grounds an unkempt man in a tattered Army field parka, homeless, Jesse guessed, stabbed with a sharpened stick at cigarette butts in the snowdrifts and collected them in a red Marlboro box. He looked toward Jesse in a shaggy, sidelong glance, not meeting his gaze. Hurriedly, Jesse shook two Camels from his pack and handed them to the man, who mumbled his thanks and shambled away.

Jesse walked across the driveway to stand on a knoll overlooking the snow-covered parking lot, its sodium vapor lights casting the covered cars and trucks in an orange glow. A Checker cab made its way slowly up the winding drive toward the main hospital and stopped at the front doors. For a long time the cab idled, as though the fare were in dispute or some other problem had come up, but finally the back door opened and a figure blundered out, nearly pitching forward. Caught by a cane thrust into a snow bank, the figure came into view: Billy, his sick, sweet, doomed brother, come out on this frigid night to pay his respects to their father. Jesse was too far away to call out to him, and even if he hadn't been, he was emptied out, with no more room for feeling, not pity or sorrow or even love.

The cab pulled into a handicapped spot to wait while Billy started up the sidewalk, on his way to the ICU waiting room, where, if history ran true, he would put the touch on their mother for return cab fare. Jesse watched his brother's pained progress, willing him not to fall, in which case he would sprint across the snow to help. But on Billy went and when he neared the building's steps the man in the field parka stepped forward and in an act that was surely compassion offered his arm to help. He guided Billy up the steps and held open the door. In the snow-blurred night his brother's voice rang out in its familiar exaggerated sociability, "I thank you, sir." An ache rose in Jesse's throat, along with a prickling sensation behind his eyes. However jaunty and brave the face his brother showed the world, it was the effort he made to be kind that was heroic.

Jesse stood for a long minute on the knoll, looking up into the swirling storm, and then he turned around to walk back the way he'd come, heading for his truck. Snowflakes, a spangled flurry in the orange light, had sifted already into his tracks so he could hardly see the path he'd made.

Five

Hattie felt herself marching along a downward path, falling into rank with her husband and her son as their situations grew worse. After Abel came home from the hospital the long prairie winter settled in, day after frigid day, and it seemed that things picked up where they'd left off, like a knitting project laid aside and then returned to after a period of neglect. She could hardly tell a stitch had been dropped. She had expected to lose Abel, and now she felt an uneasy sense of reprieve, and also a feeling that she was recovering from an illness herself. Death felt closer than it had before, her own mortality was often on her mind. Billy was tumbling down another chute, and she worried about him. She prayed she would outlive him. Who would care for him if she weren't able to? Not Abel, not Doro or Clair-Bell. Forget about the boys. The icy roads kept her from driving up to check on him as much as she wanted to. It had been a siege of a winter, one of the worst yet. Getting old was—yes, she would say it—hell.

And then finally on a day in early April there came a mild south wind that carried the scent of crocus blooms. Through the warming night the ice dams on the Big Slough thawed, in the morning the first robins, antic in their hunt for worms, hopped in the south yard, and her dormant spirit stirred once again to meet the season's turn. She had awakened with a snippet from Wordsworth on her lips, *Trailing clouds of glory do we come/ From God, who is our home.* Since her days at teacher's college, Wordsworth had been her favorite, and many a troubled night, after playing out her store of psalms and hymns in the vain hope of sleep, she had wandered among his stanzas, marveling that mere words could ease her mind. Now, with the return of the familiar phrase, she divined a desire, deeply held though only dimly realized, until the understanding broke on her like spring itself that she must see her girlhood home once more before she died.

She couldn't go alone. She no longer trusted her driving, not for the ninety crow-flight miles west toward the Red Hills country of her youth, to the Davies homestead. Abel still careered about in his Dodge Dakota, his decades on the municipal bench having immunized him against deputy and officer and even shame, but since his last hospitalization and given what she'd seen of his judgment, Hattie refused to ride with him. He was unsafe at any speed. As a passenger he was worse. He commandeered the air vents, the windows, the radio. He criticized her driving, he sprang pop quizzes—"How many car lengths required between vehicles under rainy conditions?" And his directions! "In seven-tenths of a mile you will come to a crossroads at which point you will bear east until the road curves south-southwest at an eighty-degree angle." Or "Travel along the hypotenuse of a triangle that, were it to be laid over a map, would link the towns of Winfield, Wellington, and Rock." He would hijack the day, stopping at construction sites to marvel at big equipment or jaw with any foreman or earthmover operator he could scare up.

He was best left at home in his backroom den, where in his sheepskin-cushioned recliner he could flip between reruns of *Nova* and *Victory at Sea.* Sometimes she heard him back there trying to mimic the cattle auctioneer on RFD-TV, or intoning fragments of Kansas case law, or declaiming "Invictus" with the stresses and pauses he'd used to win an eighth-grade elocution contest. "Out of the night that covers me,/ Black as the pit from pole to pole,/ I thank whatever gods may be/ For my unconquerable soul" she would hear from the room. From time to time the master of his fate/captain of his soul would shuffle into her kitchen, bathrobe belt trailing, to ask where she'd hidden the saltshaker or in which hymn could be found the line that went "Here I raise my Ebenezer."

Years before, when he was hale, he'd sculpted a two-ton Easter Island head out of Colorado limestone and winched it into place as a door guard for his Holy of Holies, his machine barn, and named it Ebenezer, this being the rock raised by Samuel to show how far, with God's help, the Israelites had come. A stone of forbearance it was, and this irked Hattie. Abel knew many biblical passages by heart—when he was a boy his parents had set him on the horsehair sofa and read him the Old Testament cover to cover—but he'd been a skeptic for decades and in their marriage Hattie, a constant believer, was the official keeper of scripture. And who was he to set such a stone? Which of the two of them, she'd like to know, had truly shown forbearance?

For a traveling companion, she would have chosen Billy. They would have laughed and chatted and sung old hymns and the songs from *Man of La Mancha* and *Les Misérables* that he loved and the hours would have flown. Her billfold would be a good deal lighter, but so would her heart. But then she remembered that Billy was at a low point. He'd been living in a basement apartment off Waco Street, a dingy, cramped space with bare bulbs. The few times he'd come home to ask for money he looked thinner, his eyes hooded and dark. She worried about his illness—his T-cell count, his viral load, numbers she didn't understand but nevertheless placed stock in—and she worried about his drug use. Methadone was supposed to help, but she wasn't sure it had. He was in constant pain because of his degenerating hip joints. She worried about him always, the groove in her brain well worn, but it was a curious thing: out of sight was, more and more as she grew older, out of mind. Too, with Billy out of the picture, she and Abel got along better; Billy was a sore spot in their marriage. Abel was apt to grouse and grumble if they crossed paths. A few weeks before, he'd accused Billy of lifting a bottle of painkillers he kept on hand for an old back injury. Billy denied it. The upshot was that Abel had banished him from the house once again, an exile that, like others before it, lasted only a few days before Hattie let him back in.

Reluctantly she left the subject of Billy and worked her way up the age ladder of her offspring. Gideon was camped out in Jesse's barn until he got back on his feet, so he was close by, but he'd be a bad bet as a companion. His politics—whatever they were—had grown dark. ClairBell called him the Unabomber.

ClairBell. Hattie lost no time at all eliminating her younger daughter, who at the moment her mother dismissed her as a possibility was lounging pajama-clad and couch-bound, watching Jerry Springer and eating Ferrara Red Hots by the handful, her recent Vicodin dose having given her a villainous headache and a sugar jones. ClairBell had an elephant's memory for slights, always accusing Hattie of playing favorites. She was jealous of her siblings. Even before the trip got under way there was bound to be a dramatic recitation of Hattie's every crime against fairness. And her shocking questions. "How long since you and Daddy had sex?" No, not ClairBell.

Her sweet Jesse. Well, sweet sometimes, but a trip with him might be a trial. You never knew the mood he'd be in. She'd thought he'd finally gotten over the aging barrel racer and rodeo queen, Patsy Gaddy by name, who for several years had broken his heart on a regular basis.

ClairBell had told her Patsy was still ensconced in Jesse's spare room and had sworn Hattie to secrecy, but she wasn't sure this was true. Abel had once said that at the Cafe ClairBell you never knew if truth was on the menu or if she was slinging hash. Still, Patsy or no Patsy, Jesse was a brooder, and it was always a guessing game to figure out which particular burr had lodged under his saddle.

Nick, her firstborn boy, was dead, buried with his head in gauze some forty years before when sepsis from a sick tooth shot through a system weakened by a heroin habit and his inborn heart defect. But she never left his name off the roll call. Maybe, from the other realm, he heard her. She wasn't sure. Neither was she sure he was in heaven—chances weren't good—but if love and prayers could boost a soul to everlasting life, hers would have given him at least a nudge. She knew it was probably wrong, but she'd worked out a theory that sometimes allowances were made. Nick hadn't been a bad boy, just lost and hurt. Another idea she'd worked out was that if in the world to come you were reunited with those you loved, then at least Nick might make a temporary appearance on her account.

This left Doro, who at the moment Hattie's thoughts turned to her was browsing at Anthropologie on Boylston Street. She'd just seen some majolica cups, thinking they would be perfect for her mother's sunflower-yellow kitchen, and this made her realize it had been a few months since she'd been home to the plains. She missed the wheat fields and the cattle and the cottonwoods, the cowboys and the Indians, the shallow brown creeks, the prairie, the very air but not the politics at all, but more than anything she missed her mother. She resolved to make a trip home soon.

Doro had lived for a long time in the east, and this was a sorrow to Hattie, for her eldest girl was nearest her in temperament. They had a spiritual connection. Not ESP or anything like that, but a mother-daughter *wooh-wooh* they sometimes talked about, giggling, half believing. A connection Hattie'd never felt with ClairBell. Although her daughters shared the straight silver hair of Abel's side of the family—a loose, pencil-fastened chignon for Doro and a Pebbles Flintstone topknot for ClairBell—and a tendency inherited from Hattie's side to pack on weight in the caboose, they were as different as sisters could be. Doro read poetry and essays and fiction; if she read at all, ClairBell skimmed the *Penny Power*. Doro worked for a college and wrote western novels under a pen name. ClairBell had wanted to be a nurse, but the plan had derailed because of poor grades and so she'd done temp work here and there—driving the Head Start bus, answering phones at a call center for Shepler's. Doro kept her own counsel unless asked. ClairBell dispensed pronouncements from a harum-scarum store of advice she gleaned from Dr. Oz and Dr. Phil and Dr. Laura and then mangled past recognition. Doro loved music and art. Though some of her tastes struck Hattie as a little hoity-toity, at least poetry and nature were important to her, at least she looked toward a deeper world. ClairBell lived for bingo and blackjack and yard sales. And the awful things that sometimes came out of her mouth . . . but why go on? Slowly, slyly, a plan came over Hattie. It wasn't in her to tell an outright lie, but she was not above a subterfuge that might seem innocent: she resolved to wait for a visit and take the trip with Doro, keep the plan from ClairBell. And of course if Billy happened to call ahead of time, why, they could zip up to town and fetch him in no time at all and he could come along for the ride. With Billy and Doro, the trip could be a lark. They were like-minded. The three of them could talk about books and music and religion and even politics. They were bent the same way on most things, though Hattie continued to vote the straight Republican ticket out of habit, except for 2008, when she staged a revolt against Abel to cast her vote for Obama. They could spend the day and not have one disagreement. With this in mind, she began to plan for the arrival of her eldest daughter, who usually came in spring to smell the Russian olive trees, which bloomed in middle May.

And so as the starkness of winter fell away and bright weather came on, Hattie grew excited. Daily in her mind she traveled two counties over to the open range, to the rugged countryside of buttes and mesas red with iron oxide, of sand draws and salt cedar and the beautiful red Medicine River. In her imagination she climbed rills to breathe the air of her youth, fashioned pretty nosegays of magenta poppy mallow, entered a bower under an elm where she and her cousin Eugene had played house, egg crates nailed to the tree for cabinets, broken crockery for cups and plates, a bed of straw covered with a saddle blanket. She was the mother and Eugene was the father and theirs was the ideal marriage. In the leafy playhouse, order ruled. At *Ding-dong, morning!* Eugene woke up and dutifully did his chores. He didn't argue with her about heaven—he was happy to believe what she believed. If she told him to say the blessing over the supper table, he obeyed. "Mighty tasty," he would say after a meal of mulberries and cracked wheat, dabbing his mouth with a catalpa leaf. At play-night they lay side by side and if she told him to hold her hand, he would do so, snoring *honk-shoo, honk-shoo* until *Ding-dong, morning!* came again. As each day passed, her desire to see the old place grew like a bud within her, flashed, and she smiled to think of Wordsworth, upon her inward eye.

From time to time as she waited for Doro's arrival the call to honesty overtook her and she considered telling Abel about her desire. Twice she'd gone as far as to walk down the hall toward his lair, intending to unburden herself. But each time when she saw him dozing in front of the television she drew herself up short. He would find reasons her trip was a bad idea and go to work on her until she forgot why she wanted to go in the first place. She would broach the subject later. There was no sense bearding the lion in his den, at least not yet.

At last Doro arrived and Hattie had only the welcome-home dinner to get through before she could take her eldest aside, enlist her support, and spring her plan. Gathered around the table were her husband, herself, Doro, Jesse, ClairBell and her husband, Randy, and the unquiet ghosts of countless awkward family dinners past when all of the assembled vied, as they always had, for Abel's favor. He was the sun around which their lesser planets circled, the god they hoped to please. He was still the Little King.

According to long habit, Hattie said grace, careful not to veer from the rhetorical formula Abel insisted on and any variation from which caused pained muttering. ACTS—Adoration, Contrition, Thanksgiving, Supplication. This from the man who refused to lead his family in prayer, forcing Hattie into the awkward position of either blessing her own hands for preparing the meal or leaving out the phrase altogether. The man who spent his spare time poking holes in people's faith and lived to catch a person in a theological blind alley. A surge of pique caused her to flush. Her heart hammered. She picked up the meat platter and passed it first to Abel. He served himself and then passed it on. Her hands shook as she passed the peas and then sent the cauliflower dish around.

Many years before, after the first five children had left home and Billy was out in San Francisco catching his death of the new plague, she'd tried to tell her husband a half-truth. This event, never mentioned in Abel's presence for it galled him still, concerned the death of his lapdog, a grandchild-terrorizing black-and-white Chihuahua–rat terrier mix named Toodles who had come to them after Nick died, a stray brought home by Billy. In her early years Toodles had been a favorite, but with age she'd grown mean-tempered, and before long no one but Abel could get close without risking a nasty bite. His was the only blood she hadn't drawn. ClairBell called her Toadles, for the way she trotted after Abel, her docked tail wriggling obsequiously, and for her stumpy little body. Abel repaid the dog's devotion with kind words, table scraps, and a patience he extended to no other being. Under his care Toodles grew fat as a football.

When Abel came home from the law office, he greeted the dog first. At the table, he used her as intermediary. "Toodles thinks the potatoes need more salt," or "Toodles prefers butter on her roast beef sandwich."

Hattie was not a jealous person, but in the years the dog had been a member of the household she'd taken Hattie's place in her husband's affections and this, Hattie supposed, was what made the creature's offenses harder to bear.

At seventeen Toodles was at the end of her days, blind, arthritic, incontinent. The living room carpet was ruined, dotted with the salt mounds Hattie sprinkled in order to soak up the uric acid. Worse, lately the beast had taken to ricketing her hindquarters into the firebox of the big stone fireplace in order to void her bowels, which were often loose. A decision was past due, but Abel couldn't bear the thought of having to make it. Finally Hattie laid down the law. She would feed and water Toodles as before, let her in and out, but she would clean up no more messes. To Abel she'd said, "I will not keep house for an animal. You have to help me, Abel."

But nothing happened and the messes grew more frequent. Abel continued to greet Toodles at the door when he came in from the barn, to feed her raisins and licorice jelly beans and chocolate cake and whatever bowel-loosening-else she begged for.

Hattie had had it. According to her temperament and upbringing and beliefs, she had submitted unto her husband as was required of her by the Apostle Paul. But she'd reached her limit. She gave Abel one last chance, waiting for a morning when Toodles had again made the firebox her latrine. "Abel," she said, "there's been another incident. Now, I believe I told you that . . ."

When cornered, Abel often fell back on cross-examination techniques. He did so then, turning to leave for his machine barn but tossing over his shoulder a question to which there was only one possible answer. Hand on the doorknob, he inquired with a maddening air of patient reasonableness, "And is there anything of a material nature preventing you from cleaning it up?" Having phrased his question impeccably, he did not wait for her answer.

Later, when Hattie told her sister Sammie of the act that nearly brought down their marriage, she would say that it was as though, around noon that same day, a voice spoke to her. "Hattie, pick up your purse and car keys," the voice said, and she had obeyed. When the voice went on, "Now pick up the dog," she had done this as well. Toodles snarled and bared her gums and feebly tried to squirm into biting stance, but she was too old and soon gave up. Next, a hand not Hattie's opened the front door, feet not belonging to Hattie walked to the car, and the will of a person not Hattie drove to the ASPCA to deposit Toodles at the front desk. "She's old," Hattie told the receptionist. "She needs to go."

When Toodles lost control of her bladder on the desk blotter, the woman said, "Looks like she's went already." Hattie hadn't remembered the woman's joke until afterward, but even after all this time, she couldn't laugh. The receptionist petted the hoary little head, looked into the milky eyes. "Not enjoying your life anymore, sweetie?"

"No," said Hattie firmly, "she's not." She signed the forms, and later in the exam room she cradled Toodles, crooning and stroking her gently as the injection went in and the breath of the little beast's spirit went out.

Only after the deed was done did she allow herself to consider Abel's likely reaction. He would be angry. He would feel betrayed. But what about *her* feelings? He hadn't listened. He hadn't respected. Wasn't a wife more important than a dog? True as these justifications were, they didn't stop her from feeling heartsick. On the way home she planned the story she would tell, and as she prepared his favorite pot roast she practiced words that would not be an out-and-out lie, only a half-truth. "In her sleep," she repeated. "Toodles died in her sleep."

At the usual hour the back door opened and Abel entered, calling in the tender voice he reserved for the dog, "Where's my Toodles-girl? Where's my little sweetheart?"

Hattie summoned her strength. "Abel, I'm afraid she died."

By then he had made it to the kitchen table, where he gripped a chair back for support. "What happened? Was she hit by a car?"

That light deer hunters used to stun their quarry, that's what Hattie saw in the glare of his stricken look, a jacklight. But even under pressure she remembered the words, "She went to sleep."

Abel's shoulders sagged as understanding dawned. In a tear-clogged voice he asked, "But she didn't suffer?"

"No," Hattie told him, grateful that the hardest part was past and she no longer had to lie. "She went fast." To hide the sudden welling of her own tears at seeing him so shattered, she turned to her dinner preparations.

When he asked forlornly from the chair he'd sunk into, "Where is she?" Hattie realized her mistake. He would want to bury his pet. Would want to see her a last time. From some inner stronghold, she was able to say, "It's all done. It's all taken care of."

"You buried her?"

Suddenly the lie could bear no more weight, and the truth tumbled out. Hattie confessed, adding that he hadn't listened to her complaints and she'd had no other recourse and it was a mercy to the suffering creature. For a moment she thought she had gotten through to him. Then she remembered the way the little body had felt as life ebbed, the sudden heaviness, and she made her final mistake, saying, "You should thank me for doing what you couldn't."

He bolted from the chair and charged toward her, palm raised, and for a dread second she feared he would do the unthinkable, that he would strike her. But instead he stalked out the back door to his machine barn, where he spent the night. He took up living in his barn, coming into the house only to shower and change clothes. For a month he refused to speak to her. Dutifully she prepared trays of food and left them at the door by Ebenezer. She went about contritely, speaking docilely to him, even understanding why he'd been so angry. In the years that followed she came to see that her solution hadn't been entirely fair. She hadn't given him clear warning. But not once had she regretted her act; it had to be done. The old dog was suffering and a swift end was a mercy. If that made her hard-hearted, then so be it. And this time, about her trip out west, she felt the same way. She would go with Doro, who wouldn't cross her, or at least not much, and leave the others behind. All she had to do was keep her mouth shut.

But years of inhabiting her own character had done their work, and at the first lull in the dinner table conversation she heard herself saying brightly, "I've just had a lovely idea for a day trip."

As they rarely did during family dinners when Abel held court, his changing moods determining the tone, all eyes turned toward her. She faltered, but then forged on, laying out her desire. "I've been wanting to go out west for a while, to the place I grew up, and I was thinking it could be a . . ."

A what? Her stomach felt queasy. Spots faded in and out before her eyes. Beside her Abel sat as stony and disapproving as his dratted Ebenezer, and she wondered if her trip into the past was partly to have a break from him, from his rules and requirements and his everlasting opinions. "A lot of fun," she finished.

ClairBell dolloped cauliflower onto her plate so violently that the serving spoon clanged against the china. "So I'm left out of the loop again?" She aimed a withering glance Hattie's way.

Passing the tomatoes, Doro laughed nervously, a nervous laugh being her habitual response to conflict. This wasn't the first time ClairBell had accused them of leaving her out. Her sister could construe conspiracy where there was none, and whether or not her jealousy was warranted had ceased to matter; the trait had taken on the strength of family fact.

There was indeed a basis for ClairBell's charge, and in fairly recent history, also involving a road trip, specifically a drive to Albuquerque in Leo's Lexus the morning after his and Billy's wedding. Hattie, Doro, and ClairBell were to follow Billy and Leo in the Skylark, stay a night or two in their beautiful house, and see Acoma Pueblo. ClairBell, arguing for the prosecution, accused Hattie and Doro of sneaking off without her. She didn't care how it happened or what their excuse was, they had abandoned her. Left her at home and gone merrily off to gamble at Sky City Casino without her when everyone knew she loved casinos more than almost life.

The defense maintained that on the morning of departure, when Hattie and Doro pulled up to ClairBell's rental house, they found her car in the driveway, the doors locked, the blinds down. Her children had already gone to their father's for the weekend. The only movement they could detect behind the blinds turned out to be a cat—or cats—toying with the window shade cords. Doro called ClairBell's cell phone.

No answer. They called the house phone. Many times. They knocked, loudly, at the front and back doors, but they couldn't raise ClairBell. They tried to peek through the windows but both women were too short. Finally, after half an hour of trying to rouse her, they gave up. "She must be sleeping hard," Hattie said. "She must have changed her mind and doesn't want to come. That's like her, you know."

Doro nodded and did not give her opinion, which was that after the big event of Billy's wedding, ClairBell had taken enough painkillers to send a grizzly into hibernation. Hattie didn't know about it, but ClairBell had done this before. Once, when ClairBell had spent the night at the Amicus house after one of Abel's birthday dinners so she and Doro could have what ClairBell called a slumber party, Doro had awakened in the middle of the night to go to the bathroom. Before she could turn on a light, she tripped over something soft. ClairBell lying belly up on the tile floor, a pool of bright red vomit beside her head and matting her hair.

Doro had tried to wake her. "ClairBell," she whispered. "Claire." She shook her sister's shoulder.

ClairBell opened her eyes. "Muh?" she muttered. "So sick. Just leave me here. I'm gup in a minute."

Doro sat on the toilet to pee, feeling profane and surreal with the heap of pink nylon nightgown that was her sister at her feet. After she finished, she went for a blanket and pillow and covered ClairBell and then stayed a while beside her, wondering what she should do.

The bathroom door opened and Billy entered, gripping the doorjamb, unsteady on his feet. He'd spent the night as well because it had gotten too late for anyone to drive him back uptown.

Doro asked, "Should we call an ambulance?"

Billy laughed. "She'll come out of it, sister-love. She just has a spot of the residue flu."

"But all that blood?"

Billy sniffed the floor. "Red hots. Last night after you went to bed SisterBell and I had a little shall-we-say potluck. A sharing of the wealth, as it were. She got into the red hots." He cackled wildly at his own wit-to-come and said in a scandalized voice, "She was scarfing them down like candy! The girl was RED HOT!"

Doro had looked at him closely. His pupils were pinpoints. He was talking fast.

"Now, if you don't mind, *ma chère soeur*," he said, snorting at his rhyme, "I must ask the lizard the time of day."

He stepped over ClairBell's body and lifted the commode's lid, preparing to relieve himself. "Or, no, do I mean bleed the lizard? Yes . . . why, yes, I do! Hurry up, please, it's time!" Doro had hurried out.

On the morning after Billy's wedding, as she and her mother stood on ClairBell's slab porch, Doro asked Hattie if they should go on without her.

"What choice do we have?" Hattie said. "Oh, this is just like her! And she's going to blame it on us!"

They had gone and had a wonderful time but ClairBell had not let them forget it, and this was the source of her accusation at the dinner table when Hattie announced her desire to see her homeland.

Now that the subject had been floated and ClairBell had made her comment about the loop, Doro cast about for a way past her sister's suspicions, a way to steer the blame from herself without shifting it toward her mother. She took a long sip of her iced tea and spoke what she realized with a start was the truth. "This is the first I'm hearing of any trip," she said mildly, conversationally, "but it sounds like a nice idea." This was why coming home was such a trial. With ClairBell you had to watch what you said and whom you said it to. You had to be on your toes at all times and you couldn't slack off or there'd be tinder for a feud. The eggshell walk was one she'd taken more times than she cared to admit.

ClairBell sat back and narrowed her cat-like eyes. "I suppose *he'll* be coming along for the ride." She meant Billy. She continued, snickering. "Or maybe I should say 'to take *you* for a ride.' "

"Just us," Hattie said, refusing to take the bait. "The girls."

ClairBell's keen gaze traveled from Hattie to Doro and back. "Hmmph," she said, and tucked into her laden plate.

Abel cleared his throat. He felt left out. Because pouting was weak and unseemly, he had found other ways to register his feelings. His mainstay was to remind his family of his power to protect and provide, but on occasion he changed his tack and staged a minor passion play to show them how sorely he'd been abused. Usually this involved food, most often salt. At hearing his wife's plan, he had at first made a show of scanning the table in an aggrieved manner for the saltshaker, planning to ask, "Where'd you hide the salt this time, Hattie?" but there they were, two shakers obediently flanking his plate. As a fallback he tapped into the genial tone he kept at the ready to say, "You girls shouldn't go all that way alone. I'll be happy to drive you." Grandly, he pulled out his pocket watch and snapped it open. "Be ready tomorrow at oh-nine-hundred hours, Zulu Time, Central Daylight."

Hattie's heart sank. Doro moved peas around on her plate. ClairBell took a sip of iced tea, and then said, "Daddy, we're grown women. I'm fifty-four and Doro will be"—she cut a simpering look her sister's way—"what? sixty-five, sixty-six?"

"Sixty-one," Doro corrected. "I'll be sixty-one." She gave out a hesitant laugh.

ClairBell deadpanned, "Is that your final answer? Do you need to phone a friend?"

Doro made herself busy quartering a tomato slice, and there was uneasy silence at the table until Hattie said, "I don't really have to go. It was just an idea."

A stranger might have concluded that the subject was closed, but Hattie's demurral was merely the opening maneuver. Not that Hattie was all that aware of her strategy, but it had played out so consistently over the years that everyone around the table understood it, except for Abel, who labored under the illusion that he had prevailed.

As she served cherry cobbler, Hattie said to Abel, as though the thought had just occurred to her, "Maybe we should go on Tuesday, when you and Big Bill are taking out that old cottonwood." Abel's kid brother, a hearty specimen in his early eighties who still went on Volunteer Fire Squad runs, came over on Tuesdays and the two men spent the day in mechanical pursuits, happiest when broken equipment required the presence of elder heads beneath an open hood.

"I can't go that day," ClairBell put in. "Business down in Oklahoma."

Hattie allowed hope to rise. ClairBell was often obstructive for no reason other than a contrary nature. Maybe this meant she wouldn't come after all.

Jesse looked up from his plate, his eyes shadowed by the graduated lenses of his aviator glasses. "Where in Oklahoma?" He smirked. "Your memorial booster chair at Kaw Tribal Bingo?"

Doro choked on a pea and had a coughing fit. It was well known that ClairBell & Co.—never mind that neither she nor her grown sons held regular jobs and that they depended on the largesse of Randy Billups—frequented the gaming palace run by the Kaw tribe over the Oklahoma line in Newkirk. But it was also well known that the bingo palace was closed Monday through Wednesday, and so ClairBell was caught in her lie. When her word was challenged she usually doubled down, taking an arrow from her father's quiver, but in this case she knew she was caught and so she floated a new fib altogether.

"We have an appointment with a relator to look at a farm." Doro winced at her sister's pronunciation of *realtor*, but the excuse was unimpeachable. ClairBell shared the family habit of driving around the countryside to inspect ramshackle farmhouses that would never be purchased. She smiled fetchingly, obligingly. "But of course I could always cancel it." She turned to Randy as if for affirmation, but he only looked perplexed. "Sure," he said.

And just like that, Hattie was going! Things would work out after all with only minor changes. That night at the hour she usually sent her worries upward, she felt no cares, no fears, only the welling of praise that led to poetry, and in her mind so many psalms collided—*O who can utter the mighty acts of the Lord? Who can shew forth all His praise? Make a joyful noise unto the Lord, all ye lands*—that they ran together. Not once in her many years of prayer had she laughed aloud during the act, but now at her jumble of words she did, and best of all, she felt in her deepest, most joyous heart that the Heavenly Father, too, was laughing to see His servant Hattie, who always and earnestly tried to be good, filled with a spirit so giddy it couldn't help being holy.

From then on it seemed that everything went right. The day of the trip dawned fair and warm. An early riser, Hattie dressed in navy blue slacks and a white cotton blouse and her bone-colored Clarks even before she prepared Abel's breakfast. She stationed her sun hat and scarf on the foyer table. As the others awakened and breakfasted she went about the kitchen preparing a lunch for Abel and Big Bill. Meatloaf that would stay warm in the oven, two well-scrubbed russet potatoes in the microwave, and in the refrigerator a pretty strawberry Jell-O mold. The table was set for the two men. She'd replenished the cookie jar with a batch of Abel's favorite molasses crisps.

ClairBell was known for backing out at the last minute, or at least stalling departures, but she arrived on time and in high spirits. Up the driveway toward the house her white Cadillac surged, ClairBell at the wheel honking the horn and waving gaily. Into the house she came, toting her signature blue train case—this stocked with pills and unguents, Ace wrap, a snakebite kit, bandages, a tube of Lidocaine in case of beesting or what-have-you, an outsized orange plastic vial filled with other more private necessities—and a giant economy-sized bag of red hots she'd stopped to buy at Costco.

In the kitchen as they made ready the girls clowned around, fixing plastic go-cups of Diet Pepsi and making jokes. Their banter was so good-natured that even Hattie, who often found their humor, especially ClairBell's, too raucous, had to laugh. The only potential blot came when, just as she picked up the dishcloth to make a final swipe at the countertop, the telephone rang.

All three women lunged. Doro feared it was Billy wanting to be picked up from the bus stop and she would have to tell him no in order to protect their mother's day, but then her mother would be upset with her and wasn't this always the way? ClairBell suspected it was Billy wanting to be picked up from the bus stop and their mother would once again abandon her to cater to her boy-child's whim and wasn't that always the way? Hattie worried it was Billy wanting to be picked up from the bus stop and that she would have to suffer ClairBell's wrath at changing their plans, which of course she would for she couldn't deny her son and anyway why should she have to?

ClairBell reached the phone first, and when Doro and Hattie heard her say, "No, thanks, not today, and please take us off your list," they relaxed. "Darn telemarketers," ClairBell said, hanging up.

Though they should have known better than to take ClairBell's words at face value, they did, and they gave no more thought to the incident. But the caller was indeed Billy, who wanted to be fetched home from the bus stop. Dismissed so rudely by ClairBell, he smoked a Maverick or two about the insult, and then he popped a Xanax, a Percodan, and a pale-blue something and started walking the five miles between the bus stop and his parents' house, intending to tell off Miss Crosspatch. He was known for zingers, was Billy, whether sedated or soaring, and for eloquence. His vocabulary rivaled his father's, and he determined to fix his sister's snippy little spite-wagon once and for all. But by the time he reached home late in the afternoon he'd forgotten his resolve. He was so exhausted and hungry that he could do little but forage for food—a meatloaf sandwich, a few bites of baked potato, a forkful of Jell-O, and too many cookies—and collapse in a recliner in front of his father's television set. But ClairBell's lie at least saved Hattie from fretting about what woe would betide when Billy came face-to-face with his father without her as buffer. And with Big Bill there to boot. There was no love lost between the two Williams, for too often Big Bill had fielded drunken late night phone calls from Billy's associates.

They were off, Doro driving the powder-blue Skylark, Hattie at shotgun, and in the backseat ClairBell and her train case. As they pulled out of the driveway they met Big Bill in his red Dodge Ram. He lifted two fingers from the wheel to greet them, flicked the switch on his Fire Squad cherry top, and *whoop-whooped* his siren as they passed.

To keep up their spirits as they drove through town, Hattie asked, "Isn't this nice, just the three of us?" She smoothed her slacks over her knees.

ClairBell rarely let an idle comment pass. Especially if the comment was of the Pollyanna variety she was compelled to prick it with pins. "Mother, can you believe that not one of your boys tried to horn in on our girl day? Will wonders never cease?" She palmed a pile of red hots into her mouth and gave them a satisfying crunch.

Even to her own ears the laugh Doro intended to sound breezy sounded false, but she was determined to keep ClairBell's invidious remarks from ruining the trip. "They wouldn't enjoy themselves," she said, signaling a turn at the two-lane that led west out of town. "We'd drive too slowly and we wouldn't stop at their salvage yards and stock auctions." She pulled the Skylark onto the road and accelerated.

Hattie smiled. "Oh, I think Billy would enjoy himself. He'd have us listening to opera and . . ."

Suddenly the air in the car changed. The aroma of cinnamon and high fructose corn syrup pervaded as ClairBell heaved a dramatic sigh. From the backseat could be heard a sharp flip-flip-flipping of a train case's catch.

Calculating that a put-down of their brother might be balm for ClairBell's injured feelings and proud of herself for walking the tightrope between her mother and her sister, Doro continued, ". . . and singing along in his horrible foghorn voice!"

Hattie tightened her lips, but she understood that Billy must be slandered as a sacrifice to the mood gods of ClairBell, who snorted and then rallied to sing in a lunatic Bugs Bunny voice, with reddened tongue and teeth, "Welcome to my shop, lemme cut your mop, lemme shave your top. Daint-i-leeee . . ." Doro joined her in burlesquing snatches of arias and soon the danger had passed.

As they made their way along the next stretch of highway the women fell quiet, settling into their trip. The road ahead, shimmering with mirages, disappeared under the tires as though into a great thresher, and then spilling out behind them. For a time Hattie remained alert for landmarks, for changes in the prairie as they moved from county to county, the dirt growing redder, the trees growing sparser, buttes and mesas rising from the plains, but soon the rhythm of the tires lulled her, and she was unhitched from the present to range from past to future and back, adrift in time. Her thoughts went first, as they always did, to Billy, to her worries about his health, his finances, his difficult dealings with Abel, but like a jarred turntable before the needle hits a groove, her thoughts jerked and skipped and instead caught on her first boy, on the highway miles she'd once driven across the state to Springfield, Missouri, where Nick lay dying in an emergency room.

This was during the awful decade when the world fell apart, the early 1970s. Abel had kept a city practice then, in addition to his duties in Amicus. He was drinking too much for her liking and he kept company with insurance men and divorce lawyers whose ethics she mistrusted. Some of them were philanderers. And in the middle of the upheaval of the so-called sexual revolution he had brought home a book called *Ideal Marriage* by a Dutchman named T. H. van de Velde who had odd ideas about marital relations. Some of these ideas were mild enough, and though she didn't much care for them, at least they didn't offend decency. But others, oh! She had thrown the terrible book in the trash.

Everything in those years was about sex or drugs or civil unrest. The old order was shattered. The war in Vietnam had split the country. The children changed almost before her eyes. Her once-studious Doro had dropped out of college and hitchhiked to Denver to work in a hotel. Nick grew out his hair and beard and spent long days at Riverside Park, doing things that made him smell like skunk and scalp and unwashed clothes. Jesse quit college after two weeks to bunk up with his high school girlfriend. ClairBell had scraped through high school by the skin of her teeth. Gideon went off to KU but seemed to drink his room-and-board allowance in beer-can-sized installments. Only Billy, twelve and still a child, had not abandoned her. Her baby was too big to ride standing up in the front seat beside her as he had as a toddler, his arm protectively around her neck, but he still rode on the bench seat next to her, and he had no problem that couldn't be solved by a stop at the Dairy Queen or a new Uncle Scrooge McDuck comic book.

Nick had been the decade's casualty. Hoping to prove himself, he concealed his condition and enlisted. Despite the blue lips and clubbed fingers that should have signaled heart defect to the military doctors, he had passed the Navy physical. Six months later, when his limitations became clear, he was medically discharged, but at boot camp he'd picked up a drug habit—uppers, downers, heroin—that would eventually kill him. Hattie and Abel had him in and out of Menninger's. After a second stint at the clinic, Nick had gotten clean enough that despite a sore wisdom tooth he was able to go with a cousin on a cross-country motorcycle trip. On the way back from New York the tooth flared and Nick's wrecked system allowed the infection to shoot to his brain.

Abel had talked to the emergency room doctor and seemed to think Nick was stable, that there would be time to fly over to Missouri in a client's Cessna the next morning, but Hattie knew the boy wouldn't last the night. She knew. There was a price for a world out of balance and this was it. Vietnam hadn't taken him, but drugs would. She pleaded with Abel to drive over immediately but he wanted to wait, and so she made the six-hour trip alone. Of that drive she remembered little. She hadn't listened to the radio. She hadn't cried. She had barely prayed, she was so stunned, so angry. She'd made it in time to see Nick still breathing, to see the smoothing of his brow when she took his hand

and spoke to him, to feel his fingers, though weakly, squeeze hers in return.

Even after all this time, though she'd never spoken of the old anger and she mostly thought it behind her, it could sometimes overtake her. Now, as the highway passed under the Skylark's tires, came the stark question she'd tried to outrun since she'd put Toodles to sleep: Was it possible that she'd done that to punish Abel?

The car had come to a stop and her daughters were getting out. They'd reached the crossroads town of Sawyer, to which railroad siding Hattie's father and his father before him had driven herds of cattle. They planned to eat lunch in a cafe Hattie remembered where the strawberry pie and fried chicken were good. She got out of the car and gathered her wits to look around, feeling dizzy and unreal in the white gravel lot and the wide blue sky.

A rust-streaked grain elevator loomed whitely, beside it an open but deserted gas station no bigger than a shack. Doro remarked that they hadn't passed another car for the last half hour. The only evidence of life festered by the roadside, a dead Great Plains skink at least a foot long, fat as an armadillo and buzzing with flies. All around them spread the red dirt prairie, the wind riffling the big and little bluestem, the blue grama grass. The town, or what was left of it, looked makeshift, impermanent, a ghost town, and the place that figured so beautifully in Hattie's memory felt mean and shabby.

To tide them over, Doro bought some PayDay candy bars from a machine, and as she handed them out, Hattie said, "I don't know what I was thinking. Let's just go home. The drive was trip enough."

Her daughters shared the patronizing look she hated for its pained patience. She well knew her reputation as a second-guesser, a ditherer, an eleventh-hour mind-changer. ClairBell crossed her arms. "You got us all the way out here to the backside of bum-fuzzle Egypt and we're not leaving until we find the old place."

Doro consulted the map and they took off south toward the Oklahoma line, toward Medicine Lodge. The farmhouse was long gone—burned to the ground during the Dust Bowl years—but they hoped to find the land. The road rose and fell as the hills grew higher and more rugged and the valleys and washouts lower. Doro thought to say something about how the landscape made her think of *Blood Meridian*, but there was no one who would know what she meant. Miles they drove, turning down one road after another, white clouds swirling at the window glass as the car's passage stirred gravel dust made of dolomite and gypsum, until suddenly there was Elm Creek Road and Hattie shouted, "This is it!"

Doro yanked the car into a sharp right turn, and Hattie felt her pulse in her throat. Things looked familiar, the lay of land, the feel of sky, in the distance the bluff that rose beyond the ground where the house had stood, the bluff where once she'd been stalked by a mountain lion. Though it would ruin her new permanent she rolled down the window and stuck her head out like a dog's. Grasshoppers spanged against the windshield and she ducked to avoid them but she wouldn't put her head back inside. The road twisted through a gully past a campground where their Baptist church had held the revival where she'd first gone forward. From the gully the road led to the upland pasture where she'd once wandered, lonely as a cloud. A covey of quail flushed and a cock pheasant whirred up from the roadside. "Stop," she cried.

Doro pulled over and they got out. Now that they weren't moving with the car the world seemed to slow down. The sky grew wider. A fragrant breeze soughed across the grass, and the ground as far as eye could see blazed with wildflowers. Mallow, dogbane, sensitive briar, coneflower, fringed salt cedar like bursts of feathery pink gauze, light as spun sugar—on and on they rolled to the horizon, where yet more blooming hills billowed like waves. Wild rose, thistle, larkspur, rue. Bluets and lupine, wild violet, deep purple locoweed and buckeye, tumble mustard, sumac and indigo, gingerbread root. Here on the empty prairie in May was the heaven of flowers, blooming for no one at all. "This," Hattie said to the wind, "is just the way I remember it."

She and her daughters walked the pasture, marveling at the flowers. The world over, their poor dowdy state earned ridicule from those who had not learned where—or how—to look, for the vastness of the land and the haste with which most people crossed it served as a veil. Prairie natives, Hattie and her daughters knew they had to stop, turn off the car, walk out a ways, and wait until the wind found them. They knew that if still they failed to feel the beating of the great slow heart of earth beneath their feet, the fault was theirs.

As they wandered they called out names of flowers and the others would come to inspect, to confirm or dispute. Doro deferred to ClairBell, accepting her names—goats beard for salsify, blister buttercup for crowfoot. This concession struck Hattie as out of the ordinary, for Doro was a shameless know-it-all, but she thought no more about it except to see that some kind of change seemed to have come over her daughters, that somehow they were easier in themselves. The three of them walked to the crest of a hill and stood, the warm wind buffeting them, quietly looking out over what had been the floor of a vast inland sea. At first Hattie thought a grasshopper had landed on her back, but as an arm slipped gently around her waist she realized the touch was ClairBell's. It occurred to Hattie that the whole long day she had forgotten to judge her younger daughter, to compare her with her sister, and she wanted, suddenly, to cry.

On the way home they stopped in Kingman for lunch. The girls kept asking her if she was all right—she seemed so subdued—but Hattie merely smiled, spooning her tomato soup. "Never better." On the last stretch of highway, Doro and ClairBell chatted in the front seat, but Hattie, who had chosen the backseat in order to commune with her thoughts, tuned them out and soon slept. At some point, though Hattie didn't hear, ClairBell whispered to Doro the truth about Billy's phone call, and though Hattie didn't see, Doro reached over to pat ClairBell's hand, mouthing the words, "You did the right thing."

At home they found the dead cottonwood reduced to a neat wall of cordwood. Big Bill's truck was gone. In the kitchen a tableau of rebuke had been arranged to make it look like starving men, perhaps on the brink of diabetic coma, had staggered through the kitchen and, finding little to sustain them, trudged on toward death. The loaf pan teetered precariously on a stove burner so the congealed grease formed an orange pool, two butter knives had been stuck in the meatloaf like crossed sabers, and a gash in the meatloaf's center looked as if it had been excavated with a trowel. A potato had been savaged, a loaf of bread defiled, the Jell-O forked into. The cookie jar was empty.

ClairBell and Doro rolled their eyes at the evidence of their father's handiwork. "Neglected Husband Attacks Kitchen!" ClairBell said.

Doro laughed. "Meatloaf Slain!"

Arm in arm the sisters headed for the guest room.

Hattie was glad it was so easy for them to cut up. All that work wasted, just to buy a day for herself. She set to cleaning the kitchen. Usually domestic tasks calmed her, but on this day she became more and more angry. After a day of beauty, of the rare and somehow unsettling gesture of affection from her usually difficult younger daughter, to come home to this! From Abel's back bedroom den the television blared, the volume set at the threshold of pain. She had a good mind to march down the hall and for the first time in their long marriage give him what-for. For old wounds and new affronts. For every time he'd criticized her driving or her cooking or her reasoning. For the way he sometimes said her name as if speaking to a child. For the way he wouldn't pray over meals. For his moods. Because he'd called a dog his sweetheart. For the way their children tied themselves in knots trying to please him. For not believing the best of Billy, who needed his love and who wanted to love him. For the loneliest drive on the darkest day of her life. For time and loss and history and sorrow, mixed. She could hear him saying patronizingly, when confronted with her accusations, "You have to learn to pick your battles, Hattie," but she would not. She would fight them all, and all at once.

As she put away the ruin of the lunch she'd prepared, as well as—mysteriously—a crumpled bag from Walt's Cheap Hamburgers, a nasty little joint Abel favored, and two Styrofoam coffee cups, she weighed the words she would say. She needed a speech his rhetorical wiles couldn't turn against her, and at length she had composed a statement. "Abel," she would say, "from now on our marriage will be a two-way street." Then she would turn and walk away before he mustered an argument.

Down the hall toward his den she went, second-guessing herself even as she neared his door, wondering if their union had always been a two-way street and maybe she'd just been trying all these years to drive in the wrong lane. She stopped at the open door and looked into the room. There, in his sheepskin-lined chair, he reclined, asleep and snoring, weary from his exertions with his brother and the chainsaw. The television's light glared onto his smudged glasses. Beside him in the matching recliner, under the afghan she'd knitted, also asleep and snoring, his mouth open and a runnel of saliva glistening on his chin, lay Billy.

Her breath caught and the sand went out of her. How had Billy found his way home? Had Abel gone to fetch him? Had there been a scene, a set-to? All she knew was that the two dozed in front of the same Discovery Channel show, peaceably inhabiting the same room while on the screen the ground around a volcano began to crack and roll.

As she regarded them, ominous music swelled, the image on the television changed, and the flickering light went red. With a rumbling bass crescendo the volcano erupted, and Hattie surprised herself by letting out a puff of air, a sort of laugh, at so crude and yet so fitting a signal for the shift of ground she felt. On the screen, lava oozed, and in its fiery glow she saw that she'd set her husband as a stone, her life's impediment, her obstacle, when maybe it was the other way around. She'd always thought she was the glue that held her cracked, imperfect family together, but—she couldn't think of a word for the opposite of glue—maybe she was the obstacle between them, all of them, not just Abel and Billy but all of them, orchestrating, always orchestrating, trying to pose them like dolls in order to make a picture of a family that they weren't and never would be.

She turned from the doorway and went back to the kitchen where she leaned for a time on the counter, waiting for her heart to slow. "Make me an instrument of thy loving kindness," she prayed. "Change *me*." She picked up the carafe and splashed cold coffee into a cup and brought it to her lips, sipped and swallowed, letting the bitter liquid cool her throat. She was tired from the day, but she set out flour and sugar, butter and eggs and molasses. About what she had seen she would not speak, not now or ever—the vision of her part in things was bleak, was terrible. But she would bake, she would fill the air with spice and warmth, refill the empty jar, and even if no one could taste the great change wrought in her, she would, and their lives together, even after all this time, might start again.

Six

In the living room between the Chickering spinet and the curio cabinet that held the senior portraits of the six children, mortarboarded and airbrushed in perpetual youth, a set of Norman Rockwell commemorative plates, Hattie's pincushion collection, Abel's gavel, bronzed, and the burnished nickel horsehead bookends Hattie had given Abel as a wedding present was a handsome Morris chair in dark mahogany and black leather, with carved lion's-head armrests and ball-and-talon feet. This was the Eliot chair, handed down to Abel by his mother, Alice, whose family had lived in comfort and plenty until her father, a fancier of fast women, blooded horses, and strong drink, drove their fortunes to ruin. The chair was all that remained of the Eliot glory, and each of the five children was desperate to inherit it, for it was more than a chair.

During the fifties when the first five were small and Abel was an insurance claims adjuster working in an office in downtown Chicago, he would come home past dark, wearing a black fedora, his thick wool topcoat smelling of city and unfiltered Winstons and snow, and the little ones would clamor to meet him, patting him down and chirping,

"Any candy, any gum?" Sometimes his pockets would conceal a pack of Beeman's Pepsin Chewing Gum or Juicy Fruit or Chuckles, anything that came in fives. Chuckles were the favorite, though one child always got stuck with the green one. Usually ClairBell or Gideon. Yellow and orange and purple were tolerable, but the red Chuckle was the prize, and the child who received it would prance about, lording it over the others, as it was taken as a token of their father's favor. All of this to say that the Eliot chair was the red Chuckle.

Doro believed she had earned it. Not only was she the oldest, but the last thing she would ever do would be to cross her parents. She strived always to please, and she was the only one who had made her way in the world without help from her parents. Sure, there had been her hippie interlude in Denver. A pot-smoking, hash-piping, Quaalude-popping, acid-dropping, war-protesting, peace-marching, free-love extravaganza. But that was 1970 and the whole country was acting up. And then there was the matter of the hamburger stand robbery she and a boyfriend had once pulled off, an inside job at a joint he worked in. Four hundred bucks she'd hidden in a box of Tide and eventually spent on she-couldn't-remember-what, probably more hip-hugger bell-bottoms and rib-knit turtlenecks and hand-tooled leather. This probably qualified her for felon status, but fortunately no one knew—she was careful to keep her mouth shut about her own misadventures—and surely the statute of limitations had run out. The chair, by rights and despite her long-ago and well-rued crimes, should come to her.

Jesse believed just as strongly that the chair should be his because he was, by default, the reigning first-born boy, and among Campbells and Eliots primogeniture carried the day. Moreover, he bore the family name, Jesse Eliot, and he had two sons—one named Eliot, to whom he could pass the chair when the time came. ClairBell's claim on the chair was that she never got anything, not one solitary thing, and she should have the chair as a consolation prize to make up for the thousand ways she'd been slighted, from the moment of birth—nay, the moment of conception!—to the present day. Gideon had no sentimental attachment to the chair, but even if he was so far down in the birth order that there was no hope of receiving it, at least he wanted his fair chance, no matter that all he would do with the chair would be to sell it, for the proceeds could keep him in tallboys for a goodly number of months. Billy believed that his well-known love of history and art and architecture and fine things in general, along with the fact that he was probably the only one besides maybe Doro or Abel who knew the meaning of the words *scion* and *ultimogeniture* entitled him to be sole heir and assign.

Although they all wanted it, most refrained from letting their desires be known. To begin jockeying before Hattie and Abel were gone struck them as greedy and crass. All of them but ClairBell, who felt no such compunction and who in Abel's waning years had begun to mount in earnest her final campaign for the chair. That her efforts were obvious to her parents as well as her siblings was lost on ClairBell, who believed she had so far and quite cleverly concealed her desire under a veil of seeming disregard for the item by making such offhanded remarks as, "Oh, that old hunk of junk? I'd take it if nobody else wanted it, of course." But at some point in every visit to her parents' house she'd make mention of the chair, find occasion to sit in it, running her hands down its smooth armrests, fingers lingering on the lion's heads, making sure to put a fond look in her eyes, and so the others knew well enough what her game was.

In all things, her hope of inheriting the chair included, ClairBell consulted her spirit guides. At latest reading the psychic signs pointed to her being the most deserving recipient. Ever since she was a child, she had known she possessed powers, the gift of clairvoyance, second sight, whatever you wanted to call it. Not to put too fine a point on it, she was pretty much a witch.

She could feel the magic deep in her bones, in the shiver that ran up her spine when a message arrived from the shadow realm. If a message came to her out of the blue on a clear, bright morning that it would rain, before the sun went down the rain would fall. If a cousin announced her pregnancy, ClairBell's mind supplied the due date. She had prophesied the birth dates for nieces and nephews, predicting sex (six out of seven), weight (within three ounces), and length (within the half inch). In addition to their vital statistics she received premonitions as to their destinies, and most of these had come to pass. One of Jesse's boys had become a pilot, the other a firefighter, one of Doro's daughters was a soprano soloist and the other two had gone into medical fields like their father, just as ClairBell had foretold. Gideon's oldest girl was in law school at Washburn, Abel's alma mater, and the youngest had just finished her first year of veterinary school at Kansas State. About her own boys' callings, she had been less accurate. She'd received no messages whatsoever, especially not about their joining the Army or managing the DoNut Dinette, but she reckoned the bloodlines were too close and this had bollixed the spirit communication. The cobbler's children with no shoes and so on. Besides, the boys were still finding their ways. They'd had none of the advantages the other nieces and nephews possessed, and this lack was solidly the fault of their father, Burton Moody, who even though he was supposed to be a big accountant hadn't been able to tolerate the demands of marriage and fatherhood. He acted like sending child support every month fulfilled his duty. Every time old Burt the Shirt tried to come around to meddle in her life under the guise of concern for the boys or to lecture her about her housekeeping or her spending or how shabbily the boys were dressed or what she fed them or whatever, she'd give him an earful on the subject of his low-down good-for-nothingness—and so what if the boys heard her or the neighbors called the police about the window she shattered with the cast-iron skillet, what did he expect?—and, after a time, he'd stayed away, which was good riddance anyway. She'd known before she even married him that he was uptight and controlling, a penny-pinching stick-in-the-mud with no sense of fun. All work and no play and rules and regulations out the wazoo. Not to mention his actual wazoo. Man walked like he had a corncob stuck up his butt. So dull you dozed off five minutes after he opened his other end to talk about actuarial tables or deductibles or whatever sleep-inducing drone-fest came spewing forth. Why she'd failed to heed her inner light and save herself a lot of trouble where Burt Moody was concerned, she'd never know.

To keep her powers of clairvoyance sharp, certain rituals were necessary. For instance, she had to count the food pieces she put in her mouth—M&Ms, cashews, red hots, whatever. One was okay and threes and fours were fine, as that made seven, which was lucky, but to put only two of anything into her mouth at the same time augured disaster. So far she'd succeeded. From time to time she made little tests for herself, making sure her radar worked, and she always passed. Once, during a period between her marriages to Burt the Shirt and Jimbo Green, when she was at a low point and had begun to doubt her abilities and no messages had visited her for a time, she turned on the television and happened onto a *Kojak* rerun from the eighties. There was Telly Savalas with his shining bald head and a lollipop sticking out of his mouth. The hair on her forearms stood up, her spine quivered: Telly Savalas wasn't long for the world. He would die soon. *Within the year,* her secret sense told her. And it was so.

Her greatest triumph had to be the inspiration she'd received some years after the assassination of Toodles, back when Abel was in his late seventies. He had stepped down from the bench, sold what was left of his practice, along with the office building on Hale Haven Road. Sold the Kansas Case Law books Doro wanted, a sale that, although ClairBell pretended to sympathize with her sister at the loss, had given her a pretty good laugh. ClairBell couldn't bear it when their father gave something to one of her brothers or her sister. Even something small. Just the year before, Doro had worn a clunky necklace with a Buddhisty-looking design, and he'd complimented it and then he'd given Doro a Chinese coin medallion he'd had since his and Hattie's trip to Hawaii. In front of everyone! ClairBell couldn't contain her tears. She clattered up from the table and yelled at Randy to take her home. Randy tried to calm her down by telling her that the medallion was a cheap tourist trinket you could get at any Honolulu souvenir shop for a buck fifty, but value wasn't the point. Her father hadn't given it to her and she took it hard.

Anyway, back to her greatest inspiration. Something had told her that after his retirement Abel was losing his rudder. Month by month he seemed to be shrinking. The Carhartts he'd taken to wearing had begun to sag in the hind end. He wandered around the property, stopping to gaze into the creek, to ponder the great chunk of white marble he'd hoisted onto sawhorses behind his barn. He saw a white whale in it, he'd told everyone, but somehow he couldn't make the first mark with his hammer and chisel to release its shape. He had lapses of judgment. At Easter, along with the jelly beans and marshmallow chicks, he'd placed in his four-year-old great-grandson's basket a .22-caliber air rifle. In fact, when she thought back, this was probably the beginning. On Thanksgiving Day of that year, at her mother's table as she'd poured gravy onto potatoes and dressing and turkey and counted out three creamed onions and four peas, it had come to her like a flash that her father was in need of something to live for.

At that time in her parents' life, the early nineties, the house was empty but for the two of them. The Boomerang Boys had at last settled elsewhere—Gid had packed up for New Mexico to begin his dual career in drink and disgruntlement, and Billy, with high hopes and at a stable point in his health with the help of AZT, had gone east to make a new life with Doro and her daughters. This left Hattie and Abel alone and for the first time in their lives with no children to worry about. They had begun to knit themselves together again.

They were happy and healthy. Hattie, knocking on wood and whispering a prayer, had begun to think their troubles were behind them and that maybe their golden years might actually have a little luster. As for Abel, he would have been surprised by his daughter's diagnosis of his lack of zest for living. He considered that his seventies were by far his best decade. He had at last outgrown the young man's competitive follies but he'd maintained the interests—welding, electronics, machinery, astronomy, stone-carving, physics, history, theology—that kept his mind agile, and he had come, finally, to understand the difference between cleverness and wisdom. He had begun to reconcile the dogmatic training of his youth with the fruits of his education to work out a view of religion and its dilemmas, an idea of creation and the order of the universe—now the multiverse—that would allow him peace. He reckoned that it had taken him a long time to become who he had always been, but now that he knew, his days were fine and full.

But ClairBell had decreed that something was missing, and so this became the fact upon which she based her operation. She cast about for the solution and it came to her with the strength of a nine-volt charge: a puppy! Abel must have a puppy to replace Toodles, a puppy to be presented as a gift so that Hattie, who had killed the poor old doggie of blessed memory in cold blood and vowed she'd never have another animal in the house, could not say no.

She persuaded Jesse to go in with her on the puppy surprise, strong-armed him into coughing up half the price of a sweet little black-and-white Chihuahua–rat terrier mix, male. She made arrangements to pick up the pup at the breeder's farm so they could present him on Christmas Eve. She found a red ribbon to tie in a bow around the dog's neck, and on the appointed day she dressed him in a doll's sweater and tied the ribbon just so. As she and her sons pulled into the long driveway and moved toward the door of her parents' house, she envisioned a blazing fire, the sequined felt stockings bearing all of their names, even Nick's, hung in stair steps from the mantel, tree lights glistening, and the folks sitting side by side on the sofa, probably sharing the snootified plaid lap robe from Maine that those uppity-ups Doro and Billy had sent as their Christmas gift. Into all of this warmth and tradition she would bring a far better offering, a brand-new, living, breathing, bow-ribboned Christmas puppy. It would be a scene straight out of Thomas Kinkade!

But her triumphal entry fell flat. She had instructed her sons, middle-school aged and balky, to go through the door ahead of her and shout "Surprise!" This they did, but in a mumble, giving the impression that a parade of oafs, a scouting party of Sasquatches had shambled into the room. She had concealed the puppy under her puffy ski coat, but he began to whimper so desperately that it sounded like ClairBell herself, or at least her ski coat, was in distress. The sound drew Hattie to the fore with concern, but when she caught sight of the dog emerging from his hiding place in the vicinity of her daughter's collarbone she threw her hands in the air. The sight of the creature was like seeing Toodles returned from the dead, and she shrieked, "No! Get that dog out of here!"

But ClairBell had already crossed the room to bestow the wriggling gift. From Abel's lap the puppy squirmed up his chest and into the crook of his neck where he began to lick madly at Abel's ears and cause him to laugh in a way she hadn't remembered hearing him laugh for years.

Hattie went to stand over him, wringing her holly-sprigged apron. "No," she cried, "Abel, oh, please. Not again!"

"But just look at this little dandy," Abel began, but then he caught a glimpse of his wife's face. The barbed-wire scar on the end of her nose had whitened, a sure sign of anger. Or maybe fear. Reluctantly he took the puppy—he, too, had hoped the golden years had come, he had his bride back after years of ginger relations, and he wanted nothing to tarnish them—and handed the dog back to ClairBell. "Sister, he's a peach, all right, and from the bottom of my heart I thank you for your thoughtfulness, but you'd best take him back."

Oh, the hurt. Once again she had tried only to please and once again her mother had rejected her efforts. She had gathered the dog, let fly some scorching words aimed at Hattie, words she couldn't remember later but which Hattie would never forget, and stormed out, the boys shuffling dejectedly, big-footedly, behind her.

She couldn't have known and, in her anger and hurt, she wouldn't have cared that across the country Billy and Doro, once they heard the story, considered the whole drama a deliberate flouting of their mother's wishes, as manipulation, as another of the traps their sister set for their mother so she would look bad. From the East Coast they had called home to wish their parents a merry Christmas and when they heard the terrible tale from Hattie via speakerphone they looked at each other with horror, with outrage and horror, made more outrageous and horrible by the fact that their sister had pulled such a ClairBellian stunt on Christmas Eve.

Billy asked, "Mother, where is the dog now?"

Hattie cleared her throat. "She took it away. It's at her house. I'm afraid I hurt her feelings. She called me some terrible names. . . ."

"What names?" Billy wanted to know, ready to spring to her defense.

In a small voice, Hattie said, "Oh . . . witch with a *B*. Bag with an *H*. I can't remember the rest."

Doro broke in. "Let the damned dog stay out there." She wanted to travel through the phone lines as avenging angel and give her sister a piece of her mind. "What was she thinking?"

Hattie's voice had taken on the wavering quality it sometimes did at times of high stress. "The puppy was cute as a button. Like Toodles when she was young. In fact the little thing was just about a dead ringer—" She stopped herself when she realized the expression she'd used, and started again. "I'm sure it was expensive, but I just couldn't . . ."

Billy leaned in to the speaker. "Don't relent, Mother. Whatever you do, don't relent. The nerve of her! She can't make you take something you don't want."

"Especially a dog," Doro put in. She could scarcely believe that the significance of such a gift—a replica of Toodles, bane of their mother's housekeeping existence, emblem of all that had once been wrong in their parents' marriage, a dog that was more than a dog—was lost on her sister.

Hattie cleared her throat, and in her voice, gone suddenly distant and preoccupied, her eldest and youngest heard the beginnings of waffling, of second-guessing, a familiar train of thought coming down the tracks on schedule. "Well, I suppose she must have had her reasons."

After they hung up, Billy and Doro lingered long before the fire in Doro's little study, drinking mulled cider and deploring their sister's reasons, whatever they were. "All dysfunctional families are ruled by their craziest member," Doro said knowingly, quoting something she'd read somewhere in her search for a reason for her family's flaws in general and ClairBell's in particular. She hoped her gambit would lead to more deploring.

Billy sipped his cider and duly deplored. He'd done plenty of time in the crazy seat but he was better now, in a period of calm, sobriety, and sanity, and it pleased him greatly that his solid-citizen sister found someone else's behavior outrageous. He was only too happy to join the dogpile on the rabbit that was ClairBell. "You can say that again," he said, raising his glass.

Doro said it again, and they laughed. Long into the night they sat in the study, a window cracked so they could enjoy their Christmas gift to each other, the forbidden and rare pleasure of smoking a cigarette in the house, dissecting and examining ClairBell's ways. How since her second divorce—from the pool hustler Jimbo Green—all she did was sleep. Billy said the trouble was drugs, painkillers to be exact, and they chewed on that for a while. How her rental farmhouse was a certifiable pigsty and she neglected her children—this was a favorite talking point of Doro's; before going to graduate school in her forties, Doro had made a career of competitive mothering. How every now and then their sister would bestir herself to slap on some makeup and a red cowgirl hat and slither out to do the boot-scoot boogie at the Coyote Club, but mostly she lolled on the couch in flannel pajama pants and a sweatshirt. And what about the time she got a bee in her bonnet about some imagined slight and engineered a boycott of Hattie's Thanksgiving table just to wound her? They reviewed in speculative detail the recent gift-giving scene—Abel in his place on the butternut chesterfield with his Asimov commentary books and his horn-handled magnifying glass, his *U.S. News & World Reports* in a stack on the end table, Hattie, be-aproned and flushed from the kitchen, perched eagerly on one of the wide arms of the Eliot chair, the tree lights a-twinkle and gaily wrapped presents arrayed on the hearth, awaiting the gathering she prayed would not end in hard feelings but which somehow always did.

"What a place," Doro said, and Billy said, "Amen to that." They congratulated themselves on finding their ways out of the tar pit that was Kansas, on being far from the heartbreaking sight of their elderly parents' attempts to mollify ClairBell's revolving-door moods by walking on eggshells, above it, in fact, and then they fell quiet, settling back in their chairs to let the fire burn to embers.

"There's no place like home," Billy broke their silence to say, aiming for wry, weary humor and a nod to waking from the dream of Oz, but succeeding only in sounding wistful.

"No place," Doro agreed.

It was late. They had smoked much and talked more and they were weary. Separately, their thoughts turned again to their sister. Doro thought of her wild blue eyes flashing in electric wit, wit that could stop the world, her kitty-cat smile, the soaring hilarity that carried everyone along on her flights of merrymaking, and her way of sometimes seizing Doro in a hug so strong and spontaneous it took her breath away. Billy thought of her long white-blond hair, piled every day into a different, whack ClairBell-do—tendrils or fountains or topknots festooned with five-and-dime bling or fake flowers—and of the sweet way she had, despite what he knew was resentment, despite the fact that she probably meant it only about half the time, of saying "Boysie, I love you," and making him know that no matter if she meant it or not, she always wanted to.

What neither Doro nor Billy would say to the other was that despite their harsh talk of their sister and the haywire ways of their family, despite their deploring of business-as-usual in the Crazed House of Home, how each of them missed it, how each of them, if a single Yule wish could be granted, would choose nothing more at that moment than to be exactly there.

Back in Amicus, after a disturbed night in which she hardly slept, Hattie had found herself stuck on the familiar flypaper of examining her actions for where she'd gone wrong. All she knew was that once again she'd injured her sensitive daughter and she needed to make things right. All Christmas Day, during which Abel was unusually quiet, spending most of the day in his ham radio shack trying to raise his old Army buddy in Djakarta, she fretted, and finally, as dusk drew nigh, she packed the unopened gifts she'd prepared for ClairBell and her children, some fruitcake, spritz, and pfeffernuss, and drove out to her daughter's tumbledown farmhouse.

Hattie didn't use strong language. She left hyperbole to her husband and children, for whom it seemed a native tongue. But if she had to put words to ClairBell's place on the Ninnescah River the words would be *hell* and *hole*. Cats, way too many both feral and tame, and their smells. Rabbits ran loose inside and out, burrowing under the slab. Cats chased rabbits. Buck rabbits humped cats. Dirt everlasting. Countertops piled high with dishes. Hillocks of dirty clothes. And now a trail of puppy piles and the stench of peed-upon rugs.

When her grandsons let her in, the puppy, which had been gnawing on a boot, scampered over to jump up and snag her knee-high hose with his toenails. She passed out presents for the boys and watched them exclaim over socks and underwear, a new shirt and a pair of jeans, something breaking a little in her heart to see their gratitude for the useful gifts. By and by ClairBell dislodged herself from her bed and frowsily entered the room, glowering, refusing to meet Hattie's eyes.

"What do you want?" she asked as she plopped onto the couch, scaring off a brindle tomcat, and just like that Hattie buckled. "I just thought," she began, meaning to say that she was sorry about her abruptness the night before and that she understood that ClairBell wanted only to please, but ClairBell interrupted triumphantly, "So now you decide you want him after all, eh? Did Daddy lay down the law? I don't blame him."

How, Hattie wondered, should she respond? No matter what she said, it would be wrong. ClairBell would take her words and use them as stones to throw, bricks to raise higher the grudge she'd erected. "Well," Hattie began, hoping to skirt any defensiveness on her daughter's part but also to make sure ClairBell knew she wasn't agreeing to keep the dog. But instead of giving the gentle and noncommittal answer she intended, she said, "I was thinking that maybe I should take him home with me and work with him. Get him paper-trained. Help you out a little."

ClairBell reached for the remote control and clicked on the television. On the screen the Tasmanian Devil laid waste to Daffy Duck's living room. "Sure," she said, pretending interest in the flickering mayhem, "whatever you have to tell yourself."

Abel took to the puppy right away, as ClairBell had foreseen, and even Hattie came around. They named him Muttley, and he became a great favorite, a low-slung, stocky, loyal little being who made them laugh. He was a rogue and a rake, a dog-about-town, siring several litters. He was named in a mock paternity suit brought by a jokester neighbor whose Cockerpoo's charms he had sampled. His finest hour was when he was featured as Pet of the Month in the Amicus *Friend*.

"Meet Muttley," ran the caption under his photo, followed by a write-up of his habits and doings, his favorite food—bacon—and his favorite toy—a stuffed fox. Like nothing else—not time, not talk or apology, not good will or forgetting or even forgiveness—it was Muttley who brought them together, sealing Hattie and Abel once more as husband and wife. For fourteen years he performed his healing offices before dying quietly of old age on a blanket in his official guard station under Hattie's side of the bed, the tattered remains of his fox under his grizzled chin. And this, ClairBell let no one forget, especially not her mother, was her own finest hour. Look how it had all turned out! Think of the obstacles placed in the way! But whose insight had triumphed and who had been right? Oh, yes, a witch, indeed. They should listen and learn.

Now, on an evening in late May all these years later, as she soaked in a bath scented with lavender in her new country house with its own greenhouse and a swimming pool and a chicken coop and everything she'd ever wanted, her third-time's-a-charm husband working nearby on his computer—an entirely new life, she reflected—it came to ClairBell that it didn't take a prophet to see that her father wouldn't live through another winter, and suddenly she had a vision so powerful it caused her to sit upright.

Not a dog this time, but something even better. Oh, Doro would scoff at her, or laugh, or else just balk when she tried to get her to pitch in, but her idea to set the world right during this time of her father's weakness and decline was perfect. And never mind Doro or the others, she would do it herself. She would send out the call to family far and wide, from stalwarts to second cousins once removed to shirttail relations and kissing kin, and they would all come because the grand party she would throw come August, in addition to being her father's birthday, would be a celebration of his long life as the family's head. He was the center, the grand old man, the beloved uncle and brother-in-law, the one they came to for advice legal and ethical and political and mechanical, his were the stories they wanted, his the approval they waited for, his the reason and logic they trusted. He was the pride of the family, and she would plan a party to tell him just that.

The bathwater had cooled, and so she ran more hot water into the tub and then settled back again, adjusting the pink zebra-print bath pillow under her neck. In her mind's eye she could see the reunion in full swing. The Campbells with their practical jokes and their antics, their hooting, braying laughter sounding like a congress of jack mules and Canada geese. Hattie's people, the quieter Davies clan, visiting among themselves about recipes, gardens, church, and trips to the Ozarks, covering their mouths demurely and saying how tickled they were when someone said something amusing. She'd have to deal with Doro and her posse of good-girl cousins, but never mind that. There they all were, her family, around her swimming pool—she'd have to get Randy to repair a crumbled spot on the coping and maybe buy some new float rings—or seated in lawn chairs on the rise overlooking the rolling hills of short-grass prairie—and maybe she could get him to finish building the loafing shed he'd started a few months back and they could rustle up a horse somewhere—maybe borrow one from a neighbor and pretend it was theirs—and have it in place in time to give rides to the kids. And, oh Lord, they'd need to rent porta potties! Either that or she'd have to get Randy to renovate the bathrooms. In her mind's eye there was the whole family standing around the big steel smokers steaming with barbecued ribs, hot dogs for the kids, eating her trademark baked beans, not Doro's gluey gourmet jobs from Boston or their cousin Carol's that tasted like tar-coated birdshot. Or wait! Home-cooked fried chicken and all the trimmings! She had forty or so hens and a few roosters and they were outgrowing their coop or was it the coyotes that were getting them? Whatever, there were plenty of them, and she'll-be-coming-round-the-mountain-driving-six-white-horses had nothing on her—she would kill the old red rooster and then some! Fried chicken it was! Praise would follow her wherever she went, circulating, chatting here with a group of cousins, laughing there with the aunts. "Isn't that ClairBell just a wonder?" she'd hear. "Can you believe she put all this together herself? So thoughtful. And when you think of how her family treats her!" And she would waft among them in a new peasant dress of white crinkle cotton. A dress she would design and sew! Maybe a wide leather belt cinched around her middle? Diamond rings on her fingers, a turquoise squash blossom necklace heavy at her breastbone. Of course before the party she would have to take off ten pounds or maybe thirty, but that was no problem. It was easy enough to cut back on red hots and M&Ms and trips to Taco Tico, maybe limit the Pepsi. Oh, and fireworks! She would get her boys to tend to this. They loved explosions. And guns, too. A twenty-one-gun salute would be moving but of course it was probably too much.

Any flies in the ointment? Yes. Billy. She didn't want him anywhere near. He would try to take over the food and instead of home cooking he'd whip up ridiculous concoctions that nobody liked—chafing dishes set on fire and raw-fish things and sauces made with shiitake (she like to died when she first heard that one!) mushrooms and capers and God knew what nasty, unpronounceable else. He'd try to cook even if he was high as a kite. In fact, that was *especially* when he wanted to cook. She tried to think where he was these days, besides freeloading off their parents. Oh, yes. He was living uptown in a grimy basement apartment, having taken up his career as a junkie just where he'd left off, only worse. How many times had she had to drive him to detox and bring him back from the brink? She couldn't keep straight all his ups and downs. Her mother and sister had been crushed by his every fall, for they believed he could change, but ClairBell had seen it coming and so had her father.

She'd been to his ratty apartment a few times, on one errand or another—once when she had a toothache and had run out of morphine and had to borrow some and another time to pick up a fentanyl patch—they were new and she wanted to try one for her arthritic knee—and it was a terrible place. She knew enough about the rabbit hole painkillers could lead you into, and the dank little room was full of signs that Billy was down pretty low. Besides, she didn't want him at the party because he was a blabbermouth. Couldn't keep his trap shut. He'd pal up to her and pretend they shared some big secret and make loud remarks about drugs and probably sell smack to her sons. He didn't understand that her prescriptions were actually prescribed; she'd no sooner buy street drugs than she'd buy her grandson the monkey he was always pestering her for. Either that or *Grand Theft Auto.* The other problem was that when Billy was around, their mother couldn't take her gaze off him and it was so painful and obvious that Daddy wasn't the most important man in her life. On this day Daddy was to be the man of the hour, not Billy. If Billy wasn't in jail or locked up in rehab or some such, she would deputize Dean Doro to bulldog him and keep him away from people. This would be nothing less than a quiet but masterful act of hospitality on her part, of kindness, really, to think of others this way. *Oh, ClairBell, ClairBell,* she thought, *you sweet little sweetheart.* How glad she was to be herself! To inhabit her skin! How glad to be just the way she was—big-hearted, generous, happy, and funny and thinking first of others!

The bathwater had grown cold, but just before she sat up to reach for the plug, she had the inspiration to end all inspirations: wouldn't it be wonderful if she could get Randy to load the Eliot chair into his truck and move it to the party so Daddy could sit in it like a king on his throne and the whole family—all hundred and how many relatives surrounding him—could pose for a portrait? Her heart thumped and her mouth went dry. From this vision there was hardly any distance at all to seeing him presenting the chair to her in front of everyone, with an elaborate speech to express his gratitude. Maybe he would even have tears in his eyes. Sudden tears of her own threatened to spring.

As she rose from the tub and reached for her towel, thinking that after she dried off she would put on her robe and go straight to Randy's desk for a pencil and paper to begin planning the party in earnest, a great sense of warmth and well-being, of outright elation, overcame her. The feeling was familiar. She tried to remember if before getting into the bathtub she'd accidentally taken one too many Lortabs. She would have to be careful about that kind of thing. Someone—most likely Doro, who fronted like She-Ra: Princess of Power and the designated driver of the world—might co-opt the party idea and take all the credit. It wouldn't do to spill her secret ahead of time. But she would call her mother in the morning, swear her to secrecy, and let her in on the plan.

Seven

On a night in late June, while Hattie lay sleeping soundly in the big bedroom, Abel was startled awake in his daybed in the back bedroom by the roar of an angry mob that milled in the south yard. The mob was bent on murder, preparing to storm the house. Doom was imminent. Calmly, with utmost stealth and a sense of mission, he rose from his bed, went to his gun cabinet, unlocked it, and took out his Sig Sauer P238. With great effort he strapped the gun belt over his boxer shorts, checked the gun's magazine, and holstered up. Then he went to wake Hattie.

"Get dressed," he whispered. "Put on your coat."

She stirred under the bedclothes, confused, only half awake. What was it now? she wondered.

"At once!" he ordered. "Put on your coat!"

She gaped at him, but gathered the bedclothes and turned them back so she might get out of bed.

Under his breath, his eyes wide, his teeth gritted, he said, "Hurry! Japanese!"

She decided to try reason. "It's summer, Abel. It's hot outside. I don't even know where my coat is. Japanese what?"

"Breaching the walls," he shouted. "Call the police! I'll cover you!"

She came fully awake and saw that he brandished a handgun. Her heart seemed to jump into her throat. "Abel! It's all right. There's no one out there."

He shushed her. He stood at the alert, gun at his side. "Listen. Hear them?"

Hattie sat up in bed. It was a warm, breezy summer night and she heard the wind soughing in the cottonwoods along the creek behind the house, their stiff, fletched leaves clattering in the usual sound they made, a bit like rainfall, but that was all.

When he repeated, "Call the police!" she realized that he was in a delusional state, that he was hallucinating. Sundowning. The horror of their situation overtook her.

"I will," she said, hoping to placate him. "Just let me find the phone." She got out of bed and started toward the kitchen.

"Company, halt!" he barked.

She halted.

"Let me go in first." He held the gun up, two-handed beside his face, the way they did in television shows. She let him lead.

The kitchen was dark and quiet. Outside the big window the trees tossed in the wind. Suddenly the refrigerator kicked on. He pivoted toward it, taking aim at the magnet-studded door.

Hattie groped along the counter for the phone. Her mouth was dry and when she spoke she could hardly get enough moisture to say, "Let me turn on the light."

"Negative. Ix-nay." When he was assured that the refrigerator presented no threat, he lowered the gun.

In the darkness she found the phone but couldn't think of what to do next.

"Nine-one-one," he provided. "Dial nine-one-one. Tell them we're under siege. I'm going to check the perimeter." Stepping cautiously around the corner, he moved toward the foyer and the front door.

Hattie made the call. "Help," she said when the dispatcher asked what her emergency was. "We need help. My husband has a gun. He thinks there are people trying to get in the house but there aren't any at all. Nobody's there. He's . . ." She couldn't find the word.

"Drunk?" the dispatcher supplied.

"Well, no, but he . . ."

"Are you afraid for your life?"

"No, he's just"—at last it came—"imagining."

The dispatcher asked some questions and she answered them—her name, what kind of gun, how old was her husband, and would he happen to be the judge who had once presided over the Amicus court?—then the woman said, "Ma'am, I'm sending the police, but they won't come near the house until the Judge puts down the gun. Where is he now?"

"I don't know," Hattie said. "He went out the front door."

"Can you check? I'll stay on the phone with you."

Hattie put down the receiver and went down the hallway to the front door. It was open to the night air and Abel was nowhere to be seen. She crept forward and looked outside. He was in the driveway, sitting in his truck with the driver's side door open. The alarm was pinging. By the dome light he was checking the magazine. She went back to report to the dispatcher.

"Do you have another door you can get out?"

Hattie tried to think. The house had five outside doors but she couldn't summon their names or think of where she was in relation to them. Finally she was able to say, "Yes, the back patio."

"Then you should try to get out and go to a neighbor's house."

"Oh, I couldn't," Hattie told her. "I couldn't leave him alone. He's not himself."

"Ma'am," the dispatcher said patiently, "you have to save your own life. If your husband . . ."

Just then Abel appeared in the doorway. "For crying out loud, tell them to step on it."

The dispatcher had heard him. "Ma'am, put your husband on the line, please. You need to move toward the nearest door."

Hattie had no intention of leaving the house, leaving him, but she held the phone toward Abel. "They want to talk to you."

He eyed her suspiciously, but then he took the phone and said into it, "State your business." After a time during which the dispatcher spoke, he said, "I will most certainly not."

Again the dispatcher spoke, and Abel replied, "I sat on the bench here for years. I suppose I know police procedure in this town." He put down the phone and held out the gun, butt first, to Hattie. "I'm handing it over to my wife right now." To Hattie he explained, as though she didn't know it, "The police are outside, down the driveway, but they won't come any closer unless this is out of the way. Put it in my top drawer." She wasn't sure, but he seemed to have come back to the world, or at least to be nearing its outskirts.

She took the gun, handling it as she would a snake, and went down the hall to his back room and placed it in his drawer. She was on her way back to the kitchen when she heard voices at the front door. Abel was greeting three uniformed officers and telling them about the siege.

A young officer entered behind the others, having checked out the house and yard. "Intruders appear to be gone now, Judge."

"And it's a damned good thing," Abel remarked. "I wasn't sure how long I could have stood them off." He peered at the lead officer. "What's your name, son? You look familiar."

"I'm Clay Ramsay, sir. Geneva and Tom's oldest boy."

"Well, Clay, did you ever stand before me on a charge?"

"No, sir, but my kid brother did. Rex?"

"Rex Ramsay. A DUI, if I recall. Nineteen ninety-eight?"

Clay Ramsay's eyebrows went up and he cocked his head quizzically. "Yes, sir, that's right."

"Well, I hope he's straightened himself out."

"He has, sir. Has two little girls."

The two men fell to talking, with the officer complimenting Abel on his quick thinking and good instincts. He fed Abel questions that allowed him to reminisce about his days on the bench and old times on the police force. Even Hattie could tell that Clay Ramsay was patronizing him, using psychology on him to get him to soften up, but Abel seemed unaware. He was happy and talkative, eager to contribute. He told his story about the outlaw El Ray Brady, dumbest criminal in Amicus, who stole a flatbed truck and took the time to change its paint color but didn't switch out the license plates before letting his teenage kid drive it down Hale Haven Avenue for the homecoming parade, carrying a load of football players and the cheer squad. Hattie had heard him tell the story many times. By and by Ramsay worked the conversation around to guns. "I'll bet you have a fine collection," he said.

Abel took the bait. "I do, indeed." He listed his guns, and when Ramsay said he'd love to see them, Abel led him down the hall to the cabinet.

"Glad to see you keep these locked up," Ramsay said. "Where's the one you had earlier?"

Abel opened his top drawer to reveal the gun, which lay where Hattie had placed it.

"May I?" Ramsay asked, indicating that he'd like to pick up the piece.

"Be my guest," said Abel. "Got that one in a manslaughter case twenty years ago. Police relieved the slaughterer of his weapon and I bid on it at the auction. Nice weight and a neat little grip."

Ramsay took an appreciative look at the gun and then handed it off to another officer, presumably so he, too, might inspect it, but Hattie saw the second officer open the magazine and unload it. "A fine piece," Ramsay said to Abel, drawing Abel's attention away by pointing toward the gun cabinet. "Do you think I could see the others?"

Abel nodded, taking the key from his ring. He opened the case wide to show the glistening firearms. A whiff of 3-in-One oil filled the room. Ramsay said, "Judge, you know that after a call like this we have to take these in, don't you? Just to run them. Routine procedure."

Abel deflated. Hattie saw his hard fall back to reality. She saw, too, that he was exhausted. He merely stood aside while the officers removed the guns from the cabinet and carried them out. She stepped forward and took him by the arm. "Let's get back to bed, dear," she suggested, and for the first time in their married life he let himself be led.

Standing at the kitchen sink, feeling spongy and blurred from so little sleep, Hattie blinked hard to trick herself into staying awake. It was late afternoon, the blue hour, and the day had been miserable. She didn't want to think about what happened in the night any longer. It was too big and too awful. She needed to put her mind on something—anything—else. So what was there? Any light spots in the day? Well, ClairBell had called. Hattie had tried to listen to what her daughter was saying, taking care to be attentive so as not to get on her bad side, but after they hung up she could barely remember a word the girl had said. Some grand plan for a birthday party.

Outside the windows a gray lady cardinal splashed in the birdbath until her swift, bright mate swooped down and startled her into flight. Hattie watched for a time as the two birds stitched the air, the male chasing the female from the box elder to the Japanese maple, squabbling as they flew, until at last they darted into the honeysuckle bower. On the grass below, the neighbor's cat toyed with a garter snake or maybe a mouse, crouching and twitching and pouncing like a mad victor. No matter which sight her gaze fell upon, she thought, the message was the same. She was the lady bird, she was the garter snake, she was the mouse, and something bigger and faster and fiercer was deviling her and it was no contest—she would lose.

She felt alone and weary. She knew she should think about starting supper but she was at a loss as to what to prepare that would please Abel, who wasn't speaking to her because of what had happened in the night.

She wondered, as she had often wondered throughout this hot and seemingly endless solstice day, if she should call Doro to alert her to the trouble. A call could be a good thing and it could be a bad thing—with Doro it was hard to predict. She might laugh it off or she might mobilize and upset everybody's apple cart and things would get even more haywire. Changes would come. Bad changes.

To untangle the thoughts that snarled in her mind, she left behind the problem of supper and went down the hall to the guest room. She turned on the television set. She tried to select a program but the array of choices was too daunting and so she left the channel where it was. She closed the door to dampen the noise from Abel's television in the next room. From the sound of things, he was watching another RFD-TV show about horses. Lately he'd been consumed with regret at having used a Spanish bit to train the horse he'd had as a boy. He watched any show about horses he could find, shaking his head mournfully, considering their beauty, nobility, and his own unwitting cruelty. He was taking it hard. He was wallowing. She wished she had the time to wallow.

She sat in her platform rocker, put her feet on the stool and started a gentle glide to calm herself. She drew a deep breath and rested her head. As they always had, thoughts of Billy presented themselves the minute she closed her eyes. She tried to will them away; the problem to be dealt with was Abel. But—really—she didn't want to think about him, either.

Since making her decision to favor her husband over her son, since praying to be changed, she had thought more than once that it might have been the most impossible promise, the most impossible request she'd ever made. It wasn't that easy to banish her worry for Billy, but she had tried. Sometimes she wondered which of the two would outlast the other. She imagined that Abel would go first—that would be the natural order—but you never knew. All she was certain about was that something had to give.

In her darkest times she worried that what gave might be her own injured heart, beating stalwartly beneath her chest. Sometimes a sharp pain pierced her and it felt as if a fist were there inside her, gripping. *Change me,* she'd prayed, but she'd meant *change* her heart, not stop it from beating. What if He'd thought she meant *that*? Oh, she was so confused. She didn't know what to do.

Abel was a good man and she didn't want to betray him by telling Doro what had happened with the gun. He'd been a good husband despite his, oh, what would she call them? Not faults, exactly, just his way of being, which could be prickly and demanding. The way he argued with her about everything. Ever since their wedding day he'd teased her about heaven. She had staked her soul on its existence, but he delighted in taking her notions apart. "How do you know?" he'd ask her, looking at her over the top of his glasses, grinning in his sly way, the better to bedevil her. If she cited scripture, he'd find a patch that contradicted it. When she recited the Apostle's Creed, with its "He ascended into heaven," Abel countered with scholarship that dated the creed's origin in the fifth century. "God did not write the Bible," he would remind her, and this would infuriate her. She knew that. But He had inspired it, she was certain. "Define 'inspire,'" Abel would challenge, and their back-and-forth would go on until she was flustered and angry and she wanted to throw his biggest Isaac Asimov book at his hard head.

She had promised to love, honor, and obey. Love was easy, honor was a matter of habit, but obey was getting harder and harder. As his disease advanced, he had made increasingly ridiculous decrees, decrees that were out of character. One day in late spring just after her trip to the Gypsum Hills he decided they would trade in the Skylark for a new Camry. They would pay cash. Up to the dealership they went and a few hours later came home in a brand-spanking-new car they didn't have the slightest use for. Hattie hadn't liked the salesman, who had no doubt seen them coming—two elderly rubes ripe for the bilking. The man had even let them take the car off the lot to drive back home to get the checkbook they'd forgotten—but Abel was intent and wouldn't see that they were being manipulated. A few days later he wanted to redeem the Krugerrands he'd stockpiled and use the money to plant a peach orchard on the front acres. A legacy, he'd said, a memorial to his father, who'd grown peaches. She'd indulged him far enough to call the nursery and place an order for a tree catalogue, though she well knew that a peach orchard was a fool's errand, as a salt seep from the oil wells around town had ruined all the other orchards many years before. He gave the five children, even Billy, out of the blue and no holiday in sight, a thousand dollars apiece. She'd gone along with this, of course. She was glad to help the children, especially Billy, but if they spent all their savings how would she live when Abel was gone? As it was, they got by on Social Security and the service disability benefit from his back injury. Abel had always been terrible with finances, and it was only through her economizing and an inheritance from her father that they'd put aside anything at all. She tried to be a good wife and go along, to let him be the man of the house. He was happier that way, and his happiness was the key to keeping the peace. That and being careful not to bring Billy's problems before him. She tried harder than before to stop herself from mentioning Billy in passing, even refraining to suggest that Abel might want to wear one of Billy's old but still beautiful ties to church on Sunday. She was surprised by how many times in a day it occurred to her to say her son's name.

On and on her mind wandered and she didn't even try to stop it. Let it blow where it listed. Billy or Abel, Abel or Billy, it hardly mattered. But Abel: an old understanding about the way he behaved when a new baby came returned. He'd acted like an old lion, stalking around the house, eyeing the babies. He didn't pick them up unless, desperate, she thrust one at him. He hardly seemed to notice them until they were in middle childhood, and she supposed that was when he had won them over and made them idolize him, at least for a while. He became their big, rowdy playmate, sitting cross-legged on the floor with them and watching Looney Tunes or Sid Caesar and Imogene Coca. He led them in raucous games, letting them sled behind his motorcycle as he rode along a country road, building an igloo from snow blocks and a cardboard card table, encouraging them to slide down the antenna pole. One winter when they'd lived in Chicago he'd emptied the gunpowder out of the rifle shells he'd saved from the war, made a line of powder along a snowy sidewalk, and then lit a match. When the police arrived he informed them they had no physical evidence, as the blast had melted the snow and consumed the residue. He thought that was hilarious. He built a go-cart with a lawn mower engine and let the children race it on the road that led to the water treatment plant. Next to the swimming pool he built a cabana with a roof that slanted upward so the boys could ride skateboards into the deep end. And those awful motorcycles. It was a wonder no one had been killed. Much of his behavior, she had decided, was because he wanted to remain a boy, free of the bonds of reality, and there rose in her a feeling—she couldn't quite name it—that felt a little like resentment, but also a little like pride. She had managed to live with this man, to love him, and that was saying something. She had grit.

The word *grit* reminded her of poor Billy. In a dim basement apartment that smelled of grime and matted carpet and his massage oils, of the vanilla-scented candles he set around. He had hopes of setting up a practice, but of course they were doomed. In the first place, he had no license, and in the second place, he'd never stuck with anything for long. To help with rent, he'd found a roommate. Who knew where they'd met. Hattie was afraid to ask, and she wasn't sure she wanted to know, as she doubted that he would be a very good influence. His name was Haskell and he reminded her of a hairy little pirate, or maybe a wolf spider—his short legs and arms were covered in thick black hair, and he made abrupt, aggressive movements. He had bad teeth, an odd metallic smell, like burnt plastic, and tattoos he showed off by wearing muscle shirts. A skull and crossbones on his forearm. Some kind of serpent's tail peeking out from his shirt neck. On one shoulder a Christian fish symbol. She couldn't square the fish with his sneaky, jerky way of moving and the way he wouldn't meet her eyes when she went uptown to help with one thing or another. Strangest of all, he had a family, a wife and two little boys who lived nearby. She had no idea why Billy had taken up with him, much less why a married man was sharing an apartment with Billy. Probably they had some kind of financial arrangement, but she couldn't be sure and she was afraid to ask. But she knew she didn't like him.

Often she thought wistfully of Billy's better years, when he was with Leo. Though the situation had been hard to get used to at first, they'd had a quiet life in Albuquerque in a lovely house near the grand cottonwoods of the Bosque, with vigas and a kiva and heated tile floors. They'd traveled to Europe, New Zealand, Peru. Those had been good times, and she had prayed they would last. While in Albuquerque he graduated summa cum laude from UNM with an art history degree and he'd undergone hip replacement surgery. She'd traveled to be there for both events, the graduation and the surgery, and she nursed him through his recovery. He'd stayed sober even through that ordeal and she'd been relieved that he was cured of his addiction. Then out of the blue he'd relapsed, and Leo had finally left.

Up and down and up and down he went. She couldn't remember all the swings. They ran together when she looked back at them. Just now he was low, and had been for a while. When she drove to town to give him money or run him around to pay his bills or take him to his doctor's appointment or bring him home to spend a night or two, he was high, although she pretended not to notice.

He and Abel were on a collision course, it seemed. Both of them going downhill fast and she couldn't tell who would win. Or lose, as the case may be. And she didn't know whose situation was most dire, whom she should care about most. Some days Abel couldn't get out of bed and then other days he was outside, trying to hammer a nail or sort screws into jars. You couldn't tell what kind of day he'd have. He had trouble swallowing. His left eye drooped. He blamed his weakness on the doctors, accusing them of some kind of malfeasance with his medicine, but Hattie wasn't sure. His myasthenia was progressing, the doctors told them. He would weaken to the point that he couldn't swallow food, and eventually he would either have to allow them to insert a feeding tube or allow his body to finish the business it had started.

He was increasingly unsteady on his feet, and several times he'd lost his balance and fallen, most recently a few nights before when he'd gone to his armillary sphere hoping to sight Polaris. When he tipped his head back to align his gaze with the arrow his body kept going, sending him sprawling backward into the boxwood hedge. One night he'd fallen on the bathroom floor and she'd had to drag him back into bed. The task had taken an hour, and it had been pitiful to see him helpless. There were other days, however, when he was as sharp as ever, and there seemed to be no rhyme or reason to it.

The worst was his habit of night wandering, when the sundowning he'd experienced during his hospital stay returned and there were whole hours when he wasn't certain where he was. The night before had been such a time. She sped up her rocking, getting the rocker going at a fast clip the better to think, for at last she had landed on the subject she'd been circling—the events of the night before.

All day he had been angry with her and he wasn't speaking. She knew him well enough to tell that he was mulling over the confiscation of his firearms, probably parsing the language of the Second Amendment and pondering how Blackstone might rule on the police's actions, but she couldn't determine if he understood exactly how the events had transpired. Time, she supposed, would reveal the answer. In the meantime, she felt the need to tell someone what had happened.

In the past, when she had weak moments, she called Doro. It wasn't like she called to complain. Far from it. She kept most things to herself, after all. It was just that she needed to hear another voice. Usually after she hemmed and hawed and beat around the bush awhile Doro would get her to open up and reveal what troubled her and then they would discuss it and laugh about it in the hectic way they'd developed over the years, shaking their heads at the futility of trying to account for behavior, usually her sons' or her husband's, behavior that often defied reason. And for a moment, at least while she was connected to her daughter, the receiver warm against her ear, she could almost think the situation was funny and that everything would be all right. Except that it wasn't. And it wouldn't be.

She picked up the telephone and dialed Doro's number in Boston. While she waited for her daughter to answer she resolved not to make a big deal about the night before, only to report it, to get it on the record. If she made too big a deal, Doro would be on a plane that very day. She'd come in and shake up everything and try to make people stop being who they were. That wasn't what Hattie wanted. She just wanted to tell her troubles to someone.

After their usual pleasantries—weather, health, work—her daughter listened quietly while she went over the night's events. At the last minute, just when Hattie was ready to tell her about Abel waving the gun around, she substituted a claw hammer. She wasn't sure why she did this. But her hiding the fact of the guns meant that she couldn't tell Doro the real reason Abel wasn't speaking to her, the confiscated firearms.

"Oh, dear," Doro said when she had finished. "That's terrible. You must have been frightened."

Hattie considered, remembering her dry mouth, the flutter under her breastbone. "Well, I guess I was."

"Have you talked to the doctor lately?"

"Your father won't let me. He's always been secretive. Remember, he's the man who had all his teeth removed and dentures fitted without my knowing it. And every time we go to the VA he goes in the exam room by himself and I hear them in there laughing and carrying on. It's like they're playing poker or telling dirty jokes or something, and then he comes out with some new prescription that he refuses to take the right way and I just don't know what . . ."

"Mother, I mean *your* doctor."

Hattie considered. "I'm not sick." She allowed herself a tentative laugh, testing the Doro waters to see if they could turn the conversation into something lighter. "I'm just old."

"Mom, it doesn't have to be like this."

"That's what you think. And what can the doctor do? She can't solve this."

"She could give *you* something that would help. You're under terrible stress. Trying to take care of Dad and Billy, not to mention your own health. Maybe something for anxiety . . ."

"But I'm not anxious! I'm tired." Just then applause erupted from Dr. Phil's studio audience. Hattie pointed the clicker at the television and turned down the volume.

"You could be anemic," Doro went on. "Or potassium-depleted. Or magnesium . . ."

Doro was as bad as ClairBell, who liked to pretend she'd been a nurse. Say you felt a little shaky, ClairBell would snatch up your wrist and pinch it, counting your pulse. Doro had been married to a doctor and she seemed to think this gave her a license to practice medicine. Both her girls were always trying to catch people and needle them with questions and then diagnose them against their will. Abel's know-it-all gene shot true through all her children in one way or another.

"I'm not anemic. I eat plenty of red meat and leafy greens and I take vitamins. And besides, I think I'd know." If she were to tell the truth about her health, she would admit that in addition to worrying about her heart she was worried about her memory. She forgot things. Would arrive in a room having forgotten what she came for. She'd begun burning things on the stove. It took her two hours to bake a batch of cookies that might once have taken a half hour to finish. And her reflexes were shot. Her driving was getting shaky. There were two dings on the new Camry already. Abel hadn't seen them and she prayed he wouldn't. He would hold the dings against her, even though his own Dakota looked like the pace car from a demo derby.

Hattie essayed a little laugh to prove her good health. "Really, I'm just fine. It's your father you should worry about. Some days he can hardly lift his head up and other days he's perking around here like that drum bunny."

"That's his myasthenia, Mom. It's unpredictable. The doctors told you that, right?"

"Well, yes, but it's hard to watch. Not that I'm complaining. I'm not complaining, Doro."

"No, you're not," Doro said to mollify her mother. "But maybe you need some help. You have to admit you're under a good deal of pressure. Let me make you an appointment."

"You're all the way on the other side of the country."

"I can use the phone, Mom."

"I don't want to bother anybody. I can handle this. Don't do anything. I'm strong."

There was strained silence at Doro's end. Finally, she said, "Mom."

Hattie bristled. "Mom what? I know what I'm doing. You don't need to worry about me."

Doro's voice grew patient. "What about Pastor Gwynn? Maybe a talk with him?"

"What could he do?" Into the silence at her daughter's end of the phone she continued, "And I'd rather not air my dirty laundry in public."

"Mama, this isn't laundry, it's your life. And there's nothing wrong with seeking help. He had a hammer, for God's sake! What if he'd tried to . . ."

"Don't say 'God' like that, Doro. Say 'gosh' if you have to say anything."

"You needed help. What did you do when he . . ."

Hattie laughed ruefully. "Oh, don't you worry. Whenever I need help I just stop what I'm doing and say the twenty-third psalm. It takes exactly one minute, did you know that? Sometimes I time things in the microwave that way. Or three-minute eggs. Just say it three times and they're perfectly done every time. Go ahead. Time me. 'The Lord is my shepherd, I shall not want. He maketh me to . . .' "

Doro struggled to retain her patience. "The Lord tells you to run yourself ragged? To put yourself in danger?"

Hattie held her tongue. She could say a word or two about people running themselves ragged. Doro was a workaholic, a *career woman* who had left town, left the state, left her mother. Doro, whom she'd always thought would be the dependable one, the one to get her through old age. Oh, her daughter talked about retiring and moving back to Kansas, getting her hopes up, but of course she never would. ClairBell said it was because Doro had to have all those books and gourmet food and trips to New York and summer rentals in Maine, and also she was ashamed of her family, and she spent a lot of energy fronting like some hotshot, pretending to be better than she was, and also she'd forgotten her roots—but Hattie believed that this was just ClairBell's unkind speculation. No, the reason Doro wouldn't retire and move back . . . well, she wasn't really sure.

"Why don't you just—" In a seizure of loneliness and need, Hattie had started to say "come home," but she stopped herself and instead said, "stop worrying."

"Dad needs to go to skilled nursing," Doro said. "He's a danger to himself and others. That's one of the criteria, Mom, the main one. What if he'd hit you with that hammer? Think about that."

Alarm shot through Hattie's chest. Her hands felt numb. "I don't have to think about it. He didn't hit me. And he'll be all right. He just had a bad night's sleep."

There was silence on both ends of the connection until Hattie broke it to say, "Did I mention that the weather here has been just beautiful? I took the bougainvillea out of the greenhouse and put it on the side porch and it shot up like a weed."

Doro wanted to protest further but she knew it was futile. Her mother had changed the subject and would reveal no more. "Sounds lovely," she said.

Hattie heard the falseness in her daughter's answer, and she, too, was done. Pretending alarm, she exclaimed suddenly, "Oh, dear, my pot's boiling over!"

Doro sighed. There was no pot boiling over. Her mother had called from the guest room phone. Dr. Phil had blared in the background throughout the conversation. But the line had gone dead.

Her stomach queasy with a sense of urgency, Doro went to the computer to look for airline flights home, but by and by she thought better of her impulse. She'd been home just a few weeks before, for her May visit, and she didn't want to get in the habit of monthly trips. Not yet. In an emergency, yes, but not just because she was worried. Her father probably needed to be in a safer place, but Hattie would prove a roadblock, not to mention the stink her father would put up if he got wind of such a plan. Things did seem to be escalating, though. After a time she calmed down, realized her nerves were on edge because this was an old story and the crisis was like the apocryphal pot on her mother's stove, brought to the boiling point and then at the last minute snatched from the flame. She went back to her book.

Meanwhile, Hattie had turned up the television's volume and tried to concentrate on the screen. A man and a woman were arguing about how to toilet train their toddler while Dr. Phil sat back with his arms crossed. The toddler, dressed in a miniature three-piece suit with a bow tie and pocket square, a suit that made her think of Billy's, was a spoiled brat, mugging and showing off for the camera. The mother egged him on, saying wasn't he cute, while Dr. Phil shook his head and the child's father frowned. Hattie should have such problems. At least those parents had someone to talk to.

Jesse. She could drive over and confide in him. She wasn't sure, though. His farm was only a mile or so from Amicus, but he rarely had visitors. His housekeeping was terrible and people had learned not to go inside his farmhouse. The boarders stayed down at the barns and when family members came to call they spent time in the barns or the tomato fields.

Hattie could look past the stained bowl in his bathroom, discolored by hard well water, and even the sulfur-smelling toilet so low to the floor that she practically had to squat. Years ago, on a pop-in visit, as she sat trying to keep contact with the seat to a minimum, she happened to look directly in front of her where a toilet plunger stood. At the tip of the wooden handle, a bit below chest level, a quick movement caught her eye. She looked away, thinking the movement was another eye floater, but when she looked back she saw that balanced on the handle tip, its tail limp and the matted gray fur of its flanks heaving in slow respirations that were obviously its last, sat a mouse.

She was not afraid of mice or insects or even snakes; but she was at midstream and the sight startled her. She tried to stem the flow, thinking to finish later, but her attempt was in vain, and so she concluded her business while looking into the creature's black eyes, eyes that seemed even as she looked into them to cloud over with a milky film, like sudden, creeping glaucoma. The creature's poor sweetness, the squalor amidst which it sat, made her soften, and memory served up Robert Burns. "Wee timorous cowering beastie," she addressed it gently, and a curious thing happened. It was though she were in sudden communion with the mouse, as though she'd pronounced its benediction, as though her utterance ushered it out of the breathing world, for it tipped over and fell to the floor and moved no more. Since then she had not been back into the house, which was how Jesse managed to pretend he lived alone and that Patsy Gaddy, his dance-away lover, was not in residence. Patsy had lost her job, her driver's license, her husband, and her children, who lived with their father. She owed money all over Butler and Sumner counties. Her life was falling—had fallen—apart, collapsing post by beam by strut, and Jesse had determined to save her from herself. Probably Patsy was there now. So, no, not Jesse.

ClairBell, then. She should depend more on ClairBell. She had her faults, but at least she hadn't flown off a thousand miles across the country. She'd stayed close by and she was around when you needed her.

Besides, since the trip out west she'd felt a change in her younger daughter. She hoped it was the arrival of long-overdue maturity, and that this maturity would bring about a diminishing of ClairBell's sense of being unloved and treated unfairly. She'd been that way since she was a tiny baby, always on the lookout for what the other children received, alert for signs of favoritism. Gideon had come along when she was only sixteen months old—maybe it was that she hadn't had enough time to be an infant—and she had refused to look at Hattie for two weeks after the new baby was brought home. Wouldn't meet her gaze. Stiffened when Hattie tried to pick her up. What broke the impasse was that ClairBell caught a cold and finally, in her misery, she accepted comfort. Maybe the idea that she'd been betrayed had taken root then. Oh, who knew? The past was the past and no going back to change it. All she knew now was that something was thawing. Billy liked to say that ClairBell was like a heraldry lion, either *rampant* or *dormant,* and Hattie thought of her as a blender with only two settings, Off and Whip. For years ClairBell had been sluggish and sleepy and grouchy, quick to anger, but now she'd inexplicably become a dynamo—bustling, ordering, putting her two cents in places Hattie hadn't asked for, asking odd questions, such as what were Abel's favorite cake and ice cream flavors and did she think he liked fried chicken or barbecued chicken better. Her mood was bright. Whatever were her reasons—and Hattie knew her younger daughter well enough to know she most certainly had reasons—she was currently set on Whip. Which of course was a far sight better than Off. Anyway, she resolved to depend more on ClairBell. With new energy, she got up from the rocker and went to the kitchen to take a pound of bacon from the refrigerator. Abel never turned down a good BLT.

They would ride this out.

Things would get better.

The situation wasn't that bad. You just had to look on the bright side.

Eight

A few quiet days later, just as she was beginning to recover from the upset of the night of the guns, Hattie was in the guest room watching *Little House on the Prairie.* It was one of her favorite episodes, the one where that tattletale Nellie Oleson was thrown by Laura's horse and pretended to be crippled so Laura would take the blame. She liked it because Nellie was so blatantly bad and Laura was so good. It was easy to tell right from wrong, and right always prevailed.

Suddenly she started up from her chair as though some invisible live wire had zapped her. She'd forgotten something! Something important, something she had meant to do, something she'd promised to do. She ransacked her mind for the day's tasks, wondering which she might have left undone, but try as she might she could not wrest from the air the forgotten thing. But it was important.

She went to the kitchen, which was the last place she remembered thinking about the whatever-it-was. As she stood opening cupboards, hoping memory would supply what she was looking for, a groan came from Abel's room, followed by violent coughing, and then a crash.

He had spent the day in his den, refusing her offer of a bowl of tomato soup and a few saltines at lunchtime. His throat felt odd, he claimed, but she wrote it off to his simmering grudge about the guns. Still, he'd been coughing ever since trying to eat the BLT a few days before. Hattie thought at first that his coughing and his indictment of the bacon were merely a more elaborate way to make her feel guilty, but as she listened to the sounds he made it became clear to her that this wasn't a performance. The bout or spasm or whatever it amounted to wasn't the usual kind of coughing, but a strangling, wheezing, deep-rooted struggle for air. She hurried to his room, where she almost tripped over the towers and piles of books he'd pulled off the bookshelves. He sat in his recliner, gasping.

"What on earth?" she asked, surveying the mess.

Between coughs he tried to speak but his voice was weak and wispy. He could only mutter, his voice seemed oddly muffled. His mouth wouldn't work right and his tongue lolled. He could scarcely hold up his head. In his distress he'd knocked over the wooden TV tray where he kept the remote control and the telephone and his notepads and they'd fallen among the books.

From the clutter she snatched the telephone and hit the ClairBell button. For a wonder, her daughter picked up on the first ring. She appeared to be on Whip. "What up, Mom?"

Hattie tried to explain, but she could only get out, "Your father. It's your father. He can't talk. He can't stop coughing."

Excitement surged in ClairBell. Her energy went from zero to sixty in a second flat. This was the moment she had waited for, her time to shine. When her parents needed her. Her pulse racing, she shouted into the receiver, "Have you called anyone else?"

"Only you," Hattie said. "Hurry, ClairBell, he needs help."

"I'm on my way," ClairBell shouted. "Call nine-one-one!"

While Abel hacked and gasped, Hattie tried to think, but she was at a loss. Vaguely she remembered the talk she and Abel had had about extreme measures. They had agreed. No heroics. They had filled out advance directives and signed them. But was calling an ambulance an extreme measure? What seemed so matter-of-fact when they'd discussed it now seemed impossible to figure out. Panic rising, she asked, "ClairBell, ClairBell, don't hang up! I don't know the number!"

"Never mind. I'll do it from the road. Does he have an inhaler?"

"A what?"

"Never mind!" She hung up.

Hattie ran for a glass of water and took it to Abel. When he batted it away water sloshed onto his chin and chest. Next she tried to get him to a seated position, but the recliner wouldn't work right and the footrest kept coming up even as she tried to push it down. Piles of books hindered her. He had a fever, she could tell, and his coughing went on and on. Finally, in the distance a siren wailed, growing loud, then louder. A clatter at the front door and then footsteps thudded in the hall. A man's voice called out, "Where are you?"

Suddenly ClairBell was there, too. She pulled Hattie up—somehow she'd gotten herself down onto the floor beside the recliner—and walked her into the kitchen. "Let them do their jobs."

ClairBell returned to the scene. She asked the EMTs a few questions about blood gases and rales and pulse ox and Cheyne-Stokes breathing and such, but they responded only with quizzical looks and so she went back to the kitchen. She collected Hattie's pocketbook and stood holding it clasped to her chest. "Mom," she ordered, "we're going to the hospital with him. I'll drive. You need to go to the bathroom before we leave."

Hattie obeyed. It was good not to be in charge. Good to have someone take over. When she came out of the bathroom she met the EMTs on their way out, Abel on a rolling bed, a green oxygen mask over his face, struggling against the restraint belt. He lifted a hand toward her and she tried to clasp it but the bed rolled on. ClairBell put an arm around her shoulder and brought her around to face her. "Now get your nitroglycerine. Where is it?"

Hattie had to think. "In there," she said finally, pointing to the pocketbook in ClairBell's hand.

"Do you have Daddy's VA card?"

Hattie brushed off her worry. "He knows his own number."

"But do you?"

Hattie thought. "No."

"Then get his wallet."

She hurried to the back room and rummaged in Abel's drawers and at last she found the wallet. Convinced the housekeeper was pilfering, he'd hidden it between folded T-shirts.

Outside, the ambulance was pulling out of the driveway, lights flashing. The Cadillac was running. "Get in," ClairBell ordered, "buckle up."

After they arrived at the hospital and got Abel through triage, ClairBell made calls. To Jesse, telling him to inform Gideon, and to Doro, telling her to let Billy know. Hattie marveled that her daughter could keep her head as she explained what was happening. Calmly she told her siblings that their father had been taken by ambulance to the VA, that he couldn't get his breath and that she suspected either pneumonia or a stroke. "It's all under control," she said to each of them. "Don't worry. I'll call you when we know something." Her manner was businesslike and patient as she fielded their questions, and Hattie was impressed. When ClairBell hung up, Hattie said, "I'm so glad I called you."

ClairBell's heart swelled and warmth seemed to pour over her body. "I got you, Mom." She reached over to pat her mother's hand, thinking that if anyone had asked her to name the best moment in the last, say, twenty years, she'd jump right over meeting Randy online and even their wedding day. She would point to this moment.

Abel was diagnosed with pneumonia and admitted for possible stroke. The doctors said he'd probably aspirated some food. "That bacon," Hattie said, remembering the day after the night of the guns. "He choked on it."

Once he was taken to a room and settled in bed, Hattie and ClairBell sat with him for a long time. He had calmed down and was dozing, but beneath his placid expression Hattie imagined she could see the dangerous glint of the look he wore when he felt betrayed.

"He looks kind of angry," ClairBell said, confirming her fears. "It's that face he makes when somebody's done something wrong but he's not ready to tell you what it is yet. He's still holding it in."

"Let's hope not," said Hattie. "He's probably a million miles away."

For a time she studied her husband, trying to comprehend the changes that had taken place in the almost seven decades of their marriage. Always when she thought of him she pictured him as he'd been in their early years—black hair thinning a little at the temples, sharp green eyes behind horn-rimmed glasses, the strong, square chin, the sly grin, the chest with its hereditary concavity just under the breastbone, pectus excavatum, he'd called it, his broad, capable hands. She thought of his voice, strong and quick, its tenor register, his wild laugh, a laugh she loved. His face had fallen, his ears had grown bigger and tufted with gray. The skin under his eyes was mud-colored. He was wattled and sunken and spotted. She put out her hand and stroked his forearm. At some point when she hadn't been looking, the skin on his arm had lost all its silken black hair.

It was around midnight when the women left the hospital and went home to Amicus, and almost one a.m. when ClairBell pulled out of the driveway for her trip home to the Flint Hills. After she straightened the den and put the disordered books back on the shelves, Hattie slipped into bed. For a long time her mind raced and she couldn't sleep. The feeling she'd had earlier in the day that she'd forgotten something important returned to her.

She got up and walked quietly through the house. The first time she'd been alone in it since . . . oh, heavens . . . ever. She'd never been alone in the house all night. Well, Abel's fishing and hunting trips, but that was all, and somehow this was different. The children had been there then and they weren't now. She thought of her early motherhood, how suffocated she'd felt in the puppy nest of infants and toddlers, when even her skin wasn't her own. And now this vast feeling of emptiness stretching out ahead of her. She walked through the house, the waning gibbous moon shedding enough light to see by, trying on solitude, trying on quiet. Her ears fairly buzzed with the silence. She touched things as if they belonged to someone else, some other woman, some other mother—the children's portraits, a lampshade, the mantel, the philodendron in its pot on the hearth ledge, the books on the shelves. She found her way to the piano and pulled out the bench and sat down, letting her fingers seek out the keys. Quietly at first and then louder as she realized there was no one to hear the surge and halt of her attempts to recover the music, she played by ear, the easy hymns of her girlhood, pieces she was too self-conscious to play when the others were around but which she loved—"O Love That Wilt Not Let Me Go," "For the Beauty of the Earth," "Blest Be the Tie That Binds." As she worked her way through the hymns she knew by heart, she found, when a warm drop struck her arm, that she was weeping, but not in loss or sorrow, but, oh, in joy, in the song of her spirit returned. She felt a dampish smile stretch her mouth, and the notion came to her that the way she felt just now might be a foretaste of what was to come, in heaven. She played for a while longer, singing along in a voice that she thought would sound small in the big empty house but instead sounded surprisingly full and rich.

She had just lain back down in bed when headlights glanced across the wall, sweeping the room in slow, kaleidoscopic movement as a car turned around in the driveway. She heard loud voices, a low, rough one raised in anger and another, higher, thick with distress. Billy's voice. By the time she made it to the front door the car was speeding off, its taillights a red glow at the end of the drive. And then it hit her, what she'd forgotten.

Billy had called earlier. In the hubbub of her dealings with Abel she'd forgotten she was supposed to fetch him from the bus stop at four o'clock. He had wanted to get away from his apartment because his landlord was acting mean. The power had been cut off because Billy had spent the bill money—there had been a tortuous explanation of his reasons but Hattie couldn't follow it.

She went outside and down the driveway, where she found him on the verge of the macadam, sitting on the stump of a cottonwood, his head in his hands. As she drew nearer she saw that he wore only his undershorts. In the moonlight the nubs of his backbone and his ribs stood out in relief. "Billy," she called out softly.

He turned toward her, his face gaunt, and finally she was able to make out that he was distressed because his glasses had slid off his face when he was pushed from the car and he couldn't find them.

She knelt to feel around him on the asphalt, on the grass, and finally she located them. An earpiece had broken off.

"Did Haskell do this to you?" she asked.

He shook his head.

"Who, then?"

He buried his face in his hands. "I don't know."

She helped him up and they started for the house.

"There should be clothes," he said. Though it was a warm night, he was shivering. His teeth chattered. "My clothes."

She didn't understand. "Clothes?"

"He threw them, too."

"Never mind that now," she said.

As they passed through the living room she snatched the plaid throw from the Eliot chair and wrapped it around his shoulders. She led him into the big bathroom off the kitchen, and with a warm washcloth she dabbed at his face until she was satisfied there weren't any deep cuts. "Can you drop the blanket and let me see if you're hurt anywhere else?" she asked.

He obliged, letting the throw fall to the floor while she looked him over. At first he appeared not to be hurt, but then she saw on his thin backside a long smear of dried blood.

Two feelings rose in her, both so powerful she thought she might either combust with anger or swoon with heartbreak. Someone had used him sorely. Someone had thrown him out like garbage. It might well have been her forgetfulness that led to this. If only she hadn't forgotten him. If only she had remembered the first time the hovering notion of having forgotten had come to her. All she could do now was continue to apply the warm cloth, rinsing it until the water ran clear.

The guest room bed was covered with fabric from a quilt she was piecing together and so she decided to put him on the empty bed in Abel's den. Hands on his shoulders, she walked him back, found him some of Abel's pajamas, and tucked him into bed. He tried to explain what had happened but he was making no sense. She shushed him. "It will be all right, honey," she said. "Just sleep now."

In the hours before dawn, at about the same time Hattie drifted into an exhausted sleep, Abel awakened in Room 309 of the VA's MICU more lucid than he'd been for several days, clear-minded, and ready to fight. Not only had his guns been seized by the goon squad, someone had called an ambulance, captured him, and delivered him into bondage.

In the past years he and Hattie had talked at length of their decision to allow no heroic measures. They had agreed to submit to whatever fates their bodies had in store for them, no matter how uncomfortable, how wrenching, how fatal. They would go the way their parents had before them. Death was part of life, and both of them, reared on farms, had practical natures. For different reasons both looked forward to the end of their days. Hattie because of her faith in an afterlife where she would meet loved ones of old and come face-to-face with the Christ of her deepest yearning, and Abel because he hoped to glimpse the mysteries of creation, to have answers, finally, for his lifelong wondering.

They had seen too many of their friends fighting against death, enduring surgeries and procedures and undergoing treatments that carried no hope, really, of making great age any better, and they didn't want to find themselves among that number. To prove their seriousness, they had filled out and signed advance directives. And even if they hadn't, Abel considered, Hattie was well aware of his desires, as he was aware of hers. Their children had been told more than once and in no uncertain terms. On the refrigerator in Amicus, secured with dancing chili pepper magnets, were two notes written on sheets from their doctors' prescription pads that bore the words "Do Not Resuscitate."

And now this. Again, onto his forearm was taped an IV line. Again, wires and patches and leads tangled across his chest and ran into and out of the loose sleeves of his blue hospital gown. Beside his bed ticked a monitor that reminded him of a long-necked sandhill crane, its digital numbers glowing green in the half-light of the room. He remembered his plan to do away with himself before things got to this point, and he laughed ruefully. There hadn't been time to do what he intended, and worse, in all the tug of life, he'd forgotten. Life was a stronger pull, but now he was going to war against it. He would have his way.

He felt around for the call button. "Nurse!" he shouted, but no one came.

He jabbed at the button. "Help! I'm in here!" Again he jabbed, and finally the door, which had been ajar, swept open, admitting a wedge of light from the hallway. A woman's voice said, "Mr. Campbell?"

"One and the same. Get me out of here."

She was young, in her twenties, he guessed. She could be one of his granddaughters, one of Doro's or Gideon's girls. She approached the bedside, hands in her pockets. From her lanyard dangled a badge with the name Jennifer Santiago, RN, followed by a train of other letters he squinted at but didn't know the significance of. She wore a smock printed with some kind of woodland animal—chipmunks they appeared to be—and pants so loose they looked like pajama bottoms. He thought with nostalgia of the snappy nurses at Tripler on Oahu where he'd lain with a broken back in 1945, their crisply starched uniforms and brisk ways. This young woman, if she was indeed a nurse, seemed to have rolled out of a pup tent. Yes, the world was changing. He was glad to be leaving it. If only people would let him.

"I'm Jenny, and I'll be taking care of you tonight." She laid a hand on his forehead. "How are we feeling? Fever's down."

The "we" irked him, but he resisted the urge to bat away her hand, held his temper, and said only, "Fine. I want to go home."

She smiled. "A rascal, are we?"

This sent Abel over the edge. "We are indeed a rascal. And we'll thank you not to patronize us. Now, if you please, Nurse Jane Fuzzy Wuzzy, kindly release us!"

She drew herself up. "I'm afraid I can't do that. Doctor's orders. You've got a bad case of pneumonia."

"And you've got a mistaken diagnosis. I have myasthenia gravis. I recovered from pneumonia months ago."

"You have it again," she said, "and you'll keep getting it until you stop eating."

He gave a sharp laugh. "Quite a prescription, that. Stop eating."

"By mouth, I mean. You're aspirating food particles and that's causing the pneumonia. You'll need to have a feeding tube put in. That will fix you up. The doctor explained all this last night but I'm happy to go over it again."

"I recall no such event."

"Your daughter wrote it all down. You're going to have a swallow test first thing in the morning and then they'll decide what to do."

Abel summoned his sternest look. "They? *They* will decide? What about me? I direct you to call my wife. At once. She knows I don't belong here."

Her voice assumed a tone of reason. "But she's the one who brought you in. And the ambulance, of course."

The mention of the ambulance set him off anew. He thought he had a memory of being driven through the night. So it was true. "I did not order an ambulance. I would not have done so."

"Would you like an ice chip, sir? I'll bet your mouth is parched. When you came in you couldn't even talk."

She had changed her tack, affecting concern, but he wasn't fooled. "I'm talking now. And I'm prepared to walk. Let me out!"

She sighed. "I'm afraid I can't do that. It's the middle of the night. We need a doctor to sign a release. Your team will make rounds about eight a.m. Now, how about a nice ice chip?"

"Call my wife." He composed himself in the bed, smoothing his gown, folding his hands over his belly. "I'll wait."

"Yes, you do that," she said, and he couldn't read her expression well enough to tell if she was mocking him or she truly intended to call Hattie.

After she took her leave he went to work, peeling the electrodes from his chest. Their leads ran down his legs as well as his arms and he had a hard time figuring their source. He worked at the task until he was clean of all wires and electrodes. Then he set himself to the challenge of figuring out the IV that ran into his forearm. A simple-enough solution, he thought, if you had a head for mechanics. He worked at the tape until it was loose enough to peel up. Where the needle ran under his skin a bruise had formed, but little by little and without too much blood he was able to work out the needle and the tube. Clear fluid seeped onto the sheets near his hip, but he was free.

A frantic beeping had erupted from the monitor. He tried to pull the thing toward the bed with the attached tubes so he could switch off the alarm but the angles were wrong. Then the door flew open and Nurse Jenny hurried in. "What's the trouble? What's going on?"

"I'm leaving," he said, matter-of-factly. He struggled to sit up and put his legs over the edge of the bed. Lightheaded, he saw stars, floating there at the upper rim of his vision. "I'm getting my coat and I'm leaving."

The girl smiled reassuringly. Probably they taught them in nursing school to be pleasant no matter what the patient did. "I'll be back.

Don't go anywhere just yet. I'll run and see where they put your coat." She turned and was gone.

He put his feet on the floor. It was an effort to bring his body to a standing position, and it made him dizzy, but he did it. Using the bed-rail to steady himself, he worked his way around the bed. His legs seemed impossibly weak, as they sometimes were in his dreams when he would attempt to walk but could make no progress against the heaviness that held him back, like trying to make headway against a swift current. He reached the closet and opened the door. No coat. Only a pair of his house slippers and the pants and shirt he'd had on the day before. Draped over a hook was the green blanket that he kept secured to his mattress at home with a row of wood clamps. For a time he contemplated it, trying to puzzle out how this blanket had come to be in this place when he was sure he'd left it on his bed. Why, in the middle of winter, he had no coat.

Nurse Jenny was back with another nurse, a woman who appeared to be even younger than she. The new nurse was tiny and sharp-featured, with short red hair. Her head made him think of an old sulfur kitchen match, the kind they used to call lucifers, and he told her so.

The new nurse spoke softly, slowly. "I'm Rachel. I'll be helping to take care of you tonight." She stepped forward, addressing him in a teasing, lilting voice. "Are you giving Jenny a hard time? You wouldn't be a troublemaker, would you?"

He eyed her. The smallest of thrills coursed through him. "Why, yes. Yes, I would be."

"I thought so," she said, laughing. "I took one look at you and knew you were trouble."

Suddenly he saw her tactic, and he summoned a glower. "Have you called my wife?"

"Don't you want her to get her sleep?" Nurse Rachel asked. "It's not even morning. The sun isn't up." She approached. "Come and let's get you back into bed and then we'll talk about this."

He let himself be led and found that he was relieved to lay his head on the pillow. Nurse Rachel asked to see his arm where the IV had been pulled out.

Proudly he showed her what he had done. "Didn't hurt a bit," he told her.

"You must be strong," she said, and this, too, pleased him.

She held his hand and gave a good impression of examining his arm but then, before he knew what was happening, she drew an object from her pocket, a metal band of some kind, and attached it to his wrist and snapped it shut.

"What the hell is this?"

"A WanderGuard. Just to keep track of you," she said, patting his arm. "In case you get lost."

"I've never been lost a day in my life," he said indignantly. "I've always been exactly where I've found myself to be. Now, unless you plan to change the Constitution of the United States at this hour of the night, you'll need to release me. You can't keep me here against my will. I know my rights."

Nurse Jenny moved forward, smiling. "We're going to let you finish the night with no electrodes and no IV, but first thing in the morning you have to agree to let us hook you up again."

"I'll do no such thing," he growled, but he sank into the pillows and closed his eyes. His exertions had tired him.

He dozed briefly and when he woke again the nurses were gone. Again he got out of bed and went to the closet. Laboriously he dressed, and when he had finished he reached for the green blanket and wrapped it around himself like a cape. He opened his door and peeked into the hall. Quiet, no nurse in sight, the coast was clear. Barefoot, inching his way so as not to make noise, he headed along the wall toward the elevators, thinking that he would take the stairs to the main floor and from thence outside.

But he'd no more pushed open the stairwell door when a terrible buzzing came from the metal band on his wrist, and before he could think of what to do two burly security officers appeared beside him. He couldn't think fast enough to fight them. They flanked him, marching him back to his room, where Nurse Jenny waited. They delivered him to his bed, settled him in it, and left the room.

A large portable nurse's station was moved into the doorway and match-headed Rachel took a seat as if preparing for a long siege. So here he was, trapped. Banded like a bird and all exits blocked. He was furious, and he planned to mount an attack if she came near him. But she kept her distance, sitting quietly at the computer station, looking up from time to time to see how he was doing. Somehow this had a calming effect, and he was able to master his emotions.

He lay back and tried to think. He closed his eyes and an image came to him, a beautiful Venn diagram, red and pulsing, intricate as a rose in bloom, enfolding him, his wife, his friends, his children, his brothers and sisters, his parents, and then the rose that was somehow his life began to spin, to whirl toward the sky, the moon and stars, the outer dark. The peace that had come to him some months before when Jeff had visited him in this same hospital returned. He, Abel, was ready to go. This time, should Jeff come around again, he would follow. There would be no feeding tube to prolong his life, to keep him here. But neither would he be truly gone, he understood. Matter didn't disappear. He wasn't fool enough to think this law meant the universe was eternal, but he had come to the conclusion that matter was just energy that was tired of happening. He determined that he would from this moment be a body at rest.

"Young woman," he called out to Nurse Rachel, who sat at the blockade's computer. "Do you believe in eternal life?"

"Beg pardon?"

"The afterlife, reincarnation, heaven? What do you think happens to us when we die?" He felt like having an argument, his body fairly buzzed with it. He looked forward to shredding everything she said.

"Nobody's dying," she said lightly. "Let's just get through the night. Things are going to look much better in the morning."

But he pressed her, engaged her in talk, and by and by she loosened up. He'd intended to trap her into admitting a belief in the pearly gates and streets of gold and then beset her with argument. He summoned his old geniality, courting her with his questions and striving to give the impression of a man in full possession of his faculties, one who was interested in her. They chatted. She told him about her grandfather, a Vietnam veteran who had died in this hospital and that was why she had become a nurse, about her mother, who was in a hospital across town, dying of cervical cancer. He told her about his parents, his boyhood, his first bout of pneumonia with Lizzie Glutz as his bedmate, of meeting Hattie at the schoolhouse corner. He told her that he'd grown up on the edge of a prairie that seemed endless and that when he was very young he thought the place where the far expanse of waving grass met the sky of the horizon was the end of the earth. He'd known, even as a child, that he was on a road that led there, and that his life would one day end. He told her many more things—of his vision of Jeff and of a saddle-dream he'd once had while riding herd on his uncle's cattle, a dream of designing a self-piloted airplane. "My sons do not love me the way I loved my own father," he told her, surprising himself.

"They will," she said. "When you're gone."

"I know," he said. "That's just it. I know. And they don't."

He told her what happened on Saipan. He'd never told another soul.

He wept soundlessly for his young self still in his poor aged body. After he calmed, she gave him a sponge bath that made his eyes well for the tenderness with which she cleansed his flesh. They went on talking until daybreak, and when the sunlight streamed through his window and the murk and shadow of night retreated, he felt good, relaxed, and though no IV line dripped into him, he felt as if a strange, strong medicine was coursing through his veins.

Nine

It's like he has radar," ClairBell told Jesse, speaking of Billy behind her cupped hand as they sat at the kitchen counter. She had arrived in Amicus early in order to drive her mother back to the hospital and Jesse had come over to check on everyone and get the lowdown before he went to work. The real reason was to cool down from the night he'd spent. He was as disgusted with Gid as he'd ever been, and that was saying something.

"The minute Daddy's gone, here comes the Boy Wonder to pitch his tent," ClairBell was saying.

Jesse nodded and pretended to listen as she went on about the way Billy used his mother. He'd heard it all before, and frankly just now the business at home with Gid troubled him more.

He'd been trying for a long time to get his brother to meetings, to slow-talk him into the program sideways, not by urging but by leading by example. So far Gid had shown no sign of wanting to be led. If anything, he was more set in his ways.

What happened in the night was that the joint Gideon had fallen asleep with had slipped from his fingers onto the floor of the barn loft where he'd set up camp. The ember apparently caught some dried hay

Gid had tracked in, and raced along the floorboards, using dust for tinder. The smoke awakened Gid and he'd either jumped or fallen out the window. He insisted it was a jump but Jesse wasn't sure—the booze reek coming off him had been strong. Broke his damn ankle and the bellowing woke Jesse all the way up at the farmhouse. He'd put out the blaze with the pressure washer. There'd been no point in calling the fire department—no hydrant so far outside town. The fire burned out before it could take the barn but it had left a great charred hole in the roof. In the middle of the night Jesse had to haul Gid to the ER to get his ankle set. Not a good time, and to make things worse, Patsy had found herself a ride to the Pay Dirt but not a ride home and so when her drunken call came he'd had to go back out and fetch her.

Hattie emerged from the bedroom wing, dressed in a trim brown skirt, a yellow blouse, and a brown-and-yellow-striped cardigan. His mother looked like a vision from a cleaner, sweeter, more organized life, a life unmuddled by Billy and the Judge and Gid and their doings. "You look nice, Mom," he said. The last thing he was going to lay on her was his own problem. He would deal with things on his own and no point troubling her. She looked pretty, and she was in terrific health for a woman of eighty-something who'd had a heart attack, but she also looked frail and small and tired. Like a little bird.

Hattie smiled at the compliment, smoothing her skirt. She liked it when the children were in the kitchen, liked the warm, industrious, and yet peaceful way it made her feel. The feeling was the same one from many years before when they'd crowded into her bed after Billy was born. It was funny, but without Abel in the house it seemed that things were somehow lighter. Quickly she banished the thought. "Have you eaten, Jess? Let me fix you some bacon and eggs. I was just going to make a little something for your brother and it's no trouble. . . ?"

"I had a burrito at the Mart, Mom. What's up with Billy?"

Hattie didn't like the way Jesse had sounded suddenly like Abel, questioning her in such . . . an accusatory way. "Well, that's not enough to keep you going. Over easy, isn't that the way you like your eggs?" She tied an apron over her skirt and set to work.

Jesse went to the carafe and filled his Reddi Mart cup with fresh coffee. "Mom, no eggs. What's going on?"

"Oh, a friend dropped Billy off in the middle of the night," she said lightly, whisking eggs and milk in a glass bowl. "They had some kind of falling-out. I'm not sure about what, but there Billy was. He's just going to stay here for a few days. Only while your father's in the hospital. I don't see anything wrong with that . . ."

ClairBell punched down the toaster button. "In Daddy's room?"

"Well, yes, for the time being. But only until I can get my quilting off the guest room bed, then I'll put him in his usual place."

Jesse and ClairBell shared a look. This was the way things happened. Their brother was like the camel with his nose in the tent, coaxing open the flap just a little wider to let him in a little farther and a little farther until he was all the way in and he took up all the room. He'd been back and forth for most of his adult life, staying months at a time, and each time had ended in grief, with their father angry, their mother hurt, and Billy skating off to whatever roller rink would admit him next.

Jesse watched as his mother moved around the kitchen, putting plates in the oven to warm, turning bacon, a happy worker bee in yellow and brown. "What does Doro think about this?" he asked. He had invoked his sister on purpose. Everyone knew what Doro would think—that harboring Billy was a mistake Hattie made again and again. She should have stopped years before. She should stop now. Jesse agreed with Doro and so did ClairBell. And certainly so would their father. But no one had been strong enough to stand up to Hattie.

With a fork Hattie poked a strip of bacon. "I have no idea what she'd think but I'm not telling her. And I don't want either of you telling her, either. She'll just get us all in an uproar. We can deal with this just fine ourselves."

ClairBell buttered a piece of toast, considering. If her older sister got wind of what was going on, she'd go into attack mode. She'd fix everything for Billy and this would make their mother happy, and then she'd be the hero again. Maybe Doro could even get the guns out of police custody. That would seal the deal. "I agree with you, Mom. We can deal with this ourselves. We handled it just fine last night, didn't we?"

Hattie smiled. "Yes, we did. I'm glad you see it that way, ClairBell."

Something hitched itself in Jesse. How was he any different from his mother? Keeping things quiet. Harboring Gid, harboring Patsy, making a soft place for them to land. Suddenly, in a way that he hadn't before, he understood his mother. It was all well and good to preach the program, to detach with love. It was all well and good to let go and let God. But when it came down to your actual family and their actual ways and the way you actually felt about them, when it came to a brother you loved or thought you loved, a woman you loved or thought you loved, things got a damn sight more complicated. He put on his hat and went outside to smoke a cigarette about it. Hattie and ClairBell waited, but he didn't come back in. A bit later they heard his Silverado start up.

"What's wrong with Brother Bear?" ClairBell asked.

"Oh, he's just in a mood," Hattie said. "I think he might be jealous of Billy."

ClairBell didn't think before she responded sarcastically. With a tone of scandalized astonishment, she said, "No!"

When Hattie looked at her sharply, she covered herself by saying,

"Well, that's just ridiculous." It wouldn't do to alienate her mother just now.

"That's what I think," Hattie said, and went back to tending the bacon.

After breakfast Hattie put a plate in the oven for Billy, should he awaken, and she and ClairBell got into the car for the trip to the hospital.

They found Abel sitting on the edge of his bed, his IVs out, fully dressed and ready to be sprung. Trying to make light, ClairBell murmured as they entered the room, "He looks like a little kid ready for the first day of school," but her mother had already hurried to his side. ClairBell swallowed hard. The truth was that the sight of her father so meek-looking was hard to take. Overnight, it seemed, he had grown truly old. She shored up the ruins of her heart, took a deep breath, and bustled into the room to stand beside her mother at his bedside. "Daddy, are you giving the nurses a rough time?"

She was proud of her quick thinking the day before and she had affected a bright, joking voice, so she was startled when in an angry growl he asked, "Which one of you is responsible for putting me in here? You knew full well what my wishes were."

Hattie stepped back from the bed. ClairBell began, "But you could have died if we hadn't . . ."

"And isn't dying the point of old age? Your mother and I have Do Not Resuscitate orders. Written and signed!"

ClairBell's stomach lurched and she couldn't speak.

"Abel," Hattie tried, "we were only doing what we thought was best at the time."

He turned his glare on his wife. "The two of you conspired to put me in here. And you knew better."

"It wasn't that way at all, Abel, we only—"

"I know my rights. And I told them they couldn't hold me here unless they plan to change the Constitution. I've determined to go home and live out my days, no matter how many or few! And I'll see those ambulance crooks in a court of law!"

The hospital shift had changed. The night nurses had rotated off and the day-shift nurse who had taken their place stood up from the station's seat and came toward the bed. "Sir, try to understand. They did what any family would do in their position. They want what's best for you. They want you to be comfortable."

"I'm hungry," he said. "How comfortable is that? No one will let me have a blessed sip of water."

"It's because of your test," the nurse prompted. "You're scheduled for a swallow test. You agreed to it last night. If you eat or drink you can ruin the results. You wouldn't want that, would you?"

"Yes, I would. I don't want the test. I certainly don't want a feeding tube or any heroic measures. I want to go home." He looked at Hattie and said, "Call Roger Blankenship and have him get a court order. Tell him they're holding me against my will." He held up his wrist to show the metal bracelet. "Unlawfully restrained."

Hattie and ClairBell looked at each other. ClairBell said, "Daddy, let's just wait and see what the doctors say."

He scoffed, refusing to look at her. "I can't believe you're in on this, daughter. I thought that you at least would respect my wishes. You were always my favorite."

Now, in addition to feeling sick, ClairBell felt two more ways, and all at once. Elated that she was his favorite—he'd never said this aloud, though her brothers and sister had long maintained it—and accused of wrongdoing when she had only done what she'd thought was right, when she was trying to save the day. "Daddy," she began, but she could say no more.

Hattie felt sorry for her daughter. The girl had tried to help and now her father was angry with her. She gave ClairBell an apologetic look, and then said to no one in particular, floating a trial balloon, "Maybe if we just take him home."

Abel said, "Now we're getting somewhere."

The nurse shook her head. "I can't let him go. The doctors have to release him. That's hospital policy. He'll have to wait until they make their rounds. I'll try to get them to start here, though."

Under her breath to Hattie and ClairBell, she said, "They'll talk sense to him." She left, taking the rolling blockade with her.

Now that the obstacle to his release was removed, Abel conceived an escape plan. To his wife, shifting his tone toward sweetness, he said, "Hattie, dear, this will be straightened out soon and I'll be home, but in the meantime will you ask the nurse if I might have a few ice chips? She offered earlier but I—"

"Oh, I'm happy to," Hattie said, relieved that the storm seemed to be over. She hurried out.

Next he turned to his daughter and smiled warmly, winningly. "SisterBell, all is forgiven if you'll run down to the canteen and get your old dad some biscuits and sausage gravy."

If this had been any other day, ClairBell would have argued with him, or pressed him to be patient or refused to do his bidding, but this day was different. She had been accused. She needed to get back into his good graces, and so without argument or further word she made her way into the labyrinthine basement of the VA to the canteen, ordered his food, paid for it, and carried the warm Styrofoam box back upstairs.

"Where did that come from?" Hattie asked when he opened the box and the smell of sausage and biscuits rose into the room. "Abel, are you sure you should? Let me just run and ask the nurse." Wringing her hands, she left the room.

Abel winked at ClairBell, and then with a plastic spoon he tucked in. He took his first bite. "Tasty," he proclaimed. "And now I've fouled up their test. All we have to do is wait for them to let me go."

Down the hatch went the next few bites of breakfast with nary a glitch, and then he must have swallowed wrong, for a bit of sausage seemed to go down the wrong pipe. He choked violently.

"Oh, shit, Dad!" ClairBell hurried to his bed and began pounding him on the back, but he couldn't stop choking. He was looking at her with widened eyes, his face reddening, hands at his throat.

"Do you want me to help?" she cried. "Tell me! I won't if you don't want me to!"

He nodded desperately, and she sat him up and crawled onto the bed behind him, straddling him to give him the Heimlich maneuver. Once, twice. His chest was surprisingly solid, strong. She had to put all her strength into her grip. On her third try, the maneuver worked and he heaved. The morsel came up. At that moment Hattie entered the room with the nurse, who arrived at his bedside just as his breakfast came up into his lap. "You need to get out of his bed," she ordered ClairBell. "What's happened in here?" The nurse grabbed the emesis basin from the bedside stand and held it until Abel stopped retching.

But there was no time for anyone to answer for what had happened, as the doctors appeared in the room, Dr. Abbas and Dr. Hakim. "We understand that you want to go home," said Dr. Abbas, flipping open the chart. He hadn't yet looked at the patient or taken in the disorder in the room. "You are aware of what could happen if you go home? You could get another pneumonia. You might not be able to eat."

"Well, I just ate!" Abel said triumphantly, wiping his mouth. "Biscuits and gravy."

"Is this true?" Dr. Hakim asked the nurse, and when she nodded he huffed in disgust. Both doctors looked around the room, as though taking in Hattie and ClairBell for the first time. "He was NPO. How did this happen?"

ClairBell stepped forward, ready to confess her part, but Hattie put a hand on her arm to stop her. "Blame him. He tricked us."

"Mister and Missus and your daughter, I presume," Dr. Abbas said, "I will put this to you simply. Either we put in the peg tube for feeding or it's the end of the line." He flipped the chart closed. "Take an hour or so to discuss it and we'll be back after rounds and we can go from there."

"I don't need an hour," Abel said, but his voice had faded and no one was listening to him. He repeated his intention. "In full knowledge of the consequences, I want to go home. This is what I want. I had things planned otherwise, you know."

The doctors left the room, shaking their heads.

Hattie sank into a chair and closed her eyes. Before her thoughts could come to rest on what was going on, on the awful prognosis the doctor had given, she thought briefly of Billy, hurt, too, and sleeping in his father's bed, of the scene Abel might make if he went home and found him there. Her heart was pounding and deep down the fist was squeezing and an aching tightness spread across her chest. She'd heard what the doctors had said the night before when Abel had been admitted, but somehow she now felt as if she was hearing it for the first time. The end of the line. The words ran through her mind.

ClairBell took a seat beside her and reached for her hand. "Sorry, Mom," she whispered.

Hattie smiled wearily. "Leave me with your father, will you?"

ClairBell got up and went out. The seriousness of what was happening overwhelmed her. She'd always known this day was coming, but somehow she'd considered her father's death in only an abstract way. The special powers had been quiet where his longevity was concerned, but now they quivered into action. She went around the corner and leaned into the corridor's wall for support. For all her sister's high-handedness, Doro's was the voice she wanted. She drew a few ragged breaths, trying to calm herself, and then she pulled out her phone and dialed the number. "You'd better come home" was all she was able to get out before her voice broke.

Hattie pulled up a chair to sit beside the bed. She couldn't think of what to say. Nothing was too much and everything was too little. And so she only looked at Abel, trying to see him truly, to see into him to the center. When they were courting she'd tried this as well, when they'd sat in the front seat of his Crosley convertible coupe, parked on the bank of the Ark River, gazing for hours into each other's eyes, but she'd never been inside him the way she'd wanted to be. She couldn't see him deeply enough, couldn't take him in. She felt that always between them there had been some strange impediment. And now he was an old man in a bed and she was an old woman in a chair beside it and the end had come barreling at them too fast. Her first and only love, her husband, looking back at her with eyes that had turned, with age, from their once-sharp green to a soft blue-gray, and yet he and she were no closer to what she'd always thought of as union.

"We agreed about this," he reminded her gently, the anger gone from his voice.

She could only nod. Despite their pragmatic approach to dying and the talking they'd done over the years, they'd not once been faced with a moment when a word could seal the future. She wasn't certain how she felt. Whether she wanted him to have the feeding tube and prolong his life and maybe his suffering for who knew how much longer—months, she remembered the doctor saying the night before—or to forgo the intervention, to take him home to let him die. Both outcomes were terrible, and there was no third choice.

The decision was his to make; on this they had long ago agreed, and she would honor him by honoring the agreement. But she wanted to say something meaningful and deep to mark the moment, something that would let him know how much, despite the way she sometimes resisted him or didn't show affection the way he wanted her to, she loved him. Her natural reserve ran deep and words were hard. It hadn't been her way to speak plainly about her feelings. She'd prided herself on her self-containment, but now she rued it. She wished she were a different kind of person, one who could cry aloud, could pound her chest in grief, throw herself on his chest, who could say what she felt rather than opening her mouth to say one thing and then saying something completely different to the point that she hardly trusted herself to speak, one who could reveal her heart clearly, without equivocation or havering or second-guessing.

A verse from James about plain-speaking came to her: *let your yea be yea and your nay be nay*. She took Abel's hand and clasped it, willing into her grip all the warmth she felt for him, all the sorrow and all the gladness, too, and most of all the love that surprised her, now, in its depth. "Abel, I don't think I'm ready," she heard herself saying, understanding even as she said the words that they were true, "to let you go."

For a time she thought he hadn't heard her. He lay quietly, his eyes closed, his chest rising and falling in slow, steady rhythm. His throat was moving, as if he were trying to swallow something back. She was just about to repeat herself, for she understood that for once she'd said exactly what she meant, when he met her gaze and said in a cracked, dry voice, "Then you won't have to."

Ten

To cut down on his night terrors, Hattie moved into Abel's hospital room and slept on a cot the nurses made up for her. After the feeding tube was inserted, she learned how to care for his stoma, a word she tried to avoid using for its ugliness. She called the narrow rubber tube that protruded from a hole in his belly a tunnel, and even though she would have to tend its dressing once they got home she did her best not to look at it too closely. He had opted for the tube for her. The least she could do was try to hide her squeamishness.

She felt dead on her feet, both at the hospital and then at home after he was released. She said the 23rd Psalm so many times as the minutes went by that she believed she could say it in her sleep, what little sleep she got. Doro had arrived to spend the remaining weeks of summer, and she and ClairBell took turns spelling Hattie, so that was a help.

Doro took on Billy duty, running her brother around on his errands, and she was saddened by the changes in him. He was as wobbly and low as she'd ever seen him, one moment at valiant pains to resurrect his old exuberance but failing and the next moment either strung out or in a dark, sad mood. No matter which state he inhabited, it was clear that he was suffering. When the word *broken* came to her, she pushed it away, but it stayed out of her mind only briefly. He could hardly walk. Sometimes bone pain drove him to his knees in the middle of a step. He'd found a discarded walker with bright yellow tennis balls stuck onto the legs and he had taken to using this rather than his cane. She'd gotten him to move back into his apartment uptown so he wouldn't be at the house when their father came home, but she could see that the situation there was bad. His roommate was a lowlife and probably a criminal. Somehow her mother had been dealing with this. Doro didn't know how she could bear it.

For all the years he'd lived under a death sentence, some kind of amnesia or scar tissue had grown up around the possibility that he would actually die, and everyone went along in a state of forgetfulness. But now Doro feared she saw the approach of his last season. He was nearing fifty. His health was shot and he, too, needed to be cared for. She wanted to find a way. She *would* find a way, but her first goal, the reason she'd come home, was to get things squared away with her parents. They couldn't go on this way, either.

They needed a plan, the siblings agreed, and so one afternoon in late June the four of them gathered at Jesse's, the better to keep the proceedings from Hattie and Abel and let them rest. They sat in lawn chairs on the raised deck built off Jesse's barn loft, looking out onto the long roll of bench land stretching south past fields of ripe wheat to the tree line of the timber.

The day had reached the golden hour when the setting sun's orange light on the swaying grain heads seemed to set the air aglow. Locusts buzzed in the catalpa trees around the farmhouse and a flock of guineas surged frantically out of the walnut grove, honking a snake warning.

In the packed dirt of the lane, Jesse's blind red setter lay on her side in the heat, from time to time raising her feathery tail and then lowering it, as if to sweep the dust.

"Just when you think things can't get any worse," Jesse said.

ClairBell finished his thought by making the sound of a toilet flushing.

"It's bad," Doro said. "Every day it's some new problem, or Dad has a new demand. She's already exhausted and he's only been home two days."

"He's agitating to get his guns back," Gid said. He took a long pull on a can of Bud Light. "Can't say I blame him." Gid had long had his eye on the collection, hoping that his father would leave the guns to him. "He wants that little Sig Sauer especially."

ClairBell said, "He tried to bully me into going down to the police station to get them back." The truth was that she'd gone on her own, hoping to make herself a hero in his eyes, but she was thwarted by regulations and procedure and the presence of her ex-husband's new girlfriend.

"Bet he didn't have to bully you very long," Jesse said under his breath. It was well known that ClairBell hoped the guns would come her way so she could pass them down to her sons.

Abel had at one time or another made the gun collection one of his confusing bequests, parting them out according to who was in front of him at the time. He'd once given the pacifist Doro a monstrous double-barrel Browning that made her queasy just to look at, but a few weeks later he'd told Big Bill the gun was his.

ClairBell made a sour face. "Don't look at me. No way I'd set foot in that station. Jimbo's new wife works in there. On dispatch." She reached up to pull at two hanks of her topknot ponytail, tightened it, then shook her head. "Thank God somebody told me that before I went down there and made a spectacle of myself. Anyway, Daddy called up Uncle Big Bill and got him to do it."

"I heard that," Gid said. "But they wouldn't let Uncle Big have them, either. Won't let anybody have them. Not until Dad's out of the house. Not while he's delusional. Fucking police state."

ClairBell looked closely at Gid. "How do you know that? About the guns."

Gid extended a pinkie from his beer can and held it delicately. "I have my ways." He, too, had gone to the station hoping to get the guns released. He'd ended up making a scene, spouting about Big Brother and the right to bear arms and the U.S. Constitution. He wasn't proud of losing his temper, but he was proud of the points he'd made speaking out the way he had, especially in a repressive government climate.

"Wait a minute," Doro said. She hadn't been able to follow their conversation. "Why do the police have Dad's guns?"

"Tell her, Bell," Gid said.

When her sister had finished the story, Doro sat back. "Mom told me he had a claw hammer."

Jesse laughed bitterly. "Of course she did."

Doro was still mulling, trying to put the story together. The day before, in her efforts to find a place for her parents, she'd gone to the Amicus nursing home to talk about the possibility of getting her father checked in. Before she'd even had a chance to describe her father's needs, the woman in charge had said, "We don't have the facilities to care for a case like his." Doro had been surprised. The woman hadn't even met him. When she pressed for an answer, the woman hemmed and hawed and seemed hesitant to provide a specific reason. Now she understood. Amicus was a small town, and word about the guns and the old judge's delirium had spread. She didn't know how she was going to fix things, but she wasn't leaving town until the situation improved.

Gid brought up Abel's threat to sue the ambulance company for ignoring the DNR on the refrigerator.

ClairBell sank lower in her chair.

Jesse reached over to pat her arm. "You were only trying to help. Don't worry about it. He's being an asshole."

Doro's throat tightened. Her brother's bitterness about their father shouldn't have surprised her—it had been going on for years—but just now it did. Anyone who watched the two men could see that the problem was that they were of the same temperament and they couldn't stop being who they accused the other of being long enough to see it. "He's an old man," she said. "He's sick."

Gid shrugged. "Doesn't mean he's not an asshole."

Doro turned the talk back to the medical aspects of the problem, and then she moved on to enlisting their sympathies. "Mom's overwhelmed with his feedings. The smell is terrible, and it has to be injected six times a day." She went on to say that treating the inflamed tissue around his tunnel opening was a long, tedious procedure. She didn't say that their father didn't shorten it any by trying to cooperate, for this would set off the boys, who were angered by their father more than, Doro thought, they needed to be. And she didn't say that their father bossed their mother, criticizing the angle at which she tried to work, the length of paper tape she'd cut, the way she folded the bandage. "And on top of all this there's Billy. He's in a bad place and he needs help, but every time he calls down to the house Mom has to wait between Dad's naps and feedings to do anything, even to talk on the phone." As she spoke she realized she wasn't really saying anything new. This had always been the way. It was just worse now. She finished with, "What's she going to do when I have to go back for fall semester?"

"Maybe they could get someone to come cook. A little nursing," ClairBell suggested, but the words had scarcely left her lips when everyone, including ClairBell, laughed. Their parents were too stubborn for this to work. Hattie hated to have anyone in her kitchen. She stood like a looming heron over anyone who tried to help, beady-eyed and alert, suggesting better ways. Abel was worse. Things had to be just so. And he feared theft. He had accused more than one workman—he had accused his own sons—of stealing.

Doro said, "They need to get out of that house. Sooner rather than later."

"I don't know," said Jesse. "You never know when things will hit bottom."

Gideon grinned, lifting his beer can as if in a toast, casting a look toward his brother. "Yep, you never know."

Doro looked away. Gid's sarcasm was sometimes hard to take. She knew he assumed the stance to compensate for his feelings of failure, but it could get old, especially as he made no attempt to change. She felt on edge, with him, with everyone. Trying to deal with her brothers and sister was a trial, like trying to line up snakes in a box. She wanted to go home.

"Mom could have a stroke or another heart attack and then where would Dad be? Or Billy could get in some kind of trouble."

"Could?" ClairBell mugged a dunce face.

"Neither one of them should be driving," Jesse said.

Gid smirked. "Try to tell that to His Honor."

ClairBell put in, "And Her Honor."

Jesse said, "The other day I saw Mom's Camry coming out of the bank drive-through. First she signaled to turn right, and then she changed her mind and signaled left. Then right again, then left. Her turn blinkers looked like some whacked-out carnival ride. Car behind her got spooked and backed up and pulled out of the lot a different way. Mom sat there a while and then finally, just when another car was coming toward her, she hit the gas and shot out. Other car stops in time and she waves her innocent old lady wave—tee-hee, little old me—and drives on."

ClairBell said, "And she drives uptown. She still tries to be Billy's beck-and-call-girl. She probably shouldn't even be driving to the Farmland for groceries."

Gid stood and leaned against the railing. "Same old same old." He crossed his arms and looked at Doro. "So have you decided where they ought to go?"

Doro had given the matter consideration, and she'd done some research online. "Well, Dad would need skilled nursing because of his tube and his other problems." She *would* say it, say the word they'd all been refusing to use. "His dementia. They won't take him at Amicus Health. I'm guessing because of the guns. Mom's a better candidate for independent living, but who knows how much longer that will last. I was thinking we might check out this place down in Clearwater. They have levels of care. It's expensive but . . ."

Jesse tipped back in his chair. "That's all well and good, but what if they don't want to move? How do we get them out?"

Gid popped another Bud Light and the hiss, coming at a still moment when the guineas ceased clacking and the locusts gave out, sounded loud and sinister. "Crowbar?"

Jesse laughed. "WD-40." He put his feet on the railing. "The place looks like ten kinds of shit. All Dad's junk around. Tape around the junction boxes. A wonder there hasn't been a fire."

When Jesse turned to look at the charred barn roof, Gid cleared his throat and looked darkly off into the distance. Doro suspected words had passed between her brothers, but now didn't seem like the right time to ask what was going on. They ran hot and cold. Jesse would get a bellyful of Gid's irresponsibility and go off on a tear trying to get him to meetings. Gid would refuse. Jesse couldn't stand being estranged, so he'd relent, and little by little they'd slide back into their uneasy brotherhood.

"And Mom's kitchen?" she put in. "She's like a pack rat. How many Cool Whip tubs does a person need? How many pickle jars and coffee cans?"

"Bread sacks," Jesse added.

Gid tittered in falsetto, "Why, a body just can't have too many twisty ties."

ClairBell took a sip of her iced tea. "She's washing plastic forks and spoons and reusing them. She brought some home from somebody's funeral. Plastic cups, too. One day I got one out of the cupboard to get a drink and there were hot-pink lipstick prints on it."

"Lord," Doro said.

"But the things that matter are on their last legs," Jesse said. "Her electric skillet's been missing a leg for the last ten years. Wobbling like a drun—" He looked at Gid and his beer and thought better of the comparison he was about to make. "Wobbling."

"She props it up with this little doodad she made that she's so proud of. An empty tuna fish can with a rock in it and the whole thing wrapped in tin foil," ClairBell supplied. "Like that makes it all right. If that thing tipped over there'd be a flood of bacon grease."

These things were true. The once-handsome house had grown shabby. And not just with time and use, Doro thought, but as if by design, as their parents, notwithstanding the money gift they'd just given everyone, seemed to grow cheaper and cheaper, their habit of scrimping refined to an art. Down in the family room wing, which had been shut off from the rest of the house in order to save on air-conditioning bills, Doro had come upon the lovely earth-toned paisley shawl she'd given her mother for Christmas. There it was, draped over a punched-down cardboard box that was being used as an end table, a vase of plastic hydrangeas, thirty years old if they were a day, adorning the surface. In the big bathroom another cardboard box had been covered with flowered contact paper and turned into a teetering toilet-side table. As satisfying as it was to bemoan their parents' ways, Doro wanted to bring the talk back around to solutions, and so she said, "Okay, so what are we going to do?"

"Listen," ClairBell said, deciding the time was right to spring her idea. She fitted her plastic cup into the holder built into the chair's arm and smoothed her terry-cloth shorts over her thighs. "What if we had a celebration? A birthday party for Dad."

Gid had been swigging his beer and he almost choked. "A party?"

"To celebrate what?" Doro said. " The fall of the house of Atreus. In slow motion?"

"Whatever," ClairBell snapped, giving her the fish eye. "Wouldn't it be nice if we did something special? I mean, he's going to be ninety-one. We could make a party of it." To soften her sharp answer she made her trademark charm-face, pertly cocking her head, folding her hands under her chin, and batting her lashes. Most of the time it was irresistible.

"I don't know," Doro said, trying to avoid hurting her sister's feelings, "this doesn't seem like the right—"

"It's the perfect time," ClairBell said quickly, powering up for an argument. "Here's Daddy feeling all left out. Not to mention mad about the ambulance and mad in general. He's got a tube in his belly, for crying out loud! And all Mom can do is chase after the Prodigal and gripe about the smell of Boost. And he did the whole thing for her."

She let what she hoped was guilt sink in before pretending to have a sudden inspiration. "Say, what if we had the party out at my place? We could swim. There's plenty of room. We could invite the whole family."

She went on, laying out her plan as though its details were just occurring to her. For a while it seemed like the others were warming to the idea, or at least not shooting it down outright, but when she got to the part about moving the Eliot chair and staging a group portrait there was a sudden chill.

The sun had set and darkness was coming on, but this chill was more than that. Doro, Jesse, and Gid were quiet. Nobody moved until Jesse shook a cigarette from his pack and put it between his lips. He dug in his jeans pocket for a lighter. Doro's mouth went suddenly dry as she saw her sister's strategy and with a sinking feeling knew that it would work. *Argumentum ad passiones*. If their father had a weakness, it was an appeal to flattery. She nudged Jesse and gestured toward his cigarette pack. "Split me one of those?"

Gid held out a hand. "Me, too."

The lighter flared, the three lit up, blew smoke.

On the tip of her tongue was a sharp remark, a dart ClairBell wanted to throw at her sister for her fall from the smoke wagon, but she decided against it. Her sister's face looked strange and stiff and stricken. Old. ClairBell realized suddenly that Doro was a dead ringer for Grandma Alice—the white hair, the same face with its string-puppet lines, same deep furrow between the eyes. Oh, oh, oh, the woman had not aged well. At. All. A brief thrill ran up ClairBell's backbone, but she remembered that underneath it all she actually loved her bossy, praise-hogging sister and so she drew up the reach of her powers short of predicting her demise.

Gid leaned forward and put his elbows on his knees. "This whole thing is bullshit," he muttered.

Jesse said to ClairBell, "You had me up until the chair part."

"Which is the bullshit part," Gid put in.

Doro stubbed out her cigarette in the coffee can Jesse had for the purpose. It had tasted terrible. "Maybe it's not a good idea to make big changes like taking the chair out of the living room, especially at a time like this."

ClairBell pounced. "But you're talking about trying to pry them out of the house. Isn't that an even bigger change?" She licked her lips. "What if we had the party first? Get them all softened up and then spring the plans on—"

Doro had recovered from the first shock at ClairBell's push to win the chair, and she picked up the opportunity her sister had provided, interrupting her. "That's what we came here to talk about, so let's make some decisions."

ClairBell allowed this to happen, deciding that she'd done enough for the time being. She'd laid down a base, and she was nothing if not persistent. There would most certainly be, she allowed her private powers full rein to foresee, a birthday party in August. And she and no one else, the spirits rose up and moved about to assure her, would win the Eliot chair.

They talked until late, deciding that the best course of action was straightforward, to call a sit-down with their parents, lay out their concerns, and give their recommendations about moving out of the house and into a facility. They would have brochures ready, and an estimate of the costs. They set the Fourth of July, when they would all be together again, as the date.

"Who's going to do the talking?" Doro asked.

"Not It," ClairBell said. Gid coughed to cover his laugh. Jesse frowned at his boots, and Doro said, "I don't want to, either." It was one thing to plan, one thing to orchestrate, but a completely different thing to confront them. They decided to draw straws. ClairBell went in search of hay straws, three longs and a short, and held them out. Jesse drew the short one.

How, they would wonder a few days later when their plan backfired, had they forgotten that their parents would stonewall them when they heard what was in store, how their father could rise to any occasion, how their mother could be a wild card, and how all it took was one rogue agent to ruin a perfectly sound plan, but on this evening with their decision fresh in their minds as they sat out on the deck at Jesse's, they hoped that this would be the time their parents would accept their help. When they finally rose to stretch and make their ways to their cars, they felt adult and industrious, that they were doing the right thing for their elderly parents. They felt saddened at the passing of the torch, sweetly beleaguered in a kind of heroic way, the responsibility heavy on them but bearable together, for they had talked themselves past their rivalrous crossfires and into believing in their own virtue. By the time they took leave of each other, the guinea flock had gone to roost in the cedars, the horses nickered softly in their stalls, and down in the timber a pack of coyotes yipped and cackled, their wild, high-pitched voices sounding like insane and far-off laughter.

Hattie had planned a cookout for the Fourth of July, easy enough, she hoped, given the upheaval the house had been in since Abel's return, and anyway it was the best she could do. Hot dogs and hamburgers, potato salad, slaw, a strawberry Jell-O salad with fruit cocktail, and a store-bought cherry pie, served on the picnic table on the back patio where they would be shaded by the sweet gum tree. The day had dawned muggy and windless and by afternoon the temperature registering on the thermometer clock outside Abel's machine barn was a hundred degrees. The American flag she'd placed in the holder by the back door hung listless.

Abel had at first felt strong enough to man the grill. He tied on his barbecue apron, which bulged at the place where his tube and its dressing jutted out. To shield his head from the sun he put on his father's straw hat. But before the burgers were ready to be turned he had to sit down. His knees kept giving out and the effort it took just to stand at the grill was too much. He turned the fork over to Gid.

To torque off Gid, Jesse said, "Hope everybody wants their burgers well done." He drummed on the picnic table and in a falsetto voice riffed the organ intro to "Light My Fire."

"Knock it off," Gid growled. If there was one thing he did well, it was barbecue meat.

Abel closed his eyes and dozed. He'd had a feeding earlier and he felt as droopy as the flag.

Billy was down from uptown but he hadn't hung around with the others, instead spending his time in the back bedrooms. He was in severe pain, Hattie explained to Doro and ClairBell, who were helping her in the kitchen. His prescriptions just weren't working. ClairBell had rolled her eyes. When Hattie called them to the table, he joined them outside, but he barely touched his potato salad and merely picked at the strawberry Jell-O. Soon he excused himself and went back inside to take a nap.

When the meal was over and the yard was cleaned up, Doro gave the signal and the siblings filed into the house, to the living room where Abel and Hattie had gone for an afternoon rest. They took seats around the room. More than one of them thought of the time they'd gathered there to confront Billy.

"Mom, Dad," Jesse began, "we wanted to talk to you about . . ." He halted. He hated public speaking. The only time he was remotely good at it was when in his drinking days he told a story at the bar or, when he was sober, he spoke at meetings. At those times he could almost believe he had inherited the quick verbal skills most of his family had—Abel, ClairBell, Billy, sometimes Gid and Doro—for the words seemed to pour out of him without his having to think about them. But most of the time he was like Hattie, his ideas garbled in his head no matter how well he collected them ahead of time, and when the time came to speak, he was stumbling and miserable and too often what came out of his mouth had nothing to do with what he intended to say. He cleared his throat and started again. "We've been talking and we're concerned about you and—"

"Have you?" Abel said, his tone sharp. "Been talking." Since his release from the hospital he'd sensed a gathering movement among his children. He suspected a putsch, an uprising. He'd seen this before, among clients who wanted to dispatch their elderly parents. To be done with them in order to get the goods. Yes, it was always about the goods. Abel sat up taller, looked sternly over the rims of his glasses. He allowed sarcasm free rein, the easiest of strategies but one that almost always worked with his children. "And you're *concerned*."

Jesse tried to overcome his father's gimlet stare. He looked over to Doro, who was nodding *go ahead* to him, and he knew without a doubt that whatever he said would be rebutted. And so he swerved. "It's just that Mom is worn out and she needs a rest."

Abel shook his head theatrically, as though playing to the jury. "You are aware, are you not, that by concluding that I'm the one wearing her out you've made a fundamental error in logic."

"We didn't say that, Dad." Then everything went out of Jesse's mind. He didn't think he'd said anything about blame, but under his father's gaze his memory went black. The old man cowed them all, except maybe ClairBell. He wished she would speak up.

Abel drilled down. "You're trafficking in supposition. Correlation does not equal causation. What proof do you have?"

Gid tried to come to his brother's rescue. "Look at her, Dad. She's gray. She's thin."

"*Argumentum ad miserecordiam!* Fallacious, fallacious, fallacious."

Doro said, "She's had to take nitro more often. There's the proof."

"*Post hoc ergo propter hoc.* I taught you kids better than that." But he turned to Hattie. "*Do* you have to take your nitro more often?"

"Yes," she said, "but it's not that bad. I'm strong. I can handle it."

Doro sighed. They were getting nowhere. They should have talked to their mother first, to prepare her and enlist her support. Then they could have laid out the case persuasively. As it was, their mother's denial had just undone any progress they might have made. She was about to call an end to the talk when Hattie cleared her throat and sat forward on the sofa.

Hattie had been thinking. Not just in the past few minutes, but for days. She couldn't do it. Couldn't be nursemaid and cook and gardener and cleaner and companion. It was too much. She'd been wondering how she could go on, and then, like a miracle, the children had stepped in on her behalf. If she did anything right in her life, it should be to speak her mind now, to say what she needed. The time was ripe; her children would back her up. "Abel," she said, taking his hand and looking into his eyes, "I think I would feel better if you went to the nursing home."

Everyone fell silent. From the bedroom wing came the sound of Billy clattering around, rummaging, it was later revealed, in Abel's shoebox collection for his cache of oxycodone, but otherwise quiet. A sense of shock hung heavily in the room.

"Where you can get the care you need," Doro interjected, moving past her surprise at her mother's statement and hoping to salvage the moment, to redirect.

Abel looked around the room, at his children arrayed against him. "Are you all of this opinion? That I'm a burden to your mother? So say you all?"

Gideon, seated on the stone ledge, said, "Dad, yes. Just until you get squared away."

Abel turned to Jesse. "I'm aware of your opinion, Jesse. Do you have anything to add?"

Of all the moments he most hated, the times his father looked him in the eye were worst. Jesse slammed on his hat, got up, and stalked outside.

Abel moved on to Doro, seated on the armrest of the Eliot chair. "Theodora? What about you? I can usually depend on you for good sense. What do you think of this?"

His eyes seemed to beseech her and it was all she could do to say, "I think it's best for both of you. Just until—"

"To be separated from each other? What about our vows? Your mother and I promised to stand by each other. I took it seriously. Had this damn tube cut into my gut. Til death do us part, we promised. I wish you kids understood that this is the goddamn death part."

Suddenly ClairBell's witchy powers kicked in, and she saw which way the wind blew. She saw clearly her title to the chair, the very chair where Doro perched, and she saw how to make it hers. "Daddy," she said, widening her eyes and making his favorite face, "Daddy, I tried to talk them out of it. I think you should stay right here. Where you're comfortable. Where you're needed."

Doro gaped at her sister. She got up and went outside. Gideon followed. They found Jesse on the deck built over the ravine and they joined him, lowering themselves onto the benches. "God!" Doro said. "That was awful."

Jesse had stopped at Gid's cooler and lifted out a tallboy. He hadn't opened it yet but was savoring the moments before he went over the edge. Now he popped the top, tilted the can, and angrily poured the golden glory down his throat.

Gid smirked. "I thought that went rather well." He, too, popped a tallboy.

Doro got up and went to fish out one for herself.

Inside the house, Hattie had gone to the kitchen, where she could think best. She decided to keep the ground beef left over from the cookout from going to waste, and so she took out a pan and began browning it to make spaghetti sauce. She gave the meat a few jabs, and then took out an onion to chop.

Billy wandered into the kitchen. "Mother, what's wrong? Let me do that for you."

She looked at him closely. Her eyes stung, but she could see enough to tell that he was bright-eyed and alert.

He took the knife from her and with a chef's ease chopped the onion finely. "You're crying, Mother. What's the matter?"

"Oh," she said, gathering a breath to have out with all of it, how weary she was, how worried she was about him, about his father, but the words wouldn't follow. She put a hand on his shoulder. "Just this onion. How are you, honey? Are you feeling better?"

"Much better. I had a good nap."

"You do look rested." She smiled. There was her boy of old.

"Oh, I am. But I find myself in need of funds. Could you lend me a hundred?"

"Dollars? I just gave you"—she lowered her voice so she couldn't be overheard—"two hundred. Where did that go?"

Billy began an elaborate tale of need, false starts, a near miss, a past-due deadline involving a certain item he needed for his massage practice and with so many twists and turns that Hattie lost sight of what he was saying. "Massage oils are really that expensive?"

"They're cheap at twice the price. I know a supplier and he'll let me have them for next to nothing. A friend is coming by to pick me up in a few minutes and . . ."

"Not that Haskell fellow."

"Oh, Mother. I'm fine. It was all a big misunderstanding with him. We're fine now."

Hattie gave up and went for her pocketbook to fish out bills. She had four twenties. When she handed them to Billy, he said, "That's all you have?"

"I'm afraid so. You'll have to wait until I can get to the bank."

He slipped the bills out of her fingers and kissed her on the cheek. "*Merci, Maman.* You can owe me the rest."

In the living room Abel had stayed in his seat to contemplate the development that had just taken place. He was furious. He reviewed in his memory the laws on involuntary committal. His children could never do it. Not only were they not determined enough—wishy-washy the lot—it simply couldn't be done. He knew the ins and outs too well. He hadn't gone to law school for nothing.

ClairBell, who had remained behind, took the opportunity to sit in the Eliot chair, caressing the wide arms. "You know," she said wistfully, "I always felt so comfortable in this chair. It makes me feel protected. Like my Daddy's arms around me."

Even in his diminished state, Abel knew soft-soap when he heard it. ClairBell was a stinker of the first water, a shameless knob-gobbler, and she was laying it on thick. He knew what she wanted, and suddenly he saw a way to punish the others. "Then by all means it should be yours."

ClairBell made a show of surprise and delight. This had been easier than she'd thought. "Really?" She jumped up and went to him and wrapped her arms around his head and delivered a loud kiss. "Oh, thank you, Daddy! I'll take good care of it. You always knew how much it means to me, didn't you?"

"Oh, no," he said wryly. "That comes as a complete surprise."

She didn't know how to take his tone, as it was at odds with her picture of the moment she'd waited for. Hoping to be told he was only being facetious, she made her fatal mistake. "So you forgive me for calling that mean old ambulance?"

The reminder sent a jolt of anger straight to Abel's carotid, and he growled, "Beat it before I take the damned thing back."

ClairBell left quickly, avoiding the others, and went to her car. She backed down the driveway all the way to the street, weeping in gratitude, grinning in elation.

Abel sat for a long time alone. He closed his eyes. From the kitchen came the smell of browning beef and onions. His mouth watered. But was that odor a hint of the garlic he had forbidden? He heard the back door open and close and the sounds of his grown children seating themselves at the dining room table, their low voices. The rasp of an aluminum can being opened.

Jesse saying, "I'll have another, too."

Gid saying, "You sure?"

Then another rasp. Jesse's voice. "Oh, shit, that's good."

"Well," he heard his wife say in a breezy manner, as though nothing out of the ordinary had taken place, "supper will be ready in a half hour. You children wash your hands. Doro, will you set the table?" She sounded bright, alive, no trace in her voice of the betrayal she'd just committed.

He rose from the sofa and shuffled outside to roam the property. Slowly he made his way to his barn. Here, among the smells of machine oil and rust, diesel fuel and solder, the souvenirs and collections and fruit of his long lifetime stored in antique hardware store bins, in drawers and pigeonholes, he busied himself by sorting gaskets and washers, screws and nails, trying with all that was in him to remember the use for any of it.

Eleven

A cannonade thundering from the History Channel's morning bill of fare, his back room darkened by drawn draperies, Abel stretched out in the Eliot chair. After much struggle he'd dragged the massive thing from the living room to the place his recliner, now shoved to the side, had held. He had decided to keep an eye on it. You never knew when ClairBell might strike, now that she had the go-ahead. As sure as he took his gaze away she'd be out in the driveway loading it into a U-Haul, along with some of the other items she'd put her name on. An antique cast-iron wash pot, a limestone relief of a Roman soldier he'd carved. No. He'd let it go, and he'd let it go to her, but he would decide when. She wasn't going to get away with it that fast. She'd called the damned ambulance on him.

His swollen feet in their compression socks propped on the raised footrest, hearing aid removed, head back on his sheepskin, he had withdrawn. He would not speak. Even when they had come to him, one by one, to apologize. For two days since their attack he had punished them, but by this day, the third one since their thwarted overthrow, the specifics of his grudge had begun to fade and he remembered mostly that he felt alone and bruised and tossed aside. But he would keep up his boycott.

Elsewhere the morning was sunny and warm. In the kitchen Hattie prepared breakfast, filling the house with the smell of frying bacon, a habit she couldn't break even though Abel could no longer eat it. She hoped the aroma alone would please him. Doro sat at the counter, spooning blueberry yogurt from the cottage cheese container Hattie stored it in while she glanced over the two-week-old Amicus *Friend*, paying special attention to the police blotter to see if the call on the night of the guns had made the paper. So far there had been no news of any disturbance, and she hoped enough time had passed that there would be none. She planned to keep an eye on things and to conceal from her father's eye, if the need arose, the public notice of the episode.

A few miles away at his place on the river, Jesse poked a pitchfork into sodden straw. He was cleaning out the chicken house and thinking that he might drive over to his parents' house to check on things. His fall off the wagon on the night of the confrontation had been hard. He'd left his parents' house and driven straight to Amicus Spirits and bought two six-packs of liquor-store Budweiser, his standby, and he hadn't stopped drinking until he fell asleep in his truck at the end of his lane. He'd been awakened by one of his horse boarders. The whole thing left him chastened and sick. He hadn't taken another drink since then and he'd been to three meetings in three days, but he still felt wobbly. *Easy does it,* he kept telling himself. *Easy does it.* But it was anything but easy. With each jab of the pitchfork into the hay he tried to forget how fricking tough it was.

Another ten miles away, in her bedroom at her Flint Hills house, ClairBell tried to shake off a drugged sleep. She'd gotten up in the middle of the night with a busy head. Sunday was the big birthday party—now back on the docket by popular demand—and she had only a few days to get everything ready. She had taken three Lortabs that took forever to kick in. In a cinder-block house on the outskirts of Amicus, Gideon was seated in his undershorts in the kitchenette of Tina, the VFW bartender, trying to coffee up enough to get going. All of them, sleeping or waking, were troubled by what had gone on in their botched family council, and all of them, except for Billy, who was oblivious to the upheaval, hoped to get back on Abel's good side. They had jumped on ClairBell's birthday party plan, and Doro had proposed moving it up a few weeks. "Dad isn't looking very good," she'd said, and they all agreed.

Four boxes of photographs and memorabilia waited on Hattie's kitchen table. The task was to sort the family photographs so ClairBell could make a collage to set up on an easel at the party. A wonderful idea, everyone said. He would love it, especially the pictures of him on his BSA 650, of him standing in the bucket of Big Brutus, posing at Waimea Falls, on the roof of the barn on the day he'd completed it, the hunting photos, the fishing photos, him on the bench, oh so many of his glory days. These would surely help to build him back up.

The night before, ClairBell had said to Doro and Hattie, "Be ready to work. I'll be there tomorrow at the butt-crack of dawn. Is seven too early?" But on this morning when Hattie's phone rang and Doro answered it was ClairBell on the other end, her voice a croak, saying, "Don't wait for me."

Hattie stood at alert, a dishtowel in her hand. It was well known that ClairBell rarely rose before noon. Hattie had had an idea that this might happen and to tell the truth, it suited her just fine. A day with ClairBell in the house, even with their common purpose, could be a trial, especially when Doro was home. The competition. The vying for the best-daughter award. Her big, bustling personality and crass remarks just didn't jibe with their quieter demeanor.

"You're not sick, are you?" Doro asked her sister. How many more times would the euphemism serve? How long would everyone pretend ClairBell's problems had nothing to do with drugs?

"No." ClairBell coughed feebly, unconvincingly. "But I think I might be coming down with something. You do the pictures without me. Just get them sorted and I'll make the collage. We've got five days before we need it done." She summoned another cough. "Has Billy called yet?"

"We haven't heard word one."

"You will. And then you'll be off on the royal runaround."

Doro ignored her sister's sourness. Given ClairBell's mood, the change of plans was for the best. "You rest. We'll get the pictures done another time."

"Well," said Hattie, cheerfully wiping the counter. "I guess this means we'll have to think of something else."

"How about shopping?" Doro suggested. "All we've done is nursing and kitchen duty. Maybe we could go to town and get something nice for"—she lowered her voice in case her father was listening—"the party." This was an appeal to her mother's vanity. Hattie was still a trim little clothes-pony.

Hattie laughed. "Well, why not? What's to stop us? We can both buy something nice." A shopping excursion meant a trip uptown and this reminded her of Billy, never far from thought. Often on Tuesdays—and this was a Tuesday—he needed to be driven around.

"Maybe I'll just check in with your brother," she said. She reached for the phone but thought twice before dialing. Should she? Was she opening herself up for trouble? Especially with Abel in the fret he was in. Did this go against her resolve to put her husband above her son? On the other hand, it was probably safe to leave Abel for a few hours. Mostly what he did was sleep. He could shoot formula into his feeding tube as well as she could. She needed the outing, a break. And the thought of a day with her two most tractable children . . . While Hattie's finger was still on the button, the phone rang, startling her.

She supposed it was ClairBell with a postscript, and so she summoned a disappointed voice, preparing to commiserate. But on the other end was Billy, talking excitedly, and so loud she had to hold the receiver away from her ear.

Never one for conversational throat-clearing, he almost always went straight for the sustained monologue, sometimes going on a full five minutes before she could interrupt him to say she was dressing, that her blouse was half on and she couldn't put her arm through the other sleeve so she was standing there with a folded wing, would he please hold on while she put down the phone?

"There's wonderful news!" he was saying, "I've found a spectacular apartment straight out of Gloria Swanson's Hollywood! Wrought-iron sconces over a stucco fireplace. Balconies. An architectural gem, Mother. You'll love it. When you see it you'll know it's meant to be mine. It could change my life, I can feel it! And the best news of all is that the rent is only a hundred dollars more than I'm paying now. I can make up for it by scheduling more massage clients so it's no problem at all. And the even better part is that the landlord will be on hand to show it to us this very afternoon. You will love it!" In French, he added, *"Vous l'adorerez vraiment."*

"Whatever that means," Hattie said, but she laughed, and she heard her voice taking on the same excitement. Her youngest and his enthusiasms always lifted her, no matter how harebrained his arrangements.

And his present energy was a welcome relief from the night he'd been dumped in the driveway.

"Does this mean you want to move?" she asked hopefully, thinking that if he had a better, brighter place to live . . .

"Yes," he said. "I've been feeling low and I couldn't figure out what the trouble was and then it hit me that I need something to lift me out of the doldrums. I have the distinct feeling that this will turn me around. This is just the place!"

Eagerly, Hattie began to plan aloud. "How about if we pick you up close to noon and go to lunch, then we'll take you for your prescriptions. You need them, don't you? Then we'll take you to pay your gas and electric and then stop by the pharmacy and then after that we can tour the new place. We'll make a day of it. How does that sound?"

When he answered, "Like you read my mind," she smiled and hung up.

In the past, Doro had tried to encourage solving Billy's problems in a way that didn't require so much of her mother, pointing out that Billy could take the bus to his appointments to save her from driving the twenty miles to town. That he could use the postal system rather than being driven around to various bill-pay sites. That he could use money orders from the Reddi Mart near his apartment rather than being driven to a bank for cash. But she'd learned after many attempts that Hattie didn't care about her carbon footprint or expediency or the waste of a day spent careening about to the point of exhaustion; she wanted to spend time with Billy and she didn't care under what circumstances. Enough, Doro thought. Enough was enough. Today she would make it her mission to straighten things out. Get Billy settled once and for all and set up new guidelines for her mother's involvement. This would take money, she knew. But she determined to spend it. The benefits would be worth the expense.

"Well." Hattie turned to Doro. "I suppose you heard. Of course he can't afford that place and this is just another wild goose chase." But she smiled. As she scrubbed at the bacon pan she went on about how a day with Billy wore her out, running from one thing to the next and always with nonstop chatter and always, predictable as dawn, a mid-stream change of plans. "But he's so upbeat. And he never complains."

Hattie flitted around the kitchen, closing drawers, tidying. "He's so excited. And he does need his medicine. Maybe if we get his business done first we can find a little time for ourselves."

"That sounds good." Doro smiled, but she could tell Hattie's heart wasn't in a shopping trip. She looked at her mother. Something was off. Hattie seemed more distracted than usual, almost hectic in her flitting. Doro couldn't figure out what was up, but she knew it was something.

Hattie indeed had a plan. It had come to her in the night, when she lay thinking of how to solve Billy's problems. She had a little money but not quite enough. She'd tossed and turned, trying to figure out how to stretch the five thousand dollars in her private account into enough to provide for him. What he needed was a nice room in a nice family house in a nice neighborhood, maybe one close by in Amicus. Maybe within walking distance. She'd prayed a little about the problem. She didn't want to ask God to solve a financial dilemma or send money through some kind of miracle—this seemed wrong—but suddenly He had sent her the solution, and it was so perfectly right that she wondered why she hadn't thought of it before. It had been in front of her nose the whole time. An antique dealer had once appraised the Eliot chair for between four and six thousand dollars. She would sell it. The children had fought over it for years, and even though he'd dragged it into his den, Abel didn't really like it. He was just making some kind of point. She would call that appraiser and offer it on the market. Spirit it out of the house when no one was looking. Give Billy a year's worth of rent so he could change his life. And who knew, maybe after that things would have settled down and he could move home. It was settled. Forgetting that where Billy was concerned, any plan she conceived was guaranteed to go awry, she hurried off to dress for the day, leaving Doro at the counter with the *Friend,* a cup of coffee, and a plate of bacon she didn't want.

As Doro sat at the kitchen counter waiting for Hattie to dress, the back door opened with its familiar squawk and thump, the displacement of the rubber gasket Abel had mis-installed in what now seemed another life. Jesse entered the mudroom, stamping his barn boots to knock off the dirt and hay. He came into the kitchen. By habit he lifted the electric skillet lid only to see the newly cleaned pan, balanced perfectly on its foil-wrapped, rock-filled tuna can, the electric cord folded neatly inside.

Hattie emerged from her bedroom to greet him. "Jesse! How nice." She was torn. She didn't want to give him the hurry-up treatment. It would be good if he'd eat a little something. He didn't eat well, always fast food. And he was as sensitive as ClairBell about getting the bum's rush. But Billy was expecting them. Quickly she made her decision. "Let me fry you a few eggs. It won't take a minute. And then we're off to town."

"Had a doughnut, but thanks." This was a lie. Patsy had made him a bowl of oatmeal, cutting up an apple to put on top and brown sugaring it just right. It had melted his heart all over again. To divert attention from his fib, he lifted the cake safe lid and spied banana bread. "What have we here?" He carved off a hunk, splashed some coffee into his Reddi Mart mug to top it off and then took a stool at the counter. ClairBell maintained that he was a moocher, intimating that he staged his visits to their parents' house at mealtimes. Doro saw things differently, having noticed that behind her brother's gruff, nonchalant manner was a careful observation of Hattie and Abel, and that in his way he was keeping an eye on them.

"We're headed up to town," Hattie said happily.

When she told him their agenda, Jesse nodded. "Off to do the Prodigal's bidding?"

Doro laughed. "Filet of fatted calf for dinner. Fresh."

Jesse made a comic grimace. "Just hold on to your pocketbooks."

Hattie scowled. She didn't like it when they mocked her dealings with Billy. Their mockery held truth, she knew that, but she still didn't like it. But she was glad Jesse'd reminded her about her pocketbook. She would have to stop at the bank to make sure she had cash on hand. In case.

Jesse nodded toward the newspaper. "Anything new in the *Enemy*?"

Doro thought to mention her plan to keep the police blotter from their father, but she decided against it. Instead she said, "Nothing new. We were supposed to sort those boxes for ClairBell's party project but . . ."

Jesse said, "She bailed, right?"

Doro nodded. "Coming down with something."

"Wonder how many milligrams of something." They shared the wry downward look that was family code, a silent commentary on the inscrutable but predictable ways of ClairBell.

"I think she's cutting down, though," Doro said. "Seriously. She's been different lately."

"Nah," he said. "It's the same old leopard and her same old spots. She wants that chair and she's in Olympic training, that's what I think. Got to keep her wits about her. Now that Dad's mad at all of us she's got to find a different way to get it."

Doro folded the newspaper. "Dad moved it into his room so he could keep an eye on it."

Jesse shook his head. He finished his banana bread. "Guess you need to go about your morning." He patted Doro on the shoulder, pushed himself up, and headed toward the back room to sit with his father.

Always he dreaded the encounter, but since the mutiny he'd made up his mind to try to repair the injury. His sister's words about their father being old and sick had struck home. As well, after his fall off the wagon and how easy it had been he'd figured that if he was serious about working a program, he ought to practice what he preached. *And when we were wrong promptly admitted it.* But he still dreaded it. He planned to open the proceedings by mentioning the Large Hadron Collider, a guaranteed gambit and fail-safe Judge-softener. If that didn't work, he'd start talking about dark matter and the God particle, and that should open the floodgates.

But when Jesse joined him in the back room, taking a seat in the recliner that flanked the Eliot chair, his father merely lifted a hand, apparently thought better of it, and trained his gaze on the footage of WWII bombers. Jesse waited for him to tell him he'd piloted them, or start in on tales he only half believed, but his father was silent. There seemed no opportunity to mention the collider. Once or twice he composed a bit of conversation, but no talk issued forth. Then, suddenly, his father said, "It's a terrible thing, to get old, son. A terrible thing. You remember I told you this when your time comes. You remember."

Hattie and Doro came in to make their good-byes. Shaken, Jesse got up and left the house with them, and when they parted ways at the end of the driveway, the women headed north in the green Camry and he in his truck headed south, driving straight to a meeting.

Up Seneca Street the women went, Doro at the wheel, past trailer parks and salvage yards, year-round yard sales, a Kmart, two Walmarts, fast-food joints, smoke shops, and liquor stores, a Reddi Mart on almost every mile section corner. Year by year the road between the city and the small towns that ringed it got seedier, the run-down businesses that flanked it evidence of hard times. The whole area, Doro thought, had gone to pot. Or maybe she'd just begun to notice. But it seemed to her that there had been a time when things had looked better, more alive, less shabby. In the 1940s Boeing had drawn thousands of wartime factory workers from Great Plains towns. In its heyday Superfortresses and Stratofortresses rolled off the lines, but in recent years the company had pulled up stakes. Outsourcing to China and Indonesia had done its damage. Still, everywhere, studded along the road margins, waving defiantly in the wind from tire stores and La Petite day-care centers and Pentecostal Holiness churches, from the easement at the turn-in to Walmart, were thousands of cheap American flags, made in China.

Once they reached the city a different vista opened, with grassy riverbanks and bicycle paths, tall cottonwoods, benches and running trails. They followed this route until it took them down Waco Street to Riverside Park and Billy's basement apartment.

He was waiting in the iron-gated courtyard of the crumbling beaux arts building. From a balcony above him and across the way, Haskell, in a red bandanna head wrap and a T-shirt, glowered.

When Billy saw Doro getting out of the car he called in his swooping stage voice, "The most beautiful women in the world, my mother and my long-lost sister!"

He grabbed his cane, shouldered his backpack, and lurched forward, crossing the courtyard in fits and starts, hitches and hobbles. Though she'd seen him only days before, his appearance was a shock, and Doro drew in a breath at how small and thin he was. He had the sunken-eyed look of a chemotherapy patient, made more noticeable by the canted eye that came down to him from their mother's side, and the fact that the skin around this eye, his blind one, had been scarred by shingles. *Boysie,* she thought. She felt a prickling behind her own eyes and then an involuntary welling of tears, which she blinked away.

"Why isn't he using his walker?" Hattie whispered.

"I don't know," Doro whispered back. "He's having a good day?"

He fitted his gear and himself into the Camry's backseat, complaining that the car was stuffy. "It's a lovely day. Let's get some air in here!" Once settled, he glanced over his shoulder. "Don't look now, but there's Gog Magog. The Family Man."

"I thought Haskell was your roommate," Doro said.

"Not anymore. He moved out and moved his family in. Right across the courtyard. So he can look down on me." He laughed gaily and then made a *pouf* sound.

Doro waited for details—neither she nor Hattie could keep track of his alliances—but Billy had turned his attention to rooting in his backpack.

"Well, just don't provoke him, honey," Hattie said. She hadn't forgotten the sight of her son on the night he'd been thrown from the car. She would never forget.

Billy laughed darkly.

Doro shifted in her seat to look at him. She would find a way to hurt anyone who hurt him. "Has he done something to you?"

Billy shrugged. "No. Mostly he yells at me if I'm outside trying to talk on the phone. Or if I happen to come home late and I make the slightest bit of noise. Or if I come within . . . he doesn't want me near his children."

"Can you steer clear of him?" Doro asked.

"Oh, I do," Billy assured her. "I only rented him a room to . . . oh, enough about me. Tell me everything that's new." Suddenly he seemed to have recovered his bright mood.

Hattie smiled. "Let's just have a nice day. Let's not let anybody else's bad temper get in our way."

The day would be arrayed around his needs, but neither Hattie nor Doro felt resentment, only that an old bond had been restored. They enjoyed each other's company. They liked the selves they were when they were together, selves that squared with who they wanted to be. Hattie dropped her reserve and became warm and spontaneous. Doro could be herself, no walking on eggshells. Billy was sweet, expansive, funny, the life of the party.

Having lived over half his life under the shadow of death, Billy had had many occasions to look back on his best times—a spun-gold evening on Prague's Charles Bridge or the green New Zealand coast or the heart-wrecking view from Machu Picchu. At the top would not be when he and Leo stood before the officiant and made their vows or any number of the beautiful meals he'd prepared for people he loved. His best time was when he was Boysie, when his brothers and sisters blanket-tossed him, giggling, into the air, when they bore him aloft through the house and everyone kissed him and kissed him. When he and his mother and sister were together, it felt almost that good.

The Copper Kettle was a down-home diner favored by Hattie for its low prices, generous use of salt, and absence of frills. At the noon hour the place was packed. They tried to find a table in the rush but had no luck. In healthier days Billy had waited tables in five-star restaurants and country clubs, and he was proud of his knowledge of the restaurant world. To hasten their progress, he snapped his fingers like an imperious maître d', commanding the attention of the other diners, who stared. His voice, bullhorn-loud in its nasality, the result of his snorting cocaine and methadone, was startling. "Table, please!"

When he tilted his head back to look over the now-quiet house, Doro spotted a white fleck in his nostril, a groove of dried blood. Although he was often flying high and garrulous and sometimes lewd and embarrassing in public, he was also funny and sweet and smart and loving. On this day it was clear that he'd taken something, but so far his behavior was within limits. She had no idea as to which way the day would turn out.

In one respect Doro was like her father in that she couldn't tolerate a spectacle. Her instinct was to flee. And so when Billy again snapped his fingers over his head and directed his voice toward the manager, shouting *"Garcon!"* she pretended an urgent need for the ladies' room and hurried away. She dallied in the stall, waiting what she thought was enough time for Billy's clamor to calm and the other diners to turn their attention elsewhere.

When she returned, feeling like the coward she'd been, her mother and brother were settled at a corner table by the kitchen doors, menus in hand. Hattie studied the choices while Billy chatted about his apartment find. "It is simply fabulous," he enthused. He seemed to be having trouble modulating his voice, which was blaring. The people at the next table—a farm couple and their teenage daughters—stared openly. His diction was slurred, and his elaborate vocabulary and his ability to speak in complex compound sentences drew looks.

He settled down to order, loudly asking the waitress about the provenance of various offerings, how they were prepared. "Does the chef julienne or chiffonade?"

"Is the oil first cold-pressed? Extra virgin? Or is it that nastiferous crankcase concoction?" At last he made an unlikely choice, given his refined tastes, a Philly cheesesteak, but only after the waitress trotted twice to the chef to be sure the prep method was one Billy approved. Hattie and Doro ordered cups of minestrone and chicken salad sandwiches.

"So"—he turned his high beams on Doro—"tell me all about your life. How are my dear nieces? How are your artistic endeavors? How is your work?"

Trying to ignore the wanderings of his good eye and its dilating pupil, Doro filled him in on the goings-on with her family. During one of the better times in his life, during the nineties when AZT had kept his system strong, he'd come to Virginia, where she'd lived for a time before moving up the coast. They reminisced about their adventures—a summer beach house on the Outer Banks, cooking together, candlelit family dinners on the wraparound porch—skirting the eventual unpleasantness, leaving out the part where he'd had to be carried from the walk-up apartment he'd rented, an apartment that in just a few months he'd made unspeakably filthy with roach-ridden food, needles and pills, piles of soiled clothing, to Doro's house where he sat through a Tidewater August lolled and incoherent on her porch in a wicker chair. Later he admitted that he'd taken a drug holiday, feeling so good in his new life that he decided to go off his meds. Once Doro got him to the doctor, he was diagnosed with brain lesions. When he was stable enough to travel, though forgetful and clumsy and out of it, she packed him up and Hattie came to fetch him home to die. That had been fifteen years before. The lesions resolved and brain function was restored, and little by little he began to improve. Protease inhibitors proved better treatment. Still, he had wide swings. After every good time, for whatever reason, either that life was so glorious and good that he sought even greater glory and goodness or that he was overtaken by a feeling of invincibility that allowed him to believe that this time he would not go all the way down but could put on the brakes before the brink, he went down. He looked almost as bad as he had in Virginia.

When their plates arrived he wanted to say a prayer. He reached for his mother's and sister's hands. Doro squirmed. "Not today, okay, Boyz?"

Hattie said, "Let's just say silent prayers." She, too, disliked the practice; it made her think of the warning against the Pharisees. And Billy's voice was truly loud today.

"Creator God," Billy began, ignoring them, "we come to You in wonder at the plenty You bestow on us, Your servants past deserving. In gratitude we ask for Your forgiveness. In Your peace"—he squeezed their hands—"amen."

His prayer was mercifully brief, but people had shot them looks anyway. "You used the formula," Doro said, eager to start conversation again and move past the embarrassment. "Adoration, contrition . . ."

"Thanksgiving, supplication," Hattie finished. While he was praying she'd thought again of her long-ago hopes for him. She'd wanted at least one of her children to go into the ministry. But as they grew up and became themselves, she realized that not one of them had the temperament or the spiritual gifts. She'd been disappointed. Until Billy.

He would have made a fine minister. For enjoyment he read Meister Eckhart and William James and Thomas Merton. His faith stayed strong through trouble. *Ad astra per aspera,* she sometimes mused, the Kansas state motto. Her son embodied it. To the stars through hardship. Oh, all the boxes checked off, except for the single unspoken, unmentionable one. She looked at her children and smiled again. "This is nice, isn't it?"

Billy set to picking apart his sandwich, enumerating the ways the creation was at odds with his orders. "One, the bread isn't griddle-toasted. Two, the beef is sliced too thickly. Three, the onions are too thin. Four, the cheese is wrong." He began to put the sandwich back together, meticulously arranging onions and sliced beef, turning the talk to his new apartment. "It's perfect for my massage practice. It has a dear little anteroom that can be a waiting room. A beautiful arabesque window." He clapped the sides of his sandwich together and took a bite. Around a mouthful, he said, "And leaded-glass mullions!"

The busboy passed by the table with a tub of dishes. Billy put out a hand and halted him to ask, "And from whence do you come, young sir? O golden youth!"

The busboy, who appeared to be a shy country kid and mortified by the attention, said diffidently, "Park City."

"Oh," said Billy, alert to possible connection. "Oh, the world is *vraiment* small! Perhaps you know my uncle who lives there. I'm named after him, you know. Bill Campbell?"

The busboy shook his head, shifted the weight of his full tub. "Done with them plates?" he asked. Hattie and Doro handed theirs over.

"What a cutie," Billy said, looking after the boy as he made haste toward the kitchen.

Hattie picked up the tab and they were on their way across town for Billy's prescriptions. He was given a script for certain of his medications in three installments rather than only once a week, experience having taught his physician that if a week's supply was given, a week's supply would be gone by the second day. They parked close to the entrance, Hattie and Doro planning to wait in the car while Billy went inside. The weather was so warm that they rolled down the windows. Just as Billy was about to enter the building, he gave a sharp yelp and then collapsed on his hands and knees. On the concrete step he writhed in pain. Doro opened her door to go after him, but Hattie said, "He'll get up. He does that sometimes, when the pain is bad. Your sister thinks he's putting on a show, but she doesn't understand. She's so hard on him." Billy maneuvered to a stand, saluted them, and then lurched into the clinic.

He was out within ten minutes. "I forgot to tell you that I have a massage client at two o'clock. So why don't we do this—you ladies take these scripts to the pharmacy and then drop me at my apartment and then go back to the pharmacy and wait to pick them up."

Doro shook her head. She was eager to see his new apartment, eager to solve the lingering problem of Billy. "All right," she said, knowing there was no point in arguing.

Hattie sighed. She'd known the midstream change of plans would come, but she was frazzled by it nonetheless. She'd left Abel to his own devices and he couldn't be counted on to feed himself. He would be rooting in the kitchen for a club cracker or a handful of peanuts and when they got home she would be treated to rebuke or a pout. When she remembered his feeding tube, a sense of freedom overtook her and the day once again opened wide. "How long do you think that will take?"

"Oh, forty-five minutes. It's just a half-hour massage. And then we'll go pay the bills and see my new pleasure dome."

When they returned to his apartment complex, Doro needed to go to the bathroom and it was not, this time, a pretense. She disliked going into Billy's place—subterranean, dirty, dark, the air thick with cigarette smoke—but she followed him down the dark stairway. The chairs were shabby and stained. Spent tubes of Androgel cluttered his table. Dirty clothes and porn magazines shared space with his set of fine German knives and his stainless-steel restaurant gear. In the bathroom she made a quick business of things, and headed to the door, which he'd left open for his client. From the back room where he'd gone to light candles and make ready, he called out, "Call before you come back!"

At that moment, a large man appeared at the doorway, dressed in business clothes, a well-cut suit, wingtips, an expensive tie. He reeked of Fahrenheit and appeared startled to see her.

"I'm just his sister," she blurted stupidly as she hurried past him to take the stairs to the ground floor and the waiting car.

Hattie had taken advantage of her absence to clean her glasses and sort the items in her purse. When Doro took the driver's seat beside her, she said, "I don't see how he has the strength to give a massage. How can he stand there for thirty minutes on those legs? Imagine the pain he must be in."

Doro had wondered about his stamina as well, and had once asked him. "I pace myself," he'd said blithely, and then confided, "THC." At her uncomprehending look, he stage-whispered, "Medical marijuana."

"I can't imagine, Mom." Doro put the car in gear and pulled onto the street. She hoped her mother had missed seeing the well-dressed man. She remembered something her daughters had told her. One summer when they were teenagers they'd gone to visit their grandparents. Billy happened to be living there, high most of the time. "It was like little birds were tweeting around his head, all cuckoo." He'd become lascivious in his conversation, his social filters gone. He'd raved about someone's gargantuan dick and pretended to swoon over a big English cucumber he'd taken from the basket on the kitchen counter. "Where was Grandma?" Doro had asked. "At the ironing board. Ironing his waiter's shirt," the girls told her.

Hattie put on her glasses. "Was that man his client?"

Doro braked the car at the Waco light. "I don't know. He was at the door when I came out."

Hattie clasped her pocketbook hasp together and then folded her hands primly over the bag. "He looked nice enough. But I don't see how Billy can give a massage to such a big man."

As they pulled out onto Waco to make the turn into the strip mall pharmacy, Hattie grew thoughtful. "Do you think," she asked hesitantly, unsure that she wanted the truth, "that he's really giving massages?"

Doro fiddled with the air-conditioning controls and vents, deciding how to answer. It had occurred to her to wonder why clients would seek out an unlicensed, self-taught masseur in a dark, cluttered walk-down apartment. But right there in his studio were a massage table, towels, a water feature played over a pyramid of smooth black stones, a CD player, oils and emollients, candles. She decided to let this evidence overtake her doubts and assuage her mother's fears, and she said, "Yes, I think he is."

Hattie was quiet, looking out the window as they steered into a parking spot at the pharmacy. She thought of the way he'd been dumped in the driveway, other signs she'd told no one. "Sometimes I'm not so sure."

"What would be so wrong," Hattie asked as they sat in the car outside his apartment, waiting for him to finish with his client and come out so they could be on their way to see the new place, "with Billy coming to live at home? He could help me with your father. He's good company. Have you ever had him give you a massage? He's just wonderful. I don't see what would be so wrong."

Doro looked at her mother. If she disagreed, Hattie would blame her. If she agreed, her mother would use her as a stalking horse, telling her father that Doro thought it was a good idea. She had to be careful. "How has it been when he's lived there before?"

"It's been just fine with me. He can be such a help. Of course your father doesn't like it but I think this time will be different." Hattie gave Doro a sudden, surprised look, at the edges of which Doro saw guile. "Why, I've just had an idea! What if you were to talk to your father!"

"I don't know, Mom," Doro said. "Maybe it's not the best timing."

Hattie pounced. She'd caught Doro on a technicality. "So you *don't* see why not. You agree with the idea. It's just the timing?"

Billy appeared at the Camry's back door. "All finished."

"Hop in," Doro told him.

"Perfect," he said as he struggled into the car, letting out a great sigh. "We're right on time. You won't believe this beautiful place."

Stewart Court was a fake-half-timbered landmark on the worst corner in the city. Druggies with backpacks, burned-out cases shambling behind loaded grocery carts and talking to themselves, toughs smoking in the alley. As Doro parked the car in the weedy parking lot, they heard, "What is this shit?" from behind a Dumpster. A man in motorcycle pants and jacket yanked the arm of a bosomy girl in a tight blue miniskirt and fishnet stockings, a child in a Cinderella nightgown crying beside them. Billy got out of the car and Hattie and Doro did the same. They headed toward the steps that led to the office when a thick-set man appeared. He wore low-riding jeans and a torn yellow T-shirt that read PARALLAX. Leading with his immense belly, he approached.

"This is Mike," Billy said, introducing them.

Without a word, Mike turned to lead them toward the apartment. Billy hurried to keep up with him, leaning on his cane. "You won't mind if I paint a mural on the brick wall in that adorable passageway, will you? I'll be establishing my massage practice and I'll want clients to know where to go. It will be tasteful, I promise."

Over his shoulder Mike said, "Not gonna happen."

Billy was unfazed. "I've told my family all about the place. Gone on and on, in fact."

Mike led them through a dank arcade piled with rags and papers, old plastic toys, a crib. A pair of city property sawhorses supported an ancient refrigerator that had been laid on its back, its door propped open like a casket. Rodent traps had been placed in corners, and over all hung the smell of dead rat. As they crossed a courtyard, things began to look up. Mike unlocked a thick oaken door to let them into the apartment.

Billy went in first and stood in the center of the main room, pointing out its features. Two-story coffered ceilings and mullioned windows. A stucco fireplace that soared to exposed rafters. Copper sconces, dark hardwood floors, a two-tiered stairway with carved balusters. "The influences," Billy instructed them, "are part Moorish, part Teutonic. Isn't it paradise?"

The kitchen was hideous. Roach droppings and mouse turds and dead flies in the windowsills. "All this will be cleaned up, of course," chirped Billy, moving quickly out of the room toward the stairway. Mike shrugged.

While Hattie waited downstairs, Billy and Doro went upstairs. The balcony railing wobbled like a rotten tooth. Doro had an awful vision of Billy either falling or being thrown from the height. In the bedroom the rachitic blinds were felted with dust, the light-switch plates black with grime. The floors were gouged and scarred, as if someone had taken an ax to them.

Back downstairs in the main room, a narrow bricked-in passageway, perfect for muggings, drug deals, and assault, lay directly outside the big window, a view giving onto trash, Colt 45 bottles, and the mildewed lid to a child's green turtle pool.

Billy took Hattie's hand. "Beautiful, isn't it?"

Hattie had reached the point in the dwindling afternoon at which she could no longer think. All she knew was that she needed to be home.

Doro hurried to her rescue. "We need to get going, Boyz. Dad will be wondering where we are."

Billy turned to Mike. "I'll come by tomorrow with the deposit." To his mother and sister, he said, "If you'd give me a minute to transact some business?"

When they were out of earshot Hattie elbowed Doro. "You know what *this* means."

Doro knew. It meant that between now and Billy's place one or both of them would be hit up for the deposit.

"I'm not going to do it," Hattie said. "Stop me if I try to. I know he wants it but I think there's a better plan." She looked meaningfully at her daughter, hoping to pave the way. She had sped right over her plan to sell the chair and use the proceeds to fund his expenses. There was an even better way.

Doro held up a fist. "Fight the power," she whispered. As she opened the driver's side door, she made a mental note to research cheap, clean housing. She'd help with that, but not with the sorry dump Billy had his heart set on, carved balusters notwithstanding. Anyone could see that a move to this place would end badly.

Across the car's roof Hattie looked levelly at her daughter. She rapped once to get Doro's attention, and said, defiantly, "Because I've decided to bring him home. You watch me. I'm going to march myself into your father's room and tell him what's going to happen."

Billy joined them at the car before Doro could respond. "Listen, my dears, I just remembered I have to be somewhere. It completely slipped my mind."

Hattie fretted. "But your bills . . ."

"We can wait a few days to pay the bills. We're nowhere near the cutoff dates."

"We can drop you where you want to go," Doro offered. She opened her wallet and took out four twenties and slipped them to him outside the window, taking care that Hattie didn't see.

"I'll cab it," he said, sliding the bills into his pocket. *"Merci, ma belle."*

He gathered his backpack, cane, and the Styrofoam dessert box from lunch. To Hattie he said, "You have my prescriptions?"

Hattie drew the pharmacy bag from her pocketbook and handed it to him. Into the bag, when Doro hadn't been looking, she'd tucked three twenty-dollar bills.

"Au revoir, ma mère et ma soeur!" He blew two kisses and then hobbled away. It would be the last time they would see him upright.

When Doro and Hattie arrived home they found ClairBell and Abel sitting at the kitchen counter, ClairBell helping to inject Boost into his tunnel.

"Daddy called me," she said. She smiled her kitty-cat smile and Doro immediately suspected mischief. She hadn't spoken to her sister since her defection at the intervention and to see her now, currying favor with their father, set off alarms. Jesse had told her that ClairBell was working the Eliot chair angle hot and heavy, but Doro didn't want to believe her sister would stoop that low.

"I believe I'd like some chocolate ice cream, ClairBell, dear," Abel said. "Just a taste."

Doro walked straight past her sister. "I need to make a call." She went outside where cell reception was good and called Jesse. "We have to do something about Billy. He's killing himself and Mom's in huge denial."

"So it's standard operating procedure? Business as usual?"

Doro allowed herself to speak an uncharitable thought. "When will this ever end?"

Jesse knew the answer. Never. It would never end. The Big Book talked about lost causes. He didn't want to think it, but from what he could see, their brother was at end stage. There wasn't much behind his eyes anymore, or at least Jesse couldn't see any sign, and he knew what to look for.

"Rehab again," she was saying. "I don't see a choice. But we should wait until after Dad's party."

"Makes sense," Jesse said, thinking that for all the two of them could do to change their brother's fate, Doro might as well be talking to herself.

Twelve

Party morning dawned hot and overcast, the sky thick and white with humidity. At the kitchen sink Hattie peeled boiled eggs for potato salad. Doro sat at the counter, reading the *Friend* and finishing a bowl of Grape-Nuts. ClairBell had decreed that the party was to be a surprise, and she'd put them in charge of getting Abel to her place without revealing the reason.

"Billy hasn't called," Hattie worried. "It's been almost a week since we were up there and we haven't heard from him." In the flurry of preparations there'd been no time for a run uptown to check. "You don't think he found the money for a deposit on that apartment, do you?"

"I doubt it. It was seven hundred, I heard that Mike person say. Where would he get that kind of money?"

"I worry." What she was truly worried about was that he'd used the money she'd sneaked to him on the day they'd gone to see his apartment to buy street drugs and was on some kind of spree.

Doro, too, had had that thought, wondering how complicit she was in his activities. "You've tried to reach him?"

"His phone must be out of minutes. Or else he lost it again. I don't know if he'll want a ride or if he plans to be there at all. Oh, I wish that just for once he'd think of others."

To calm her mother, Doro said, "You know Billy. He loves a get-together. He's probably planning to make a big entrance."

Hattie plopped the last peeled egg into the bowl. "We did tell him about the party, didn't we?"

Doro walked her empty cereal bowl to the sink and rinsed it. "Twice. You told him twice."

Hattie dumped the eggshells into the Hills Bros. coffee can she kept to make garden compost. "He forgets things. I just wish he'd call."

Doro opened the dishwasher and started to load her cereal bowl. Hattie put out a hand to stop her. "Not that way." She took the bowl from Doro, deliberated for a moment, then made a space for it on the lower rack and fitted it snugly. "There, that's better."

Doro turned away and allowed herself an eye roll. Another week and she would board a plane for Logan, leaving the prairie behind. She was ready. Past ready. She loved her parents and she knew they wouldn't last forever, but it was time for her to go. After the party was finished she would arrange for rehab for Billy, even if she had to put it on a credit card, and then she was done. She turned around and picked up a dish-towel, preparing to dry the silverware. "Have you talked to Dad about Billy coming home?"

"I was waiting until after today. I didn't want to ruin ClairBell's party. You know how your sister gets, especially when it's something to do with your brother."

Doro was going to say, "No need to stir up a hornet's nest," but she stopped herself. What her mother had said was true. ClairBell took it badly when anyone else got attention, especially Billy. But it was also true that the pleasure Doro took in hearing her sister's shortcomings spoken of was a habit just as bad. She wanted to break herself of it, to rid herself of the need to be better than everyone else. It was hard-enough work just trying to be better than she knew herself to be.

From the hall the women heard Abel making his way to the kitchen, tapping his cane along the baseboard in the Morse code pattern for SOS. *Dit dit dit-dah dah dah—dit dit dit.*

"What stinks?" he said by way of greeting.

"Good morning, Dad," Doro said.

"Eggs," said Hattie. "I'm making potato salad. We're invited to ClairBell's for barbecue."

"Today? This is news to me. Nobody told me."

Doro put in with a quick lie, "It's spur of the moment, Dad."

"If that's the case, that same nobody shouldn't mind if I stay home." He grinned at his verbal turn. Enough time had passed that he'd either grown tired of maintaining his grudge or he'd forgotten the reason for it.

"She wants us to see Randy's new tractor," Doro hurried to add, though this lure was a lie. But it was true that Randy had a vintage tractor and that her father loved to keep up with the restoration work on it.

Abel perked up. "The little Allis Chalmers?" He took a seat at the counter. "Maybe I'll change my mind." He looked at Hattie and Doro over his glasses. "If *nobody* minds."

Dutifully, Doro laughed.

From the sink Hattie said, "I'd like it if you went with me, Abel."

He smiled, brought down a palm on the countertop. "Then say no more. It shall be done."

Hattie and Doro shared a look. He was in a good mood; with any luck it would be one of his better days.

By afternoon the skies cleared and a pleasant breeze came up. ClairBell had specified three o'clock, but people began arriving at her place shortly after noon, and by two o'clock the long front lane was two deep in parked cars. Uncle Big Bill stationed his truck on the county road in order to direct overflow into the pasture. Doro drove her rental out early in order to help set up, and by the time Hattie, carrying a yellow Tupperware bowl filled with potato salad, and Abel, leaning on his cane, arrived that afternoon, the party was in full swing.

ClairBell was pleased with the way things turned out. Streamers on a line that ran from the purple martin house to the yard light pole fluttered in the wind. The pool sparkled aquamarine. Her new red market umbrellas shaded the tables around the patio and paper lanterns bobbed from shepherd's crooks planted here and there. She hadn't been able to rustle up a horse, but no matter. She'd sent Randy to Walmart to buy two big trampolines, and now nieces and nephews and grandchildren bounced with abandon. She'd scotched her idea about the Eliot chair. It was too fraught a reminder of the abortive family council and as well it wouldn't do to call attention to it. Her claim on it, though still her secret—she hadn't told a soul except for Randy—was strong enough to hold, and she would defend it to the death if need be. Plus, she'd knocked herself out making this party; anyone could see that. Who could begrudge her the chair? Maybe, she thought, this would be a good day to tell her siblings that it had been given to her. That would put her mark on it. Seal it for good. There was no need to mention it again to her father. It was a done deal.

Four generations of Campbells and Eliots, Davieses and Hensleys gathered on lawn chairs and blankets. They milled in visiting clumps around the tables that held the potluck offerings. Cakes and pies and casseroles, platters of homegrown tomatoes and sweet corn, all the favorites from family reunions past—Aunt Sammie's pink angel food loaf cake, studded with walnuts and cherries, the Eliot family's burnt-sugar cake, the Ennis corn casserole, zucchini bread, macaroni salad, pickles, olives, chowchow, hand-cranked peach ice cream. To ward off imposters, ClairBell had placed an embargo on the baked beans of others, and she'd put together a hundred-year-floodplain batch—double brown sugar, extra molasses, two pounds of applewood-smoked bacon—in her Nesco roaster. She'd decided against fried chicken and instead was serving ribs and brisket, hamburgers and hot dogs. The huge sheet cake she'd ordered was in place on the center table, concealed in its box, which she had taped closed and further tented with sheet after sheet of foil so it would be a surprise. Everything was ready. She had tried to get a head count but people kept moving around. She thought there might be a hundred.

The elders congregated in lawn chairs in the shade of a catalpa, a breeze from a box fan riffling their cloud-white hair. Occasionally one or the other of them threw back a head and gave out with the Campbell laugh as they told stories patinaed with age and telling. Uncle Big Bill and doddery Aunt Jewel, Uncle Joe and Aunt Nadine, lonely Uncle Ed, married four times and each time a dud, the widow Aunt Grace. In the center sat her father and from the look of his satisfied, easy posture, and the fact that his was one of the laughs she heard raised, he was happy.

When she went upstairs to find a bathing suit for someone who'd forgotten to bring one, she looked out the back window at the party spread below. The kids in the pool and on the tramps, the old folks in their chairs, the tables, the lanterns, smoke from the grill, the line of coolers. Out near the rise some of the cousins gathered around Randy's tractor. Gideon stood off to the side, his arms crossed, his ATF ball cap drawn forward so that his eyes were hooded. So far he was on good behavior, though he sometimes disappeared over the hill to a stand of cedars. He'd brought along his guitar, and she'd heard him singing in his Neil Young voice about lying in a burned-out basement with the full moon in his eyes. Jesse had called from the road. He'd be late but he'd be there. Down in the kitchen Doro and her gang of cousins had set themselves up, calling themselves the Marthas and gabbing about whatever the four priss-pots gabbed about. Hair dye, Botox, boob jobs—who knew? Maybe clothes. She wouldn't know; she had never been part of their circle. But in the interest of peace she set this old wound aside. All of this, this glorious day, was because of her, and everyone knew it. People thanked her left and right and she was Queen for a Day. And her biggest worry hadn't come to pass. No one had heard from Billy.

Billy had every intention of being at the party. He loved a gathering, especially when it was his family. He'd had a rough week and he needed something to look forward to. After he left his mother and sister on whatever day that was he'd gone . . . well, he couldn't remember exactly where he'd gone and how he'd gotten there . . . but the upshot was that he had scored some extra methadone. And plenty of it, thanks to the windfall cash his mother and sister had slipped him.

Later that night when he tried to get into his apartment he discovered he didn't have his keys and so he'd had to knock on Haskell's door, which was a big mistake. Haskell had yelled at him and Billy yelled back and then out of nowhere and for no reason Haskell clocked him, hard. But after that Haskell threw the key into the courtyard so at least Billy was able to get inside and go to bed. He holed up for a while, waiting for his bruised jaw to feel better. It was a good thing he had the extra methadone. Things had a way of working out, he reflected.

He was looking forward to going to ClairBell's. He loved it when his brothers and sisters got to clowning around, when they got loud, they got silly, and he would laugh until his belly ached and his cheeks hurt. They would cease to be parents, grandparents, uncles and aunts, they would cease to be the tired old fogues they'd become, and they would go back to the way they were when they were young, before the long siege of grief that set in after Nick died, back when he was their golden one, their Boysie.

Each had a different kind of wit. Doro's ran to silliness and wordplay. Sometimes she spun out of control into the ridiculous, but occasionally she spooled off a golden riff. Nick had been a satirist, inclined to irony, but no one spoke of this now. Jesse told homespun tales of the cowboys and drunks and drywall apes he worked with, his laconic delivery spaced by artful pauses that had listeners thinking the story had ended. But then Jesse would pick up the tale again, twirling the story in a lazy lariat circle. ClairBell was bawdy and comic, antic, colorful, a natural mimic. She was the quickest and the most cutting. She reminded him of Roseanne Barr; she had the same growly, crackling sharpness. Gideon loved to tell shaggy-dog stories, putting an iconoclastic spin on things so you never knew where his sympathies, if he had any, lay. He wrote sad-sack laments that he sang in his high lonesome voice. Billy's favorite was, "You drank her wine, you ate her cheese, and now you've got her-pees." Billy's stock in trade was a story of his own well-known pretensions. Like Doro, he got carried away into silliness, but he loved to tell "The Teacup of the Aga Khan," a tale about the porcelain demitasse he had stolen from the Harbor Club because that worthy, whom Billy had waited on, had sipped from it. He would have them all rolling.

Hattie didn't participate. She saw her children as cynics and smart alecks, not to mention she couldn't tell a joke if her life depended on it. She'd tried to breed their father's wild streak out of them with Bible verses and her dry English humor, but her side's mildness and understatement and devotion didn't take, or took only spottily—in Doro's conciliatory nature, in Jesse's reticence, maybe in Gid's haunted hermit behavior, in ClairBell's . . . well, nowhere at all in ClairBell, she was a mad Campbell/Eliot hybrid. Abel was a storyteller, but he preferred an audience of cronies and so he took a backseat when the brothers and sisters went at it.

Billy never felt more himself than when he was in the middle of family noise, and he'd planned a grand entrance, guaranteed to make a splash and start the party off on a comic foot, no matter that the guest list had on it more than a few family members—especially among the elders—who believed that he was a walking spokesmodel for sin. They also loved him, he knew, and over the course of his life they'd probably sent up more prayers on his behalf than could be counted. Depending on how he looked at it, their prayers had either worked or they hadn't. And sin or not-sin, it was hardly their business. It was God's, if He should care to meddle in such things. Billy believed that He did not trouble much with sin, that He was a creator god who didn't intervene to punish or reward. As for Jesus, Billy had long ago worked out an answer that allowed him to hold two ideas at the same time, his love for the redeeming Christ his mother taught him and the prevailing prejudice held by most churches: if his was sin, it could be redeemed, and if divine forgiveness depended on contrition, he'd been contrite in one way or another every single minute of his adult life.

A friend had a vintage convertible Mercedes and Billy saw himself arriving in style, a rooster tail of dust spinning behind them on ClairBell's dirt road. The pal wasn't a romantic interest but he could be talked into tooling down to the gathering on the promise of barbecue and a few doses of THC. Billy was looking forward to seeing everyone, but for the past week he seemed to keep losing track of time. When Saturday night rolled around and he remembered that the party was the next day, he realized he had nothing to wear.

He knew the look he wanted. He wanted it to appear that he had just breezed in from the Hamptons—either in tennis whites or some Ralph Lauren, a pink shirt, maybe. Or if he could find a straw boater and a string tie he'd go Gay Nineties and wouldn't that be a hoot? He was well aware of the silliness of showing up for a prairie barbecue in such getups, but that was part of the fun. He would carry it off and be charming. He prided himself on his ability to poke fun at himself before anyone else had a chance.

Once he realized he needed an outfit, he set out on the long walk to the Goodwill. To be safe, he used his walker. He'd been feeling wobbly all week. When he arrived, he found the store closed. A look at the clock on the corner of Broadway and Waco told him that somehow it had gotten to be midnight. It was dark outside, so this meant it wasn't noon, he deduced. As he made his way back to his apartment, he was careful to walk in the nearly deserted street to keep his walker from catching on the crumbling sidewalks and buckled curbs, and so he didn't hear the car coming up behind him until just before it struck him.

On the party went, afternoon fading to dusk. After the meal, which he couldn't eat, though he tasted his daughter's sugar-coma baked beans for old times' sake, Abel made his way through the crowd to Randy's barn to inspect the tractor, the 1959 Allis Chalmers his son-in-law was restoring.

Feeling the need to get away from gab and small talk, endless questions about his farm and what his sons were doing and blah-blah-blah and everything except what was actually on his mind, which was Patsy and what he should do about her, when and how to let her go, Jesse had walked out that way himself. He found his father sitting on the tractor's front wheel, hands folded over the cane between his knees, holding forth about the tractor's specifications to a group of cousins. The men listened respectfully, but Jesse could tell by their stiff faces and lowered eyes—or at least he thought their eyes were lowered, maybe they were just looking at the ground—they were humoring the old man.

"You see," he was instructing them, "your tie rod cylinders are held together by four rods. Cost less than a welded cylinder and they're easier to fix. For your welded cylinder, the fixed end is welded in place. Stronger. Lasts longer. Better for a high-pressure operation. You've got an open system here, by the way. More common before 1960."

When he caught sight of Jesse he drew up short. He gave a smile Jesse didn't know how to take, and for a minute Jesse feared he'd walked into a trap. But his father seemed as earnest and unguarded as he'd been back in the winter when he'd told him about Jeff.

"Gentlemen, here's the real expert," his father said. "Son, what do you think? Which system do you favor? Open or closed?"

The listeners shifted their attention Jesse's way and widened their circle to make room. His father's question was simple, a nothing-question, and the answer didn't really matter, but his father had made the move to build him up. Jesse's impulse was to step back, to deny that he knew anything, to rebuff his father's gesture and leave him hanging. He'd almost done so when his better nature—or maybe, he thought later, his Higher Power—overtook him, and he answered the question straight, explaining the difference between systems in the way his father once had explained it to him, outlining the benefits of each. "So I'd say it depends on the nature of the job. Wouldn't you say so, Dad?"

They were small things, answering kindness with kindness, yielding the floor, letting his father have the last word, but they seemed to make the old man happy.

Abel grinned at the other men, his brother, his nephews, his nieces' husbands. "Have you met my son?"

The others passed it off as though Uncle Abe was making one of his jokes, but Jesse saw the lapse. His father's mind had just made one of its hairpin turns, traveling from clarity to blur in no time at all.

Jesse went to stand beside his father. He put his arm across his shoulders and turned him toward the house. "Mom wants you for something," he said.

"Oh, she does, does she?" Abel replied amiably, and then summoned from distant memory a line from Emerson. "'When duty whispers low, *thou must*, the youth replies, *I can.*'"

Walking slowly, Jesse took his father's elbow and guided him back to the catalpa tree where the others sat.

As he went back out toward the barn, from a stand of cedars came the smell of cigarette smoke—Gid sequestered in his secret He-Man Woman-Haters hideout. Jesse didn't want to put himself anywhere near a beer cooler, but he was drawn to maybe the only other person who would understand what had just happened. He found Gid sprawled in a camp chair, cigs and lighter in one pocket of the webbed cup holder, a tallboy in the other. His feet rested on an orange Igloo cooler. Gid reached behind him for a second folding chair and shook it open. "Take a load off, brother."

Jesse took the chair, set it up, and sat.

Gid field-stripped his cigarette and ground the butt into the grass. He put the filter in the chair's mesh pocket. "Looks like I'm the only drinker in the place," he said. He jerked his head toward the gathering. "Bunch of holy rollers."

"Yeah," Jesse said, shaking his head, "they're pretty bad." He glanced at Gid to see if he'd laugh but apparently the sarcasm was lost on his brother. Most of their family, on both sides, led sane, serene, productive lives, free of addictions and the wild whatever-it-was that had afflicted his.

Out on the prairie a coyote howled. In return an owl hooted from the hedgerow.

"I was thinking about quitting," Gid said, apropos of nothing. "And then I decided it'd be better if I'd quit thinking." He tipped his can Jesse's way and grinned. "Plenty more where this came from."

Jesse shook his head. "I'm good."

"Much Pepsi in there, too." Gid took his feet off the cooler's lid and opened it.

Most of the ice had melted and the cans floated free. Jesse fished in the frigid water for a can of something-not-beer. He selected a Sprite and popped the top, seeing how slowly he could release the gas.

Gid rested his head and looked up at the sky, now turning orange with the setting sun. "You think we'll ever get over it?"

"The Judge?"

Gid laughed. "Well, him, yeah. But I meant booze."

Jesse took a long pull. It was peaceful in Gid's arbor. From time to time they heard bursts of laughter. Shrieks from the diehards still in the pool playing Aqua Bull, a game in which a kid would jump onto a plastic oil drum floating under the diving board and try to stay on as long as possible, which was usually a hot second. "Not likely," Jesse said.

"What's not likely?" Gid's voice was slurring, guttural, as if his tongue had swollen.

Classic drunk voice, Jesse thought, and it made him feel two things at once, nostalgia and disgust. "What you asked me," Jesse said patiently. "If I thought we'd ever get over booze?"

"Oh. Oh, yeah. Didn't think so." Gid raised his can to clink with his brother's. He was in his cups and he was feeling sentimental. "I love you, man," Gid said.

His brother was down for the count, Jesse knew. There were all the signs, the unfocused gaze, the numbed speech, the sloppy emotion. He felt a rush of pity. For Gid, for Patsy, for himself, for anyone who had to fight the awful fight. He had been there, he knew how his brother felt, and he knew that the drunken love that was overflowing in Gid, for all its sloppiness, was as genuine as any other love and maybe more, for it contained all the forgiveness stone-cold soberness couldn't quite muster. "I love you, too," Jesse said, knowing Gid would keep repeating the words until he returned the favor. "But when this is over I'm driving you home."

Gid attempted a level gaze. "You have every right, sir."

Jesse drew back. The way Gid said this had sounded just like their father. Clipped, reasonable, matter-of-fact, on the edge of a challenge, the complexity of tone that was Abel's.

Gid had heard it, too. "Oh, no," he said. "Oh, hell no."

"Don't say hell, Gideon," Jesse said, imitating their mother. "Say heck." They laughed, and for a shimmering moment before it closed again Gid thought he felt a hairline crack in his heart, a fleeting beam of light.

The lanterns were lit and the fireflies were out. It was time for the cake. Doro was sitting in a lawn chair, chatting with a cousin, when ClairBell found her and asked her to cut and serve. "I thought you'd want to have a part in things," ClairBell said. "Not that you haven't already," she was quick to add, "but I mean it might be nice for us sisters to do the honors. Daddy's little girls. Besides, you'll just love the cake's theme. It's right up your alley. Bookish, what I mean is."

Doro got up. She winced inwardly at the "Daddy's little girls" bit, but when her sister was feeling expansive you had to go along. She wondered if ClairBell had taken something and then she laughed at herself. Of course she had. Trying to puzzle out the reasons for her family's addictions and thinking she'd found the answer, Doro had once asked if ClairBell believed that people smoked or drank or took pills to blunt their feelings of loss. ClairBell had given her a look, and then snapped. "You still think it's some kind of moral horse race, don't you?"

Doro went with her sister to the center table and stood by while ClairBell removed the foil sheets that had covered the cake box. With a pair of kitchen shears she cut the tape that sealed the box. "Where did you order this?" Doro asked, more to make conversation than for any other reason.

"Lady works out of her basement," her sister answered, busy lifting the lid to reveal the sheet cake. "I told her what we wanted and . . . oh, wow, it's just beautiful!"

It was all Doro could do not to gasp. The cake was a glossy, garish, gel-covered horror. In frosting, amid a border of muddy-looking sunflowers was the design of an open book, also in frosting, with the words "Book of Life" in bright green cursive. The book's pages were studded with plastic toys, a galloping horse, a motorcycle, a tractor, a shotgun, a tiny scale of justice, a green army man with rifle raised, a telescope, a radio, a miniature Easter Island head that looked uncannily like Ebenezer. Above the book, which looked more like a tombstone or the tablets of the Ten Commandments than it did a book, an inky blue night sky held unidentifiable heavenly bodies made of silver dragees and the words "Happy Birthday Daddy" in orange. The name only ClairBell called him. No comma to offset the proper noun.

"Pretty, huh?" ClairBell said, admiring the cake. Everything had gone as she had hoped. She had mended her torn family. She decided to share some of the credit with her sister. Doro was a stuck-up piece of work, with snooty notions, and she'd always left ClairBell out of things. Wouldn't share a bed with her, claiming ClairBell kicked. Paid less than no attention to ClairBell's overtures of friendship. Still, they were sisters. She put a hand on Doro's arm. "Let me get the candles. You round everybody up and tell them it's time to sing."

Doro felt her heart constrict, but she did as she was bidden. The less she had to do with the awful cake, the less it would seem that she'd had a hand in it. With every announcement she made, she resisted her impulse to disown the monstrosity and said simply, "Time for the cake," or "Birthday cake time."

When everyone was gathered, ClairBell led the group in the birthday song. Everyone applauded. Uncle Big Bill stepped forward. "To ClairBell, our hostess!"

A cheer went up. ClairBell had hoped for this and so she'd prepared a few words to say about her father and how much she loved him, but when the time came to speak the words she couldn't get her throat to work right. Instead, she made a deep curtsey and blew a kiss before turning away from the crowd to hide the sweetest tears she'd ever cried.

Doro had thought that maybe when it was cut into pieces the cake would look less awful, but when she scored it the creation looked worse than it had before. The way the colored gel bled at every knife cut made her think of the tacky paint-swirl pictures kids made for five dollars at the state fair. As people came through the line she tried to make her expression bland and smiling, and that kept her going until one of the more waggish cousins came through the line and, teasing, said, "That's some cake you got there, Dorito. You bake it yourself?"

Suddenly she could take no more. She plopped the piece of cake she had just cut onto a paper plate and opened her mouth to disown everything that had to do with the tasteless mess, but just then ClairBell appeared with a stack of paper plates and Doro couldn't badmouth the confection in front of her.

ClairBell saw what was going on and she determined to ride to her sister's rescue. It was clear that Doro wanted to take credit for the cake. Probably would have, if ClairBell hadn't shown up to witness the moment. On any other day ClairBell would have called her out and set everybody straight. No uncertain terms. She wouldn't have shared the credit, but today she had credit, in abundance. To the cousin she smiled, and making her voice louder so it would carry and everyone around could hear, she said, "She didn't bake it, but she did design it!"

Doro smiled stiffly, smiled miserably, and lowered her gaze.

It was a clear evening. Abel wished he'd brought his telescope, but he'd left it at home because the last few times he'd tried to set it up he couldn't get it to work. Something seemed to be wrong with it. On the southern horizon Sagittarius was rising, the familiar teapot shape that was the first constellation other than the Big Dipper that he'd learned as a boy. He'd once known the names of the stars that formed it, known the secret language of the heavens, but now he'd forgotten. Beyond the teapot's spout he knew lay, but he could not see, the numberless stars of the galaxy and the path to its very center.

The day had been good and he was touched by it. His daughter had done this to show him how much he was loved. Truth be told, he had needed it. His ouster as the family's head had hurt. As if he needed them to tell him what he already knew. That he was an old spent star. One foot on the ground beneath him and the other in the great beyond. He saw the way they looked at him when the wrong words came out of his mouth, and in their looks he saw pity. There was a time when he would have disdained the pity and tried to overmaster it. Not now. Now he understood that its wellspring was love. Love notwithstanding, he was tired. He had lived a long time.

Hattie, who was rounding the corner of the house to toss table scraps into the dog pen, saw him silhouetted against the sky, his wide, big-eared head, his bowed legs, the third leg that was his cane. She picked her way across the uneven ground. She thought that maybe this would be a good time to broach the subject of bringing Billy home. The night before, she'd had a premonition that Billy wouldn't last much longer. She'd missed him all day. It wasn't right that he wasn't here. She wasn't superstitious about omens and such, but the feeling was so strong that she thought it might be God, preparing her.

"My bride," Abel said, raising his free arm so she could slide in next to him. When they were courting he'd tried to teach her the constellations, but she couldn't hold the names in her head and finally he'd given up. And now, he reflected, he couldn't remember them. They were gone from his mind. Somewhere he'd read that the Osage or the Kiowa or maybe the Kaw—he couldn't remember which tribe, either—made a distinction between the Near Sky in which birds flew and trees rustled and from which snow fell, and the Far Sky, the home of the old ones, invisible from earth. But he couldn't recall if the moon and the sun and stars and planets were part of the Near Sky or the Far Sky. It didn't matter, he supposed. All he had tried to know and to understand, all of it gone, his mind whitening, losing its salt. He thought of the Hubble photos, world upon nameless world billowing up like great glistering clouds. He was glad he'd lived long enough to see them and he was sad that he'd never know more than he knew at this minute and would, as time went on, know less and less.

Hattie felt good standing beside her husband. Beneath the pabulum and soybean smell of the Boost he'd just injected she caught a whiff of his smell of old—his soap, bay rum, his scalp, his breath—and it struck at her heart. She wanted to say something about it, but she couldn't, for this wasn't the kind of thing she said. She slid her arm around his middle, careful not to disturb the peg tube, and leaned her head on his shoulder. A line of Wordsworth's came to her and so she recited that instead. " 'The Soul that rises with us, our life's Star, Hath had elsewhere its setting . . .' "

He was silent for a long time and so she asked, "What are you doing out here?"

Without thinking he answered, "Having a look at my new home."

She looked at him to see if he was trying to start an argument about the afterlife. But he appeared to be serious.

"Do you mean heaven?" she asked hesitantly.

"Call it that if you like." He pulled her closer. "It's where we're all headed." He kissed her hair. "And you're in for a surprise, Hat. You don't have to be good to get in the door."

"Well," she said, but nothing else would come. She wasn't sure what he meant—probably his old theory that everything was made of stardust. She'd lived with him long enough to know that his contrarian impulse was most easily triggered by a direct question, and so she didn't ask him if he believed in a heaven after all. She wasn't sure, in a sudden heave and shift of belief, that *she* did. And she wasn't sure it mattered, what she believed. Heaven either was or it wasn't, and no amount of wishing or will on her part would change things. What a time, she mused, for the bottom to fall out of a lifetime of certainty. In the space of a moment she felt oddly light, oddly young, oddly free, but then suddenly old and alone and bereft. She would not let this happen. She collected herself. "Well," she finally said, "think whatever you want, but I know what I know." And just like that she was back in the fold.

A great warm memory came to Abel then, and he considered telling her about his visit from Jeff, but then he thought better of it. She was a literalist, might take his vision as apostasy, you couldn't know. And the old vision was tangled anyway. Jeff, Jesus, Allah, God, Jehovah, Yahweh—what did the name matter? He lifted his cane and pointed it toward the teapot's spout, directing Hattie's gaze toward the thickest part of the Milky Way. "I'll meet you right there. I'll have a carnation in my lapel." He gave her hip a pat. "And a reaction."

She made a *pfft* noise, turning away so he wouldn't see the rise of pleasure and then—inexplicably—a sudden ache. She walked back down the rise.

Around two in the morning when the phone rang the only one still awake in the Amicus house was Doro. Hattie and Abel had gone to bed long before. Doro hadn't been able to sleep for thinking over the day's events, not so much the party itself, which now seemed a blur, but the upsetting confession that came as she and ClairBell stood in the yard saying their good-byes. ClairBell had taken her hands in hers and looked at her so directly that her blue gaze made Doro uncomfortable. "Now, we're sisters and I don't want any hard feelings between us," ClairBell had said, "and I just hope and pray you understand."

Suspiciously, but like the gaping fish she was, Doro bit. "Understand what?"

"Oh," ClairBell said, affecting surprise. "I thought you already knew."

Doro waited, heart racing. The exchange had the marks of a ClairBell coup and she suspected it had to do with the Eliot chair. She was supposed to ask "knew what?" but she wasn't going to give her sister the opening. She waited.

"That Daddy told me I could have the chair," ClairBell finally said.

Later Doro would think of stinging things she should have said, but at the time all she could come up with was silence.

ClairBell wouldn't be denied her moment. "So no hard feelings?" She made her sweetest, most fetching face and held her arms wide. "Sister, I need a hug."

Doro stepped back, unable to speak. She got into her rental car and shut the door and locked it. She started the engine and backed down the long driveway, waiting until she turned out onto the road before she punched the gas pedal to the floor and let out a throat-scouring yell. For miles she yelled that ClairBell Campbell Moody Green Billups should fucking fuck her fucking self, until her neck glands hurt and she thought she might give herself a stroke, and then the rest of the way home she cried like a child.

Now, prowling through the quiet house, she turned up nary a stray cigarette but in the kitchen she discovered, wrapped in a foil tent, a few pieces of the terrible birthday cake that Hattie had saved in case Billy showed up. The cake was still awful, but she was ravenous, gritting her teeth, in need of something to fill the gnawing in her belly. In the kitchen, by the light of the fridge, standing over the counter, she wolfed it, shoving cake and clots of frosting into her mouth with her hands, washing down mouthfuls of Crisco and corn syrup and red dye #40 with gulps of milk from the carton until the roof of her mouth was slick. She ate her fill and still there was some left, liquefying brown gel drooling down the side. She dug her fingers into the cake, drew a glop of it toward her mouth thinking to finish it off so it would be gone, but then, seized by anger that wouldn't die, she flung the mess hard at the refrigerator door.

When the phone rang she was on her knees, wiping the floor tiles with wet paper towels. Her mouth and throat went dry when she heard a woman who identified herself as a unit clerk at Saint Francis asking if she was related to William Campbell.

Her knees weakened. "I'm his sister," she answered.

The unit clerk said, "Your brother has been hit by a car. A hit and run. I can't tell you any more than that. The police will have to. I'm just supposed to let you know that he's here in the trauma unit."

Doro found her voice. "When was he brought in? Can you tell me that?"

"Early yesterday morning. I can check on the exact time for you."

Anger rose. "You're just now calling?"

"Sorry, ma'am. He didn't have a driver's license or any ID and he wasn't conscious when they found him."

Her wits returned. "So he's conscious now? He's awake?"

In the background phones rang. The clerk said, "He's conscious but he's sleeping. He's stable."

Doro hung up and called Jesse, who drove over. They decided to let their parents sleep. "He's safe," Jesse said. "There's nothing anybody can do. Especially not Mom and Dad."

Doro said, as though struck for the first time by the idea. "They're old, aren't they? Really old."

Jesse nodded. "Let's tell them first thing and then we can drive them up there. They won't be able to manage."

Quietly, they made a pot of coffee and sat in the living room. "This makes me think of when Nick . . ." Doro said. "When we were waiting for word. I was sitting on the sofa, the one that used to be here, that old plaid one with the fringe. Grandma was in the rocking chair and her face looked broken. It was the first time it hit me that she was really old. Funny to think we're almost the age she was then."

They were quiet until Jesse said, "I was in the kitchen, at the counter with Billy. He was about twelve, I guess. He didn't really know what was going on, I don't think. He was drawing mansion floor plans on graph paper the way he did and he wanted to show them to me. He was proud of himself. Talking fast—that birdie-chirping Boysie-talk of his. He'd designed this castle with twenty rooms and ballrooms and libraries and conservatories. But he hadn't put in any doors between the rooms. There were just boxes of rooms with no doors. And he didn't put in any bathrooms. I joked with him about it. Where was His Highness supposed to take a crap, you know? Drop the royal load in the banquet hall behind a potted plant? A litter box? I ragged him pretty hard. It made him mad and he started waling on me with these little Richie Rich slaps and that's when the phone rang and we heard—" Jesse broke off. He bent over and looked at the floor between his knees.

Doro said, "I shouldn't have said anything."

Jesse looked up. "No, it's not that. It's something else." He thought of telling his sister about his trials with Patsy, how he didn't know what to do. In the time between the birthday party's ending and Doro's call, Gid had brought Patsy home from the Pay Dirt, the two of them staggering into the farmhouse kitchen like cartoon drunks, slaphappy and foolish. Jesse had been asleep but he'd heard them banging around, trying to make a midnight breakfast, falling over each other. He'd not been able to go back to sleep, and he'd resolved to tell her she had to leave, that he couldn't take it anymore.

"It's just . . . damn Boysie," he said after a time. "Why couldn't he be a jerk?"

Doro shook her head.

Jesse collected himself. "Do you remember what Dad did? After Nick."

Doro repeated the legend. "He called up his buddy and they got on the private plane to Missouri."

"No, before that."

She didn't.

"After Mom called and told him and he told us and all of us were crying and screaming, Dad came to our rooms with that bottle of pills he had for his back injury. Darvon, I think. Whatever they had back then. And he gave a pill to everybody, even Billy. He told us it would take the edge off. It would help us calm down."

Doro said, "I don't remember that."

"Maybe you were outside." Jesse closed his eyes and rested his head on the back of the sofa. "I'd had two beers already. Stole 'em from Dad's barn. I wasn't tanked but I had on a pretty good buzz. When that pill hit, I thought I'd hit nirvana. I always kind of wondered if that was when it got into me."

They talked through the night, dozing off and on. They agreed that their sister was a grade-A horse's ass.

"I'm not going to speak to her again," Doro said. "I quit. Trying to be nice and tiptoeing around her."

Jesse nodded, waiting for his big sister to sort herself out. She was like him—hot talk when angered but nothing much behind it. He wouldn't be surprised if by morning when ClairBell joined them at the hospital the hot talker and the grade-A horse's ass would be locked in a big fleshy white-haired sisterly embrace and boo-hooing to beat the band. He wouldn't be surprised if when he got back to the farm there'd be Patsy, standing at the stove, frying him a ham steak, a bruised, sweet look on her face, a table set for two, and his heart would be wrecked all over again.

Around sunup they heard their mother stirring in the kitchen and they got up and went to her.

"Why, what are you two doing?" Hattie asked pleasantly, happy to see them first thing in the morning. Then her face fell. "No," she said. "No."

"He's all right," Doro said. She told what she knew. Jesse stood by to catch his mother in case she went down, but she didn't.

"I'm fine," Hattie said. "Don't wake your father. He needs his sleep. Just let me put some clothes on."

While Hattie dressed Jesse called ClairBell, waking her. She said she would be over to wait until Abel woke and then she'd drive him to the hospital if he was up for it. They couldn't rouse Gid but they decided it was probably just as well.

Billy had a compound fracture in his femur, a broken arm, some cracked ribs, a head injury, and no memory of what had happened. What they knew about his accident, they learned from the police report. The nurses were keeping him snowed on morphine.

"Did Haskell do this to you?" Hattie asked him at one point when he opened his eyes. "Was he driving the car that hit you?"

Billy gave her a blurry smile. "He doesn't even have a car. Somebody stole it. Don't worry. I'm going to be fine."

A healthier man might have been able to mend, but Billy had spent decades of his strength in fighting T-cell counts and viral loads, pneumonias, medicines, surgeries, and years of compromising his heart and lungs and liver, veins and arteries and gray matter. He ran fevers and was in excruciating pain. A resistant staph infection set into his hip joints, and no amount of antibiotics would touch it. The plan was to keep treating for infection in the hope of curing it. Then he might get replacement joints. "They're completely degenerated," the doctor told Hattie. "It's a wonder he went so long on them. He must have been in a lot of pain."

He was released to a surgical rehabilitation facility a few miles north of Amicus, where he stayed for the forty-day period allowed by Medicaid. Hattie visited every day, fitting in her trips while Abel napped. She grieved to see that Billy's natural cheer had gone out of him. He was a husk of himself, thin and sallow, his skin blighted with open sores. He tried to put on a show of being brave and optimistic, but his reserves were gone. She saw his old spark only twice—when she bought him a new laptop and when Doro, who had gone home to Boston, sent an extravagant floral arrangement, birds-of-paradise in colors Hattie thought outlandish but which pleased him. Sometimes she fibbed to Abel in order to sneak in a visit, telling him she was popping out to the grocery store, so as not to hurt his feelings. And she believed. Or wanted to. Believed that her son would rise again as he had each time before.

One day when she went to Abel's room to tell him she was just running out to pick up some more surgical tape, he said, "Hold up, Miss Hannah."

"I'll be right back," she said, turning away. She wondered if he had guessed where she'd been going.

"I want to go," he said, so quietly she barely heard him. "I want to go with you."

It was an effort for him to dress, and so she helped.

In silence they made the drive through the browning fields of September. Hattie concentrated on the road, at first careful that her driving technique conformed to Abel's instructions, but when she realized his attention wasn't trained on her, loosening up and doing things her way. As they approached a stoplight, she stole a look at him and then began to ride the brake rather than waiting to perform the controlled stop he insisted on. She let up pressure, then tapped again, to see if he would notice.

He gazed out the window, thinking at first of nothing, then of the way the world sped by as he, encased in the capsule that was their rocket car, made his way through the future toward their son. How had it happened that almost fifty years had gone by since the boy's birth? Where was the man that he, Abel, had been? Back there in time at the start of his life, an infant, a boy, a young man, then in age at full power and strength, and now old and as near to death, he considered, as he might be aware he could be. And who was he? It seemed urgent that at this moment he know, as it was late, getting later. His light might go out at the next stop, or a second from that or a second from that. Who could know? He didn't know what he would say to his son.

At the door to Billy's room Abel put out a hand to stay Hattie. "Let me," he said. "Alone." He pushed open the door and went in.

Hattie stood nearby so she could overhear what they said to each other. She inclined an ear toward the door Abel had closed behind him. Then, suddenly, she held back. What was between them was theirs.

When Abel came out his shoulders sagged. He looked wobbly and drained. All the way home he was quiet, and when they got to the house he went slowly up the walk while she put the car in the garage. Inside the front door he waited for her, holding out his arms. "I'm so sorry," he said. Stunned, she stepped into his embrace. They rocked each other.

At the end of forty days Billy's infection hadn't cleared. He was sent home with a wheelchair, a urinal and bedpan, and a PICC line, an open portal near his collarbone where pain medicine and antibiotics could be given quickly. There was no question about his coming home—there was no choice, no money for private care. Hattie settled him in the guest bedroom. It was obvious to everyone, and most obvious of all to Billy, that he had been sent home to die.

On his third morning at home he awakened with a strange sense of mission, of relief, and to the beautiful truth that he could choose not to live any longer. For years people had told him he was killing himself. He hadn't thought of his habits this way. He might have accidentally overdosed more than once, but ending his life was the last thing on his mind, and courting death was not what he'd thought he was doing. He had not yearned *toward* death but *away* from it. Had yearned toward immortality, he now understood. With his attempts to lift himself higher, he was seeking wholeness and union, chasing after the spirit that was always flitting just ahead. Carl Jung had come right out and admitted this could be so. *Spiritus contra spiritum,* he had written to Bill W., who knew it, and Dr. Bob S. knew it, too. And now Billy did. Whatever was beautiful, shimmering, loving, and warm, he wanted to keep going toward it forever.

All day as he dozed, sleeping to pain and waking to pain, he thought about the end. What was he waiting for? He had done each of the twelve steps at least twice, some many times over. Step One, admitting he was powerless over—what? The answer in part horrified him and in part made him laugh: everything.

He'd done the first step thirty times if he'd done it once, the second and third, too. He had confessed to God, himself, and another human being (twice this human being had been Doro, tender of the grave wherein his saddest sins were laid) the exact nature of his wrongs. He had made amends and then amended the amends and on and on and on heaped high toward eternity as he wronged and wronged and wronged again. He was tired. Tired of wronging. And there was no decision to be made now that he hadn't made decades before.

He spent the late afternoon, as the sunlight moved from his window and dusk began to fall, dozing and praying. Adoration, contrition, thanksgiving, supplication. He smiled inwardly at the famous formula, glad even now and despite all their cross-purposes to be following his father's method. He would not forget that his father had come to visit him, that after a long silence during which he stood by the bed with his palm on Billy's forehead, he had at last taken away his hand and bent to kiss him where the hand had been, and this stood for something. He thought he might be ready.

For all the harm he'd done, he begged repair. He prayed to be forgiven for what he was about to do, should it be another of the sins he couldn't seem to help committing. Somehow he didn't think so. God, he thought, cared less for judgment and more for mercy. He prayed for his sister Doro, that she might someday come into herself. For years he'd waited for her to confide. At first he'd been hurt by her failure to open up, but as time went by he came to understand that there were certain boundaries she couldn't cross, that she'd spent too much time building the story she told herself, and it was probably too late.

For those who withheld mercy for his kind, he prayed their hearts would open to receive hearts different from and yet the same as theirs. That those he was leaving would be comforted. They knew he loved them; he'd made no secret of it. Not in all the years, however down he'd been, however up. He had told each of them outright when they visited him in the rehab hospital—his father and mother, Doro, Jesse. Why ClairBell and Gideon hadn't come to visit him—not once in forty days—he didn't know. *Why,* he had written in anguish across the foolscap pad he used to keep track of his medicine doses, *have C and G abandoned me?* For a time he contemplated what he had written. It was a stark, terrible question, and there was no answer to it. In the end he tore off the sheet and crumpled it and tossed it in the wastebasket so no one would see it after he was gone, and in this act he understood for the first time the reason his sister couldn't admit who she was. He wanted no pity.

When Hattie entered his room that afternoon with his medicines, he told her the doses weren't touching his pain and that at rehab the nurses often doubled down when he needed it. "Usually that takes care of it," he said. "For a while at least." He summoned a smile. In a curious way, this was like the old days when he would lie to her or try to fast-talk in order to get more drugs so he could go to Joyland.

"Are you sure you need more now?" What a stupid question, Hattie thought even as she asked it. That time was past. Were there limits to mercy? Boundaries to love?

"Mother, it's bad," he said.

"Wait just a minute, then," she said. "I'll be right back." She hurried to the kitchen for sterile water and then returned to draw up a chair beside his bed. With the mortar and pestle she crushed the big methadone tablets into powder the way he specified and made a solution. She drew the liquid into a syringe and prepared his PICC line to fit the syringe in place.

"Thank you," he said. He lifted a hand to pat her arm, but he was careful to make no sentimental or telling gesture that would alert her to his purpose.

Hattie smiled, convincingly, she hoped. "You'll feel better in a little while." Slowly and carefully, as she'd been taught, she pushed down the plunger and watched with relief as his tension relaxed, the furrows on his forehead smoothed, his stricken look vanished, and he closed his eyes.

Peace overtook him.

"Hold off a minute before you go to sleep," Hattie told him, glancing toward his bedside table at the water glass that had grown smudged and cloudy. "Let me get you a better glass so you can take your other pills."

When she got back from the kitchen the room felt different. Without watching for the rise and fall of his chest, without taking his pulse, she knew. She held her breath, waiting for a sign that he was alive. But she knew.

She lowered herself to the chair beside his bed. She bowed her head and waited to feel something. Finally she lifted her gaze and looked toward the ceiling, slowly releasing the breath she'd been holding and allowing the words to flow through her. *Thank you,* she said. *Thank you.*

She sat for a time with him, and then she rose and went to the kitchen to stand at the sink and stare out the window at the Japanese maple, its rustling crimson leaves like living fire. From Abel's room came a surge in the television's volume. A frantic commercial for Celebrex urged him to dance to the music. She turned toward the sound and made her way down the hall.

Abel lived through the winter, occasionally enjoying a good day but for the most part enfeebled. Not himself, Hattie would tell visitors. Toward the end, as spring came on and the weather warmed, he might get out of bed on a good day and she would see him sometimes in the sunshine of the south yard where the pool had been, stretching his arms like wings, as though he were preparing to fly, a scrawny, wizened old fledgling.

One day, seemingly out of the blue, he asked her, "Whatever happened to that book? That marriage book I brought home? I've looked for it everywhere. I always thought we could read it together."

"The one with the pictures of people"—she didn't know how to finish—"doing things?"

"Yes, that one. *Ideal Marriage.* By that randy Dutch doctor."

She affected a pensive pose. "Why, I don't know where that thing could have gotten off to."

He lowered his gaze and made busy with his feeding tube, arranging the bandage. "Hattie. Hannah. I always wanted to ask you something."

Shyness had not been his way. It was odd to see him so hesitant. She said, worrying that she sounded too flip, "Well, ask away."

He tried to clear his throat but the effort was too much, so he spoke through it, hearing as well as feeling the quaver and catch of his voice. "That part of it. Did I let you down? Were you disappointed?"

"Not once," she said quickly, truthfully, "not even once."

And so they went on. The old irritations didn't die but they seemed to trouble less, and in their place had come a sense that there were no more storms to weather, only these long last days. They had forgiven each other everything. "You have a beautiful spirit," he told her once as she trimmed the gauze bandage around his tunnel.

Marriage, she sometimes said to herself, marveling. Theirs was not ideal and sometimes it hadn't even been good, but it was good enough and it didn't need an adjective. It was marriage.

One afternoon as she lay trying to nap the thought came to her that it was through Billy's sacrifice that at last she was able to devote herself fully and without stint to her husband's care, that through her son's death she had been released to attend to Abel, but she quickly pushed the idea away. She would not make Billy's suffering her life's redeeming.

When Abel died—a peaceful quiet death at home in his back room with hospice care and Hattie and the children ranged around—she was sad, and she knew she would miss him for the rest of her days, but for the first few weeks of her widowhood, before the reality of his absence overtook her, she was also secretly giddy. She felt as if she'd become unmoored from earth, had become small and buoyant, airy as a puff of thistledown, a feather, and was drifting upward through the clouds, following him aloft. Then, naturally, literally, she fell. Stepping off a curb outside the post office where she'd gone to buy a book of stamps, not even thinking about the many sorrows of the past year, she turned her foot wrong, or misjudged the drop, and down she went, scraping her knees and banging her forehead, and it was only when a passerby hurried to help her to a sitting position on the curb and asked if she was all right and she heard the tenderness in his low voice that she allowed her grief out into the world, wailing like a baby to a stranger on the street. She cried for Abel, for Billy, for Nick, then back again for Abel and so on around until she didn't know for whom she wept, only that it hurt and that there was no greater or lesser, no comparison, no favorite, only loss.

She lived on in the big house, alone. Every now and again her children carted her around to various places, trying to spark her interest in independent living or assisted living or whatever euphemism they were calling cold storage by these days, but Hattie was wise to them. She stood fast. She would stay in the house. It was her life's work, or at least the vessel that carried it. The children were put out with her because she wouldn't do what they wanted, but she didn't care. They thought they knew best, especially Doro, whom she suspected of long-distance badgering and getting the others to spy on her—twice she'd caught Jesse following her car as she drove home from church—but the truth was that they didn't know anything. They were nowhere near old enough to know anything. Sometimes she even laughed to herself at what the lot of them had yet to learn—that good stories did not always have happy endings, for example, but that you could make a story happy by looking back and taking those small moments of love or joy or grace and adding them together. That even in great sorrow you could find peace. That old griefs could be changed, with time, into a feeling of boundless tenderness. That the shape of anybody's life, even the most ordinary, was anything but regular, and that the lines that connected hearts to heads rarely traveled straight.

Whether it was that Abel was no longer around to temper her rising power or that she had simply, almost suddenly, grown into what felt like wisdom, in her new knowledge she became garrulous and outspoken. For most of her life she had yielded to the will of others, she had done what others wanted, but now it was her turn to be obstinate and she resolved to enjoy it. She waited until Doro came home for a visit and then summoned everyone to a family dinner. *This worm has turned,* she planned to say.

She hadn't cooked for months, but all day she'd worked on pot roast, mashed potatoes and gravy, Jesse's favorite creamed cauliflower, green salad, and yeast rolls. Remembering dinners past, she at first set the big oval table for eight, thinking as she laid out the Eliot china and the Ennis silver of their seating order of years gone by. She laid a place for Abel at the table's head, at twelve o'clock. At his left hand she put Clair-Bell, then Nick, and then Gideon. At six o'clock, facing Abel, was Jesse, because he was left-handed. Rounding the turn and next to Jesse she set a place for Billy, and then Doro in the middle. At Abel's right was her place, closest to the kitchen door. For a time she stood to survey her work, satisfied with her centerpiece of bittersweet and oak leaves, firethorn and red sumac from the yard, with the glimmering crystal in the amber light of the chandelier.

She wasn't muddled or mixed up or confused, she was at peace and remembering, but Doro, passing through the dining room, said worriedly, "Mother?"

"I know," Hattie told her. "I'm just playing."

Doro moved closer and put an arm around her mother, who looked at her, eyes glittering. "But wasn't it *something*? All of us?"

They went to work taking away place settings. Neither of them said, though both of them thought, how empty the table looked.

Hattie wound up at the head, in Abel's place, for no one else wanted to take it. Jesse kept his seat at the table's foot. Gid and ClairBell took one side and Doro the other. ClairBell cupped her hands around her mouth and called across the table. "Yoo-hoo. Anybody out there?" No one laughed.

The dinner went beautifully, Hattie thought, with Jesse even taking off his hat and everyone on good behavior until about midway through the meal, and then something happened out of the blue, sudden as a thunderclap, a ball of lightning, something.

ClairBell pushed back her chair and slapped her palms on the table. The china and silver rattled. Iced water in the crystal goblets sloshed. "That's it!" ClairBell shouted, her voice breaking into a sob. "I can't take it anymore!"

Hattie flinched. Jesse was dumbfounded. Gid made a dubious face. Only Doro knew what the uproar was about.

She had been true to her word—she'd hardly spoken to her sister, not through Billy's or Abel's funerals. Just the necessaries—yes, no, maybe, I don't know—and nothing more. She'd been cool and distant. It hadn't been difficult, as she'd distanced herself long before. Because of her sister's capricious moods, her jealousy, her general crackpottery, her temper. Doro wasn't proud of this, but there it was. She loved her sister, but she didn't like her very much. The chair had clinched it.

"Look," ClairBell was saying, her face pink and inflamed, "you can have it! Take it! I don't care about it anymore. Just please be my sister again!" She slid her plate to the side and put her face on the table and cried.

Gid, beside her, patted her on the back. "What's the matter, Bell? Nobody knows what's going on."

Doro said, "I do. It's the goddamn chair."

Hattie said, "Doro, don't swear at the dinner table." She thought a while, testing the application of the law, then shook her head. "Or anywhere."

"Just take it," ClairBell blubbered.

Everyone looked at Doro, who had been surprised at her sister's reaction to her snubbing. She wouldn't have guessed that anything mattered to ClairBell but getting her way. She knew she should be moved by her sister's pain, but instead she felt a kind of cold, sick hardness.

"Will you take it?" ClairBell asked. "I'm giving it to you."

Hattie geared up to put in, "Well, it's not really yours to give, ClairBell," but Doro, who suddenly saw that she couldn't take the Eliot chair now, not in good conscience—because the gain would have come from her own pettiness—and not after such a heart-rending public drama, whether or not the display was genuine, said, "Nobody should take it. Mom should do what she wants with it."

ClairBell peered at Doro. Her powers, like a cartoon alarm clock shrilling, alerted her that this could be a ploy for Doro to actually end up with the chair. What she'd been counting on was for her older sister to see her misery and then tell her it was just a chair—just a thing—and there was no way a chair would come between blood sisters. She would have bet next week's Bingo money as well as her yard sale allowance that old Dorcas Do-Right would have said those exact words. She, ClairBell, was screwed. "Okay, all right. Now can we just go back to normal?"

Doro forced a smile. "This is normal."

"No, really," ClairBell insisted. She sniffed. She pushed out her lower lip and made a petulant face.

Doro knew what her sister wanted, and so before ClairBell could utter the dread sentiment about needing a hug she got up from her chair and went around the table and embraced her sister, whose face was wet with tears, whose soft flesh was hot and clingy.

Something in the hug undid Doro, who had intended to be firm and matter-of-fact. It was her sister's need and their shared griefs, how soft she was, how short, how good she smelled—like grapefruit—maybe because for the first time since ClairBell had started on the painkiller road Doro felt she actually might have a sister and not merely the shell of one.

Over the course of their long embrace, Doro's mixed feelings sorted themselves out, at least as much as they could be sorted out. There was wariness still, both sisters felt it, but somehow this was a tension that had become tangled in their history and there would be no changing it. The moment lasted briefly, until ClairBell gritted her teeth and hissed into Doro's ear, "I'll never forgive you for this."

"Well, at least that's settled," Hattie said happily, wiping her mouth and placing her napkin beside her plate. "I never liked that chair. Not from the first. And I know just what to do with the dratted thing. We'll donate it to the church library in honor of Billy. We can have a plaque made with his name on it."

Gid and Jesse grumbled assent. Doro busied herself heaping her mashed potatoes into a nest in order to keep from showing disappointment that the chair was truly lost to her and that once again ClairBell had seized the upper hand. She nodded.

Thinking already of ways the chair's eventual destiny might be recharted in her favor, ClairBell wiped her eyes with her napkin, shrugged, and said, "Whatever."

Now that the upheaval was over, Hattie announced that she'd called them together to get a few things straight.

Everyone looked toward her with worried expressions. Thinking his mother planned to speak of wills and inheritances and eager, to tell the truth, to see if what lay in store for him would provide him with another start, Gid asked, perhaps a bit sharply, "What things?"

Under her son's sudden and hostile interrogation everything flew from Hattie's mind. He sounded like his father. Oh, why hadn't she made a list? Flustered, she felt the way she had when cross-examined by Abel.

But then suddenly she blurted, having discovered, like a gift bequeathed by him through his beloved mysteries of time and matter, a reservoir of quickness from which to draw, "From now on I'll be the jerk."

She hadn't meant to be funny. She had meant to say "head of the family" instead of "jerk." She probably said "jerk" because Gid was sitting there with his mouth cockeyed, looking like a tinhorn despot, being one. But her children laughed. They imitated the way she'd slammed down her fist beside her plate, they imitated the words she'd said and the way she'd said them, cracking themselves up again and again.

"You children stop this!" she said, but they didn't, or couldn't, and they went on hooting and snorting. She feigned a show of exasperation, pursing her lips, but she discovered, through the offices of a rapid message from her deepest heart, that she was pleased.

For the rest of her life she would stay in the old house, big and empty and going to seed though it was. Abel and Billy were there, not as ghosts but as living memory. Sitting at the kitchen counter spooning up ice cream, drawing plans, tinkering out in the barn, in twin recliners in the den, each in his place at the big table, in the gloomy and maddening visage of Ebenezer, in the bed of tulips Billy had planted on the day he'd told her of his diagnosis, bulbs so long in the ground now that the once-red blooms had blown white. Oh, everywhere. Nick had been gone such a long time—could it be forty years?—that he was no longer present in material things, and so she had to look harder to find him, but he, too, was here.

Of all the fates she'd imagined for herself, loneliness had not been among them, and yet here it was, her daily companion, like a little follow-dog. Ruefully she remembered that once she'd dreamed of time and quiet enough to hear herself think. She'd finally gotten what she wanted, she supposed, but it turned out there wasn't that much left to think about. She tried to reflect on her life, on what she'd done and hadn't done, on those she'd loved and those maybe she hadn't loved enough. Marriage, she decided, was not a pairing of two people but a sum of all the ups and downs and ins and outs. She wondered if it was possible that what people called true love was seen only through time, and backward, when you couldn't change a thing you'd done or try to be someone you weren't, when what was done was done and you understood, when all was gone and still and quiet, you'd been living in it all along.

Her eyes had gone bad and she could no longer see to read or sew, but her fingers could still find the notes of simple hymns, a little Schubert, some minuets and marches, and so she entertained herself this way throughout the winter. And there was Free Cell. And Dr. Phil and Oprah and Ellen and reruns of *Little House*. Long visits from Doro, who had finally retired and seemed less on edge than she'd been in the past. Every now and then her daughter would mention "a friend," but Hattie didn't pry. Jesse stopped by on his trips through town. He'd brought a new woman friend to meet her, a florist she halfway knew through a friend of a friend. They'd had several pleasant visits. The woman knew her flowers. Jesse seemed happy. ClairBell buzzed by once in a blue moon, but mostly kept to herself. Hattie would have liked a few more visits, but she knew that if she called her daughter would be there. Gideon would drop in, smelling of beer, to borrow small amounts of cash, saying he was strapped. What he did for a living she had no idea. She had decided not to ask. Her children had their own lives. In the summer she gardened, slower at her tasks than before, but at least she could be outside. The seasons passed serenely. Her health held.

A curious thing had happened to her heart—a small miracle, she thought it was, though her doctor told her such a thing was fairly common. Still, she considered it a wonder that in all the turmoil of the past years, in all the worries and loss, when she hadn't been thinking about it or trying to heal and not even taking vitamins as regularly as she pretended to Doro she was or even aware that such a thing could occur, her heart had grown another pathway around the blockage, quietly fixing itself.

She was happiest when morning broke, when the earth felt newly born and her spirit rose to meet the coming day the way it always had and she could almost think she had the strength to live another lifetime. When this notion overtook her she would shake her head and stop herself before she went too far. *Oh, Hattie, no,* she would say to herself. For all its trials, hers had been a fine life, but once would be the greatest plenty.

Evenings were most difficult. When shadows fell and darkness took her too deeply into the past—where there were moments she could not unlive—or too close to the mysteries of the world ahead. Sometimes, eager for what was to come, she willed herself not to wake up come morning, to hold herself adrift in sleep until she was no more. But of course she couldn't keep her mind from springing back to life, at least so far. Still, to pave the way and reassure the One who had heard every prayer she'd uttered since she was a child and knew already, she believed with all her heart, what would become of her, she sent up the all clear, *I'm ready,* and as an afterword she put in, *Anytime,* should there be doubt.